PRAISE FOR BESTSELLING AUTHOR

HELENA HUNTING

AND HER PREVIOUS NOVELS

"Fun, sexy, and full of heart...a laugh-out-loud love story with explosive chemistry and lovable characters. Helena Hunting has done it again!"
—*USA Today* bestselling author Melanie Harlow

"The perfect combination of sexy, sweet, and hilarious. A feel-good beach read you won't want to miss!"
—*New York Times* bestselling author K. Bromberg

"Characters that will touch your heart and a romance that will leave you breathless."
—*New York Times* bestselling author Tara Sue Me

"Heartfelt, hilarious, hot, and so much sexiness!"
—*New York Times* bestselling author Tijan

"A love story like no other."
—*New York Times* bestselling author Alice Clayton

"Emotional, sexy, captivating. A beautiful story."
—*New York Times* bestselling author Emma Chase

"Helena writes irresistible men. I loved this sexy, funny, and deliciously naughty story!"
—*USA Today* bestselling author Liv Morris

"The story came alive so vividly in my mind....My heart raced, I laughed out loud, I just was completely drawn in from the very beginning." —*Aestas Book Blog*

I FLIPPING LOVE YOU

HELENA HUNTING

St. Martin's Paperbacks

This is a work of fiction. All of the characters, organizations, and events portrayed in this novel are either products of the author's imagination or are used fictitiously.

I FLIPPING LOVE YOU

Copyright © 2018 by Helena Hunting.

All rights reserved.

For information address St. Martin's Press, 175 Fifth Avenue, New York, NY 10010.

ISBN: 978-1-250-18397-2

Our books may be purchased in bulk for promotional, educational, or business use. Please contact your local bookseller or the Macmillan Corporate and Premium Sales Department at 1-800-221-7945, ext. 5442, or by e-mail at MacmillanSpecialMarkets@macmillan.com.

Printed in the United States of America

St. Martin's Paperbacks edition / June 2018

St. Martin's Paperbacks are published by St. Martin's Press, 175 Fifth Avenue, New York, NY 10010.

10 9 8 7 6 5 4 3 2 1

For my sister and your beautiful soul

ACKNOWLEDGMENTS

I couldn't do any of this without my husband and daughter and my family and my friends. Your love and support make this all possible.

Debra, why can't they create a portal so we can have three-dimensional lunch every day?

Kimberly, you go above and beyond every time. Thank you for being amazing.

Huge love to my team at SMP who make the hard work feel easy.

Nina, Jenn, and my SBPR team, you all need superhero names and costumes. You're incredible women and I'm proud to call you friends.

Sarah, Christina, and my Hustlers, you're such rock stars. Thank you for the time and love you've given me over the years. I'm blessed and honored to have you on my team.

Beavers, you're always a highlight to my day. I'm continually amazed by your passion for romance and reading.

To my Backdoor Babes: Tara, Meghan, Deb and Katherine, keep being fabulously talented women.

Filets, Nappers, Holiday Readers, Pams, Ruth, Kellie, Erika, Jenn, Tijan, Deb, Leigh, Marnie, Susi, Melanie, Sarah, Kelly, Shalu, Kristy, Shay, Teeny—I'm so lucky to have such inspiring women to share this journey with. Thank you for always being my support team.

None of this would be possible without the readers and bloggers who give their time, energy, and support to share their passion for stories. I am beyond grateful to be part of this community. Thank you for being such voracious, dedicated readers.

CHAPTER 1

ANGRY HOT GUY

RIAN

I flip through my stack of flyers, checking for a sale on the jumbo box of Cinnamon Toast Crunch cereal so I can price match it. I'm a conscientious price matcher. I mark the sale with a big circle before tucking the red Sharpie into the front of my shirt. If I'm going to wheel and deal at the cash register, I want to make it as easy as possible for the cashier and the people in line behind me. Nothing is worse than getting stuck behind an unorganized price matcher.

I shimmy a little to the song playing over the store intercom as I toss boxes of my most favorite, unhealthy cereal in my cart. A prickly feeling climbs the back of my neck, and I shiver, glancing over my shoulder. A mom rushes past me down the aisle, her toddler leaning precariously out of the cart in an attempt to grab a box of Fruit Roll-Ups. I can't blame him. They are artificially delicious.

But the mom-toddler combo isn't the reason for the prickly feeling. Halfway down the aisle is a suit. A big suit. Well over six feet of man wrapped in expensive charcoal-gray fabric. He doesn't have a cart or a basket. And he's staring at me. Weird. I can't look at him long enough to decide if he's familiar or not without making it obvious that I'm staring back.

I have the urge to check my appearance, worried I have his attention because my hair is a mess, or there's a sweat stain down the center of my back. I'm not particularly appealing at the moment. I've just come from a boot camp class at this new gym my twin sister forced me to try out.

Marley bought an online two-for-one coupon for forty bucks, so now I have to attend six of these stupid classes with her. I managed to get out of last week's class, but she wouldn't let me escape two weeks in a row. My tank is still dewy, post-exertion, I have terrible under-boob sweat, and my thong is all wonky. If I were alone in this aisle, I'd for sure fix the last issue, but suit guy is here so I must leave the thong where it is for now, wedged uncomfortably between my vagina lips.

The suit quickly shifts his attention to the shelves and picks up the jar directly in front of him, which happens to contain prunes. He inspects it, then maybe realizes what it is, because he rushes to return it, exchanging it for another item. I bite back a smile, pleased that even in my disgusting state I'm being checked out.

As suit man gives the shelf in front of him his full attention, I return the checkout favor. His attire and his posture scream money and a twinge of something like longing combined with jealousy makes my throat momentarily tight. At one time, price matching was a practice I would've laughed at—like an entitled jerk—now it's a necessity.

Suit man must be warm, considering it's late April and we're experiencing temperatures far above average for this time of year. Based on the tapered fit of his suit, I'm guessing it's a high-end brand. He's complemented it with black patent leather shoes. Very impractical for this weather and location. Does he realize he's in the Hamptons?

He's wearing a watch, and from his profile, he can't be much beyond his early thirties. I have to assume the only reason for the watch is because it's expensive and he wants to show it off. In my head, I've already profiled him as a pretentious, rich prick who probably commutes to NYC a few times a week where he bones his secretary and has a penthouse with the barest of furniture. The rest of the time he works from home.

I return to shopping and continue down the aisle, in the opposite direction of the suit—it's my way of finding out if he's actually creeping on me or not. I keep tabs on him in my peripheral vision as I scope out more sales and more delicious, unhealthy food items. My job is to balance out all the fruit and vegetables my sister, Marley, is currently picking out in the produce section.

I grab a jar of the no-name peanut butter since we're out and the good stuff isn't on sale, dropping it in the cart. My phone keeps buzzing in my purse. It's distracting, so I give up ignoring it and check my messages.

It's my sister.

We're in the same store. It's not particularly huge, so I don't know what could be so pressing that she needs to text four thousand times instead of finding me.

ABORT SHOPPING
LEAVE NOW
Meet me in parking lot
RIAN??????

Jeez. What the heck is going on? Maybe the grocery store is being robbed. *Holy Hot Pockets.* What if there *is* a grocery store heist going down? I'm about to abandon

my cart in a bid to find Marley and escape the mayhem
I've created in my head. It's all very dramatic. As I turn,
I come face-to-face with the suit.

I suck in a breath and slap my hand over my chest. The
tank is still damp, and my skin's a little gritty with salt-
sweat, so I drop it quickly, because *ew*.

"Hi." His expression is hard to read. He seems . . .
smug.

"Hi, hey. Uh . . ." I wave a hand around in the air, a little
flustered, and conflicted, because it's not often I get approached by a guy this hot—and in a grocery store of all
places. Maybe he'll be here again next week. "I'm sorry,
I'd like to stare at your pretty face, I mean . . ." Crap, why
are words so hard? "I have to go."

I try to step around him, but he mirrors the movement,
taking a linebacker stance, as if he's considering tackling
me. Which is an odd way to stage an introduction.

"Recognize me?" he asks, one perfect eyebrow arched.

As I take him in, I wrack my brain for a time or place
I might've run into him before. I don't think so, though.
His light brown hair is neatly styled, and the cut of his
suit highlights all of his assets. Well, the visible PG ones,
anyway.

He widens his stance and crosses his arms over his
chest. His very broad chest. The sleeves of his suit jacket
pull tight, biceps bulging and flexing. He's a bit intimidating based on his size alone, but we're in a public grocery
store, so I feel relatively safe. And he's just so gorgeous.
Which is a silly reason not to be concerned, some of the
most notorious serial killers are attractive men. Also, I
need to find my sister, in case the grocery store is really
under attack—although maybe this suit could save us.

I adopt his crossed arm pose, but I don't think I look
intimidating. All I succeed in doing is awkwardly squeez-

ing my boobs together inside my damp sports bra and jabbing the right one with the Sharpie. "Should I?"

He looks me over, a slight smirk tipping his mouth. His gaze gets stuck on the Sharpie for a few seconds before they come back up to my eyes.

It's possible I met him in a bar, but I swear I'd remember his face if I did. The bar scene is also more my sister's speed than it is mine. Oh God. It's also possible he's mistaking me for her. It's happened before.

While we look nearly identical at first to most people, we're actually fraternal twins. After a few interactions, most people can tell us apart. I have a distinctive Marilyn Monroe mole on the right side above my lip, and my eyes are amber, where Marley's are closer to green. My mouth is too big for my face, my lips a little too full and my nose too small. At least that's my perception. Marley's also the more outgoing of the two of us and an inch taller. And about ten pounds lighter.

Marley is a little less cautious than I am with men, so there have been a few uncomfortable occasions where her previous hookups have approached me, asking why I haven't returned their calls. It's too bad if this is the case, because this guy is inordinately attractive and it would be nice if he wasn't one of my sister's castoffs.

His face is a masterpiece of masculine perfection; straight nose, high cheekbones, an angular jawline that could cut glass, full lips. Especially the bottom one. The kind of full that makes me think of kissing, with tongue, of course. He's all-American handsome with a shot of alpha hotness. It's a lethal combination for the state of my already damp panties.

"I recognize *you*." He has a low, rough voice, like the delicious scrape of fine grit sandpaper.

He breaks me out of my ogle daze. He must think I'm

Marley. I'm actually rather disappointed. "I think maybe you've mistaken me for someone else."

"Oh no, sweetheart." His gaze rakes over me again. I feel very naked all of a sudden. And hot. It's really hot in here. "You drive a powder-blue Buick."

"How the heck—"

"I knew it!" he shouts, eyes alight with some kind of weird, victorious satisfaction as he points a long finger with a blue-black nail at me. Maybe he slammed it in a door or something. Or based on the way he's rudely pointing, maybe someone slammed it for him. "I fucking knew it! You hit my car."

I definitely would've remembered hitting someone's car, especially if a guy this good looking was driving it. He should probably come with a warning, like: Panties may combust if you get too close, or something. I take a step back since he's all up in my grill and clearly he's not looking to flirt like I originally thought. "I have absolutely no idea what you're talking about."

"Don't play dumb with me! You think you can flip your ponytail"—he reaches out and flicks the end, which is rather startling—"flash a smile and some cleavage, and it's going to get you out of this. Well, think again, sweetheart. I guarantee my paint is still all over your bumper." He's leaning over me, face way too close to mine. So close I can see tiny gold flecks in his deep green eyes. They're an unusual shade. Dark like pine tree needles.

And he's chewing gum. Juicy Fruit. I can smell it when he breathes in my face. I would've expected a man like him to chew something more along the lines of Polar Ice, or Arctic Ice—strong mint.

I put a hand on his chest and take one deliberate step backward as he opens his mouth to resume his tangent. It's a solid chest. Extremely hard. His gaze darts down, brows furrowed. I use his distracted state to my advantage. "First of all . . ." I point my finger in his face, like he did to me. "Don't 'sweetheart' me. That's condescending. Secondly, I'm sure I would've noticed if I'd hit another car. Thirdly, there are literally hundreds of powder-blue Buicks in this stupid city. It's not an uncommon car. And I'd like to point out, that the cleavage comment was completely unnecessary and unwarranted and actually, pretty damn sexist."

He blinks a couple of times, possibly taken aback. That expression doesn't last long. His lip curls in a sneer and that pretty all-American handsomeness morphs into downright malevolent hotness. "Nice try, *sweetheart*. But there's no way I'd forget you." His gaze sweeps over me—it's not in an unappreciative way either.

I poke his hard chest. "Stop leering at me, you pervert. I don't know what kind of drugs you've been snorting, but I assure you, you've got the wrong person."

"Oh shit!" my sister's voice comes from behind me.

I turn to find Marley doing an about-face, and then she breaks into a little grapevine step as she moves back toward me. Her eyes are wide, mouth contorted into some kind of grimace as she grabs my wrist.

"What the fuck? There are two of you?" hot-crazy guy asks, eyes bouncing between us.

"We gotta go." Marley latches onto my hand and drags me down the aisle, away from crazy-hot suit.

"Whoa! Wait a damn second!"

Hot suit makes a grab for me, but Marley yanks me out of the way and shoves my shopping cart at him—hard. He's not quite quick enough to get out of the way, and the corner of the cart slams right into his crotch. He doubles over with a groan and aggressively pushes the cart aside. It ricochets into a display of canned peaches, which spill into the aisle with a deafening crash.

"What the heck, Mar?"

"Come the fuck on!" She sprints down the aisle, dragging me behind her. I'd protest, but I don't think I have much choice in the matter, considering the death grip she has on my hand, or the fact that she's assaulted the sexy-crazy suit with my shopping cart.

Marley fast-walks to the exit, glancing over her shoulder. "Act natural."

"Will you tell me what's going on? Who is that guy?"

She flips her hair over her shoulder and smiles as we pass the cashiers and the automatic doors open. Marley fast-walks down the sidewalk toward our car. "I may have tapped that guy's car last Saturday when I was shopping."

I stop walking, which brings her to a jarring halt. She yanks on my arm. "Seriously, come on. I'll explain when we're in the car."

"Nope. No way. You explain now."

Her eyes are bouncing all over the place. "It's not a big deal. I just grazed his bumper." Marley spin and tries to push me forward from behind. "Now let's get out of here before he finds us again. We should probably shop somewhere else for a while."

I stumble forward a step and then spin away from her. "You *hit* that guy's car?"

"It was more of a graze. At least I think it was." She wrings her hands and makes her *oh crap* face.

Now crazy-hot suit guy seems a lot less crazy and much more justified in his reaction. Except for the cleavage comment. That was still unnecessary. "It sure didn't seem like nothing with the way he freaked out in there."

"He's probably overreacting. Where are your keys?" She's still wringing her hands.

I pat my hip with the intention of keeping my purse safe and away from my sister. Except all I end up patting is my actual hip. I look down, running my hands over my stomach, searching for the cheap, faux-leather knockoff. "Oh fudge."

"What?"

"My purse. It's in the cart. I have to go back and get it."

Marley grabs the back of my tank. "You can't! What if he's still in there?"

"It has my identification in it, Marley. And my bankcards, and my money, and keys to the car and the apartment. I can't leave it in there!"

Marley flails and paces around in a circle. "What if he's waiting for us to come back and get it?"

"You can stay here if you want, but I'm going back for it. I'm not leaving my purse behind because you hit some guy's car in a parking lot. I can't believe you just drove away!"

"I thought I tapped it, and then I panicked." Her fingers are at her mouth now. "I didn't want to drive up our insurance premiums over some guy and his Tesla."

"You hit a Tesla?" This keeps getting worse.

"Anyone who has the money to buy a Tesla has the money to fix it, right?" Marley says.

"So you drove off! Jeez, Marley. What were you thinking?" I shake my head. I'd like to say I'm surprised by this, but sadly I'm not. Marley doesn't always use common sense in day-to-day life.

"I don't know. I wasn't thinking. That's the problem, I guess."

I'm about to go back into the store, but stop short at the sight of the suit leaning against the side of my car, one ankle crossed over the other, all calm like. Dangling from a single finger is my knockoff, hot-pink Coach purse. "Forget something?"

CHAPTER 2
DOUBLE TROUBLE

PIERCE

Getting hit in the nuts with a full grocery cart hurts like hell. But I keep the smug smile in place as one of the twins walks toward me. The one who apparently *didn't* hit my car. The other one—who *did* hit my car—stands about twenty feet away, nervously twisting her hands.

The twin making her way closer seems fairly embarrassed. Her cheeks are a fiery shade of pink as she approaches, full lips pressed into a line that almost looks like a pout. Her eyes are on her purse, which is hanging from the end of my finger. Since she's not looking at me, I have the opportunity to check her out. Again.

Last week, I stopped at this grocery store on the way to my brother's after a meeting I had in Manhattan. It hadn't been a fun meeting, so I'd already been in a salty mood as a result. I've never been to this store before—but it's not too far from his place on the beach, and I was in a bit of a rush at the time and in need of a bathroom. I figured while I was there, I could pick up some steaks for the barbeque and a whole lot of beer. As I was standing in line, waiting to check out, I noticed a woman with a belt full of vegetables and a box of Cinnamon Toast Crunch—one of my favorite juvenile indulgences.

Once I cashed out, I headed to the parking lot, where I noticed the same woman slip into the driver's seat of her car—parked beside mine. And then I proceeded to watch her scrape the front of her car across my rear quarter panel when she pulled out of her parking spot. I stood frozen in horror as she ruined the paint job on my two-hundred-thousand-dollar car. I was expecting her to jump out of her car to check on the damage, or even to leave a note, because that's what a decent human being would do. But no, she stopped for a moment, looked around, saw me standing all the way by the entrance of the grocery store, and drove off.

And now here she is again, except there are two of her. I hadn't notice her then—she was just a woman who liked Cinnamon Toast Crunch and hit my car. But when I saw her in the cereal aisle and really got a good look at her, I noted how gorgeous she was. The kind of beautiful that numbs your tongue and jacks up your heart rate. It's odd, but despite them being nearly identical, I'm only attracted to the one approaching me. It's also good to know that I'm not into women who pull hit-and-runs.

She stops when she's about three feet away and motions behind her, to her sister. "Mar told me what she did. I'm really sorry about that. And about"—she gestures to my crotch and her nose wrinkles in a grimace—"getting hit with the cart. But in all honesty, I thought you were some weirdo who was stalking me through a grocery store, and you knew what kind of car I drive. You have to admit it's kind of creepy, plus you made that inappropriate comment about my cleavage, which was completely uncalled for." What begins as an apology quickly turns into righteous indignation. She snaps her fingers and crosses her arms over her chest. "You're looking at my boobs."

I lift my gaze to her face. "You were talking about them." She does have a legitimate point about the cleavage comment, but I'm not admitting to that yet, not when her sister pulled a hit-and-run.

She plants her fists on her hips, eyes narrowed. They're a pretty honey color, framed with long, thick lashes. She's not wearing makeup, clearly the exercise wear is authentic, and she's not one of those women who walks around in spandex all the time pretending she's been to the gym. Based on the curve of her backside, which I'd been checking out in the grocery store, she definitely puts some work into it.

"Can I have my purse back, please?" she snaps.

"Sure." When she takes a halting step toward me, I hold it out of reach. "As soon as I have your insurance and contact information."

She blows out a breath and her eyes fall closed for a few seconds. When she opens them again, she plasters on a sweet smile and holds out her hand. "It's in my purse."

"Nice try, sweetheart, but that's not going to work."

She purses her lips and her nose wrinkles. "Would you stop calling me sweetheart?"

"Give me a name I can use if it bothers you so much." Antagonizing her is ridiculously fun. I recognize I'm being an asshole, but then, I feel justified considering the three thousand dollars in damage that's been done to my Tesla. I've had to resort to driving my truck most of the week, which is not as easy to park.

She sighs. "Rian. It's Rian, and you are?"

"Ryan?" I try to fit the name with the woman standing in front of me.

"Like the boy's name, except it's spelled with an 'i'

instead of a 'y,' in case you'd like to write that down somewhere." She shoots me an annoyed smile. "And you are?"

"Pierce."

"Of course." She rolls her eyes. I don't know what that's
all about, and I don't get a chance to ask because she bar-
rels on, "Well, I'd like to say it's nice to meet you, *Pierce*,
but under the circumstances that'd be a lie, so . . ." She
gives her head a shake and mutters something else under
her breath.

Beyond my ability to appreciate her appearance, I think
I might be even more attracted to how prickly she's being.
"Not big on tact, are you?"

"Not really, no. Surprising I'm single, huh?" She looks
up at the clear blue sky. "So, Pierce, why don't you take
down my contact information so we can deal with the
scratch on your steel baby, or whatever, and we can all be on
our way."

"It's a three-thousand-dollar scratch."

She blinks a few times, mouth dropping open. She
shoots a glare over her shoulder. "For the love of Golden
Grahams. She couldn't have parked beside a Civic or
something. Had to be an expensive car that's expensive
to fix."

I dig my phone out of my pocket, pull up my contact
list, and add her name. "Your number?" I consider how
differently this might've played out if I'd approached her
under alternative circumstances.

Rian rattles off a number, and as soon as it's added to
my phone I call it. Muffled lyrics come from inside the
purse dangling from my finger.

She arches a brow. "Satisfied?"

"I will be when I have your sister's license and insurance information."

"Mar, get over here," she calls over her shoulder.

Her sister trudges our way, looking more than a little cagey, and angry. Which is ironic since she's the one who hit my car, not the other way around. "What?"

Rian motions to me. "He needs a picture of your license and insurance information."

"My license is at home. You drove." She's still doing that hand-twisting thing. "I really thought I tapped it."

"Tapped? Feel free to check out the missing paint." I motion to the side of my car.

Rian's eyes go wide as she takes in the long scratch gouged out of the side. "Oh, for frack's sake. Look at this!" She drags her sister over to see the damage.

"That could've been there before. Maybe I really did bump his car and someone else did that and he's using us so he can get our insurance to pay for it."

"My paint is still on your car." I point to the streak of black marring the front bumper.

"Maybe you put it there," Mar says.

"Seriously? Well, if you had bothered to stop and get out of your car to look at what you did instead of driving off, you would know. You fled the scene. That's a crime," I point out. "Punishable by law."

That gets her back up. "I panicked! And obviously you can afford to have it fixed. Look at you." She motions to my suit. "What is this, an Armani?"

"It's a Tom Ford, actually, and I could've called the cops and reported it. Do you have any idea what the fine is for that?"

Rian holds a hand up in front of her sister's face. "Can you stop talking and get the insurance card out of the glove box? This is so embarrassing." She directs her next comment at me. "I appreciate you not calling the police on my sister."

"Especially since it was an accident," her sister chimes in.

Rian grabs her sister by the arm and hauls her about fifteen feet away. They have a brief whispered, but heated, conversation. When they return, Rian passes the keys to her sister. "Get in the car, please."

"What? Why?"

"Because I'd like to avoid making this situation worse." Rian has a stare down with her sister that lasts all of four seconds. She heads for the driver's side until Rian stops her. "Passenger side." There's a lot of huffing and muttering of profanity as she rounds the hood and throws herself into the passenger seat.

I feel a little bad for Rian as she rummages around in the glove compartment and produces the insurance card and her license since her sister doesn't have hers, especially considering how stressed she seems to be over the cost of the repairs. I have her number now, which is nice, although it's come with quite the price tag.

Rian rubs her forehead with a sigh. "If you can forward me the quote and the bill for the repairs, we'll work something out. I don't know if it's possible to avoid going through insurance, but we'll manage it, however it suits you best, considering the circumstances."

"I'll get everything to you in the next couple of days." I hand her back her purse.

"Great." She gives me a smile that in no way matches that single affirmative word. "I'll just wait until you leave before I do, you know, to avoid further potential damage to your very pretty, very expensive car."

"Your thoughtfulness is much appreciated." I give her a wink, to which she responds with pursed lips, flushed cheeks, and a muttered *right*.

I motion for her to get in her car before I get in mine.

I even go so far as to hold the door open for her, like the gentleman I can sometimes be. She gives me a strained, slightly frustrated smile as I close her door, then get into my own car.

Her windows aren't tinted the way mine are. So despite her best efforts, I can clearly see she and her sister are having some kind of tight-lipped argument. Her sister is also flailing her arms all over the place. Which is quite entertaining. I'm only half paying attention to what's behind me as I back out of my spot, and nearly end up getting hit by a little old lady, also driving a powder-blue Buick.

Rian's eyes are wide, one hand covering her mouth as I slam on the brakes and narrowly miss losing the back end of my car.

Once the old lady passes, and I'm sure I'm in the clear, I back the rest of the way out and give Rian a jaunty wave as I pass her car.

Her sister is right. I don't need the money. In fact, if I wanted to, I could replace this Tesla with a brand new one. But that's not really how I do things. Just because I have access to excessive funds, doesn't mean I want to fritter them away on unnecessary toys. Well, more than the ones I already have. I secured three quotes for the repair to make sure my dealership wasn't trying to scam me.

Regardless, it's the principle that matters. Hitting someone else's car in a parking lot and driving away is a shitty thing to do. And while I feel bad that Rian seems to be the one taking the heat for it, someone needs to assume ownership for the mistake.

Besides, it'll give me an opportunity to talk to her again. And despite her prickly demeanor, or maybe because of it, I'm hoping it's going to be her I deal with.

CHAPTER 3

NEGOTIATIONS

RIAN

"I seriously can't believe you!" I keep a tight grip on the steering wheel so I don't end up flailing, as my hands want to do when I'm agitated like this.

"That guy was a total asshole." Marley slouches down in the passenger seat with her arms crossed over her chest like a petulant teenager. Which isn't far from reality some days. It's hard to believe she entered the world before I did, considering her lack of maturity in this current situation. Those three extra minutes of life haven't made her any more aware of the repercussions of her actions.

"You hit his car! He had every right to be an a-hole." I'm still going to perseverate on the cleavage comment, and maybe find a way to use that sexist remark to my advantage when it comes to managing paying for the paint job.

"He was parked way too close to me. It's his own damn fault I hit his stupid, pretentious car."

"Well, I guess you should've waited him out and told him about his subpar parking job instead of ruining his paint job. Like we can afford three thousand dollars in repairs right now!"

"We'll have the money when we sell those two houses on the beach in a couple of weeks, and the trust comes due soon, so it's not even really an issue."

"The commission and the trust aren't supposed to be for some guy's paint job."

"Well, he seems to like your rack. I say you use your boobs to get some kind of Tesla repair discount so we don't have to use the commission money." Marley pulls out her phone and taps away on the keypad.

"I'm not using my boobs to get a discount." I'd like to say it's odd that my sister and I often have the same train of thought, but it's not. Being twins means that we frequently already know what the other one is thinking, or planning, before it happens. The more I think about it, the more I consider the validity of her suggestion, regardless of how abhorrent it seems.

She gives me her bitch brow. It's the expression where she arches a brow evilly, with a knowing look. "Why the hell not? That asshole was hot, which are two of your favorite qualities in a man. And rich. He's a rich, hot asshole. And he thinks you're hot."

"I do not like hot a-holes, and he does not think I'm hot." The truth is, I have a very bad track record when it comes to dating attractive men; they always turn out to be grade-A jerkfaces. I hit the brakes when the light turns yellow and come to a stop before it changes to red. It annoys the person behind me, but I'm nothing if not a safe driver, unlike my sister.

"I saw the way he was checking you out. You need to capitalize on his hormonal impulses. Use it to get us out of having to pay for his scratched paint."

"Are you suggesting I sleep with him so we don't have

to pay for the repairs?" I don't know why I sound appalled. I shouldn't be the least bit surprised that Marley has intimated this. It's totally something she would consider.

"I didn't say anything about sleeping with him, but I find it interesting that's where your head went."

"That's what you were implying!"

"Actually, no, it wasn't. I'm just saying he's smokin', and he clearly thinks you are too, so you can use that to cut our paint-scratch bill."

"Well, if he thinks I'm hot, he thinks you're hot. So maybe you should sleep with him." I pull into the driveway of our duplex and come to a jerky stop.

"Not true. He doesn't want to hump my rack; he wants to hump your rack."

"Our racks are nearly identical, much like everything about us."

"Again. Not true. I'm a B cup and you're a C. You have way more curves and your butt was made for twerking."

I glare at my sister. "Are you quite done?"

"Based on how angry you look, I'm going to say yes. It's not an insult, Rian; it's a compliment. I'm a stick with boobs. You actually have a shape."

"Please stop."

I'm more than a little annoyed by this whole situation. I'm also concerned about having to part with thousands of dollars for an unforeseen car repair. We have financial goals we need to meet in order to execute our plan, and this is going to cause a setback. I don't like setbacks. Especially the financial kind. We've had more than our fair share of those over the past decade, and we're finally getting our lives on track. I don't want anything to mess that up, especially not an antagonistic suit.

For the past few years we've been making a decent living in the real estate market, but the real money is in flipping, which requires a lot of capital and a fast turn-around. The quicker the flip the better, and the right piece of property can mean big profits. The kind that can make a bank account sing "Hallelujah." As long as Marley doesn't hit any more Teslas.

I get out of the car, slamming the door a little harder than necessary, and round the vehicle, popping the trunk. It isn't until I get a load of the whole bunch of nothing in-side that I remember all my groceries are still in the cart in the store where I left them, my hour of price matching wasted.

I bang the trunk closed and walk around to the front of my car, where smudges of black paint mar the bumper. My car once belonged to an elderly person who could only tell if she was close to something when she hit it, so it's no wonder I didn't notice the paint smudges until now, since all the edges have dings. None of which are my fault.

"I think you need to look at the positives in this, Ri," Marley says as she follows me up the driveway to the side entrance. "At least I wasn't driving the good car." She pats the Acura on the hood as we pass.

It would be smarter financially to have only one car, but the truth is, we need two. And one of them has to be nice. Arriving at a showing in a beater doesn't scream success, and in the real estate market, driving a nice car says very loudly: *I'm successful, buy from me, sell through me!* It's a fake-it-till-you-make-it world out there.

So Marley gets to drive the Acura to all the open houses, and I drive around in an old Buick previously owned by a person who hit stationary objects on a regular basis.

I key in the code and drag my poor, already achy legs to the second-floor apartment, Marley following close behind. It's a far cry from the home we grew up in. But when you're orphaned at eighteen, left with a mountain of debt and an army of enemies, you learn to appreciate what you have, even if it isn't much.

This little duplex was a gift from our grandmother, God rest her beautiful, intelligent soul, because without it, Marley and I would've been homeless a decade ago. It's the only thing we have left from Deana Sutter. Thanks to our fraud of a father, everything else we had was either repossessed by the bank or put in foreclosure.

Marley is an excellent agent and I'm very adept at the money-managing side of our venture. But this bill for the paint is an unexpected expense and puts distance between our financial position and our house-flipping goal. And the ones in the Hamptons are incredibly desirable, particularly the properties surrounding the Mission Mansion.

It's a beautiful, although rundown, estate in the more affordable part of the Hamptons, if any of it can actually be considered affordable. Anything on the beachfront boasts prestige and exclusivity, but this unique property and its location make it a desirable piece of real estate, despite the work it needs.

From what we've observed over the past few years, it's the homes owned by elderly couples or widows and widowers surrounding the mansion that make the best investments. They're tired of the maintenance, of the busy beaches on the weekend, and the inevitable changes that come with time. They want the warmth from down south, where the temperature never dips below zero. They're also the same people who last updated their home in the early eighties or nineties, so everything is out of date. And surprisingly for the Hamptons, the prices of some properties aren't as astronomical as one would think.

Once we have the capital on hand, we want to buy one of those houses, bring it into the twenty-first century with a facelift, and flip it. Between our savings and our trust, we'll finally have enough to make cash offers so we don't have to worry about mortgages and credit. Our ultimate plan is to continue to sell real estate, but to move in the direction of flipping more houses until we can afford to buy the Mission Mansion—the gorgeous, neglected estate in Hamptons Bay that was once owned by our grandmother.

I don't want to flip it, though. Ideally, with enough financial backing, we could renovate and turn it into a bed-and-breakfast. Convincing Marley that's a good idea is where the challenge lies. She's not attached to it the same way I am.

Besides, it's a crapshoot since we don't know when, or if, it will go up for sale. But it's been empty for years, and the market is crazy right now, so I have a feeling it's just a matter of time. It's a big dream and an even bigger numbers game. I love numbers. So much. They make me happy. They give me peace. But not when they're in the form of dollar bills being drained out of our bank account by rich, Tesla-driving, a-hole hotties.

After a quick shower, I throw on leggings and a T-shirt and settle on my bed with my laptop. I have notifications from the online dating profile my sister set up for me, without my permission, as a joke.

They make you take a survey—which Marley kindly answered for me. I went back and adjusted all the information because I was curious who I would match with, and what algorithm they use to determine the compatibility score. I'm most interested in looking at the men who are incompatible, rather than the ones who are—just to see who would be bad for me. Unsurprisingly, it's all the really hot guys.

My history with hot guys hasn't been particularly promising, so I tend to steer away from them. They're generally unreliable and fairly self-absorbed—both in and out of bed.

The guys with a higher compatibility rating tend to be less attractive, but also less likely to screw me over. I went out with a guy named Terry the other day. We had coffee. Well, I had coffee and he had decaffeinated herbal tea.

He asked me out again yesterday. This time for dinner. I'm not 100 percent convinced there's much of a connection there, but we're supposed to be a nine out of ten on the compatibility score, so I said yes mostly as a social experiment. Maybe the awkwardness was first-date jitters and the second one will be better.

I'm not sure I want a man in my life, regardless. They make things complicated. I already have daddy issues, and my last long-term relationship went up in flames—that was years ago, right after the rest of my life took a giant crap. I haven't had a lot of time or energy to invest in another person who isn't my sister. Also, getting dumped is the worst. If I could get more comfortable with the whole casual fling thing like Marley is, that'd be ideal.

At midnight, as I'm getting into bed, my phone buzzes with a message. I give it a cursory glance, sometimes I get messages on that dating app at this time of night. I assume all the lonely losers are lying in bed, wishing they weren't alone. Not me. I'm happy to have my entire double bed to myself. Most of the time. And I have a pretty decent vibrator to take care of my physical needs when the loneliness takes its toll and dating is too much effort.

Except it's not the dating app. It's a message from a number I don't recognize. I slip under the covers and key in my password.

Hi. It's Pierce, the guy you nut smashed with a grocery cart and whose car your sister scratched.

Can you shoot me your email address so I can forward you the quotes?

I debate whether or not I want to respond at such a late hour. I decide to wait until the morning. It is midnight, after all. Most people who have to work in the morning are already asleep. Maybe he's the kind of suit who makes his own hours.

The following morning I wake up to the wisps of a very X-rated dream, which takes place in a grocery store. I also wake to new messages from Pierce—who incidentally was the star in my dream. My imagination has decided he's very well-endowed.

Pierce: Guess that's a no.

That message is followed by three pictures, each a quote from a different body shop. They're all very similar in price. I fire a message back, and blame my lack of forethought on the fact that I'm only half awake.

Rian: My sister was the nut smasher, not me. Do these quotes include the sexist comment discount?

The humping dots appear, indicating he's composing a message. But after two minutes the dots disappear and suddenly my phone rings, making me jump. I pull the covers up to hide my stupidly hard nipples—not that he can see them.

"Hello?" My voice is still sleep raspy.

"Hi. Is this Rian?" Why does my name have to sound so sinful coming out of his mouth?

I cover the receiver and clear my throat before I answer. "Yes."

"It's Pierce. Did I wake you?"

"Yes. I text in my sleep."

"What else do you do in your sleep?"

"Isn't it a bit early for innuendo-laden conversation be-tween virtual strangers?" I don't give him time to answer that question. "So I've done some thinking."

"And what kind of thoughts have you been having, Rian?"

Dirty ones, about you and me in the produce aisle. I keep that inside my head. "I think it's only fair that you discount the repair bill on account of that sexist comment you made about my cleavage."

"Is that so?" He sounds amused.

"Mmm. Also, Marley said you parked way too close, so it's your fault she scratched your car in the first place."

"Ah. That's some interesting logic."

"If you'd left her more room, maybe your car would be fine." I don't honestly expect him to discount the bill, but I figure it's worth a shot.

"Do I need to remind you that your sister fled the scene of an accident and I was kind enough to refrain from call-ing the cops on her?"

"But can you even prove it was her in the first place? What if you're scamming us? And really, you kind of stalked us in a grocery store, I'm not sure that's much better." Why am I engaging with this guy? I mean, other than to keep him on the phone so I can listen to his sexy voice. Also the lower half of my body has started pinging.

"Well, considering it's a custom paint color and there's still lots of it on your bumper, I'm not sure it would be all that difficult to prove. Unless you've taken your luxury se-dan to the car wash since our introduction yesterday."

Sarcastic turd. "Maybe I have. Maybe this alleged proof doesn't exist."

"Doubtful. I'm willing to negotiate terms, though."

"Terms for what exactly?"

"The repair bill. We could discuss them, say over drinks?"

"Excuse me?" I can't imagine I heard that correctly. "Can you repeat that please?"

"We could negotiate the cost over drinks. Just a couple hours of your time during which I'm sure we can come to an amenable agreement."

"Are you asking me on a date?"

"We can call it that if you want."

It suddenly clicks what he's trying to do. "Hold on a second. Are you trying to blackmail me into having sex with you over a car repair? Because if that's your angle, I'm sorry to tell you, but you can't put a price tag on my vagina. She is not for sale."

Half of me is flattered that he thinks sex with me would be worth trading for a three-grand car repair. The other half of me is disgusted that I'm flattered at all.

Three grand is a pretty hefty price tag, but still. Only a few cars have parked in my garage. I'm not interested in letting another one in there simply to avoid paying for a repair, even if the car is a nice one and is owned by a seriously hot man.

"Whoa. Simmer down, sweetheart. I'm not trying to blackmail you. You were the one asking about a sexist comment discount. All I'm suggesting is that we discuss how to proceed over drinks. They can be of the nonalcoholic variety if you're worried about being under the influence around me. And for the record, I neither said nor implied that sexual favors would be involved, but I'm quite intrigued that you've automatically assumed it would be included in the deal."

I *pfft* into the phone. "Oh, come on. The implication

was totally there. I mean, who trades a three-thousand-dollar car repair for a date unless they have money to burn and are too much of an a-hole to get laid without black-mail? There will be no sexual anything and there will be no date. I don't even know you. You could be some crazy sociopath who's been stalking me and my sister at grocery stores, waiting for the right time to strike." That crime story marathon I watched last week probably wasn't the best idea.

"I can assure you, I'm definitely not a sociopath. If you change your mind, you know how to get in touch with me."

And then he hangs up.

I stare at phone in complete disbelief. "What the heck?" This has to be some kind of weird game. Maybe the date thing is to throw me off. Maybe he thinks he's being funny. I have no idea. I don't even have a last name for this guy. Just Pierce; hot a-hole in a suit. I hope I never hear from him again, although I realize it's unlikely since Marley and I still owe him money.

Much to my dismay—sort of—Pierce messages me again the next day.

Pierce: Reconsider drinks yet?
Rian: No.
Pierce: You sure?
Rian: Yes.
Pierce: Okay. Just checking.

Of course I've reconsidered, probably a hundred times in the past two days. But I can't say yes now. Not after I automatically assumed he was bartering for sex. Not that someone like him needs to barter for anything, especially not sex. I'm sure women regularly fall for the *sweetheart* business and his pretty smile. Which is the exact reason I won't say yes. It's on principle. I also have that date with Terry next week and I don't like to date more than one guy at the same time because it gets confusing.

For the next two days it's more of the same from Pierce.

Pierce: Root beer float?
Rian: Isn't there a dirty song about that?
Pierce: Why is it always about sex with you?

I don't respond to that one. Later that evening I get another message:

Pierce: Do you like tea?
Rian: Are you going to make a joke about tea bagging?
Pierce: Such as bag in or out?

I ignore that message. It's been days since he sent the quotes, and I'd like to get it off my conscience and my plate.

Rian: I'd like to wire the money to your account. Can you send the details, please?
Pierce: Sure. Meet me at Frescos on the beach. 7pm work for you?
Rian: Not happening. Bank details please.
Pierce: I'd prefer that this transaction takes place in person.

I look up Fresco's. It's a five-star restaurant. That place is designed for romance and seduction. The cheapest dish on their menu is a thirty-five-dollar chicken breast. I don't know what this guy's game is, but I don't want to play. Mostly. Sort of.

But I need to get this money situation sorted out and for him to stop messaging me. Because I'm starting to enjoy all this banter, which isn't good. So I relent, even though I shouldn't.

Rian: Meet me at the Starbucks on the corner of Montauk and Ponquogue in an hour. I'll bring a check.
Pierce: It's a date.
Rian: It's a transaction, and a way to get you off my back, don't read anything into it.
Pierce: See you soon ;)

I don't understand why this guy is pushing so hard to see me when all I've been is difficult with him. He probably likes the chase.

I would like to say I make zero effort to look good for my anticipated meeting with Pierce, but that would be untrue. I only make half an effort. I pair jeans with a long-sleeved shirt and fix my makeup—but just the basics, mascara and some lip gloss. I wear flats and I put my hair in a ponytail so as not to seem as if I care what he thinks of my appearance.

I go armed with his quotes, my checkbook, and a vague plan to whittle him down for his sexist comment. My goal is to set this up like a business meeting so he knows it's not a date. Even though I'm fifteen minutes early, he's earlier. A-hole.

He's sitting in one of those comfy chairs, with his hand wrapped around a grande something or other. He's not dressed in a suit this time. Instead, he's wearing a pair of distressed jeans and a T-shirt with a hot dog on it. I wouldn't have thought it possible, but he looks as good in jeans as he does in a suit, maybe even better.

It's horribly unfair. And all my girl parts are reacting accordingly. Which is bad. I have to remind myself that hot guys are always a bad call.

He lifts his eyes from the phone in his hand when the bell over the door tinkles. He sets his coffee on the little table and motions to the empty seat across from him as he rises. Why does his smile have to be so pretty?

"You're early." It comes out sounding like an accusation.

Pierce's smile widens. His lips are so full; his teeth are so white and straight and perfect. "So are you."

I drop down in the chair across from him and immediately produce my checkbook. "Shall we discuss the quotes?"

He ignores my attempt to get right down to business. "What can I get you to drink?"

"I'm not thirsty. Thank you for the offer, though." I should be somewhat polite considering my plan to haggle a discount.

I wait for him to take a seat, but he doesn't. It means his crotch is at eye level, and it's difficult not to allow my eyes to drift in that direction. Especially when he stuffs his hands in his pockets. I finally yield and meet his amused gaze. "I bet you're a caramel macchiato woman."

I frown. Maybe he really is some kind of crazy stalker. "How would you—"

"Your grocery cart was full of sugar. Lucky guess. Any modifications, or just the way it is?" He takes a step toward the barista.

"You can't buy me a coffee. I already owe you money. I don't want to owe you more."

"Technically your sister is the one who owes me money. I'm just lucky I get to deal with you instead." I can't tell if he's being sarcastic or what since I don't think I've been a particular joy to deal with thus far.

I lurch out of the chair and duck around him with a complete lack of grace so I can get to the counter first. I place my order and attempt to pull up my app, but Pierce reaches around me and scans his first. I mutter a reluctant *thank you* and wait for the macchiato I had no intention of purchasing, but am very much looking forward to drinking—even if it's on Pierce's dime.

He stands right beside me while I wait. "You look nice," he says conversationally.

I glance in his direction. "Thanks."

"What're you doing after this?"

Probably going home to masturbate to the image of your pretty face. "I have to work."

"Do you do that from home?"

"Sometimes." I don't enjoy being asked questions about myself, partly because my family history is less than ideal. It's one of the reasons I struggle with dating. The whole let's-get-to-know-each-other part is a problem. For most people, banal questions about family and employment are easy to answer, but not for me.

"You're a real talker, aren't you?" Pierce asks, that wry smile still in place.

"Sometimes." The barista passes me my drink and I follow Pierce back to the table he's secured for us. I notice we're tucked into a corner.

"You sure had a lot to say last week in the grocery store."

"Well, you were throwing out accusations, and making sexist comments, so of course I had something to say, which brings us to the reason we're here." Using that as a way to bring it back to business, I pull my checkbook out and the quotes. "I'm willing to cut you a check for the dealership quote, minus twenty percent for objectifying me."

"Do you work in sales or something?"

"Or something, not that it has anything to do with you being sexist or my sister hitting your car. Your quote is for $3122. A twenty percent discount would bring it down to roughly $2500."

He sips his coffee, or whatever it is, regarding me from over the rim. "If you think that's fair, you can go ahead and write a check for $2500."

I can't believe he doesn't even argue over the 20 percent. Or that this could be so easy.

"On one condition," he adds.

Of course. I set down the pen. "And what would that condition be?"

"You agree to go out with me."

I frown. I'm sure it's an unbecoming expression.

That ever-present grin widens and his eyes, quite literally, twinkle as he clarifies. "On a date."

"No."

"Why not?"

"Because."

"Because why?"

Because you're gorgeous and I'm attracted to you and it makes you exactly the kind of guy I should definitely not *go out with.* "I don't understand why you want to go out with me. It's not as though I've been particularly friendly, or even a little nice or encouraging."

He leans forward, as if he's going to tell me a secret. "I find you attractive, and I like that you're sassy and not a pushover. I also like a challenge."

"I'm seeing someone." It's not exactly a lie since I have a date with Terry later this week.

"Oh." Pierce's smile disappears, and he leans back in his chair. "Why didn't you say something before?"

"It's new, and I didn't feel as though I owed you an

explanation." I'm not sure why I feel as though I owe him one now either.

"Are you exclusive?"

"I don't date more than one person at a time."

"Why not?"

"I just don't." This guy is super-insistent to the point of being unnerving.

"Okay. Fine. I like that you don't want your attention divided. I don't like mine divided either, so when this thing with this current guy doesn't work out, you can go out with me."

I take that to mean he's accepting the 20 percent chauvinist-remark discount, so I fill out the check. "What makes you think it won't work out?"

He hitches a shoulder and motions between us. "Because there's chemistry here, and I doubt you'll be able to ignore it indefinitely."

"Wow, it's surprising you can fit through a door with the size of your ego." I pass the check over and give him my sweetest smile. "I added four dollars and seventy-five cents for the coffee."

He may be right about the chemistry, but there's no way I'm going out with him. That's a recipe for certain disaster.

CHAPTER 4
DATE

RIAN

Two days later I'm standing in front of my closet, surveying my dress options. I'm going out with Terry tonight. I'm not excited. At all.

Marley flops down on my bed. "Wear the green dress. It brings out your eyes."

"I wore the green dress last time." I pick out a hot-pink wrap. "What about this?"

Marley cocks her head, her long, wavy ponytail skimming my comforter. "Is that new?"

"I've had it for a while." The neckline is pretty low, though, which is why it has yet to make an appearance. I shimmy into the dress, adjusting the top so the girls are mostly contained.

Marley nods her approval. "You should definitely wear that."

I inspect my reflection in the mirror with a critical eye. "I don't know. I think there's too much cleavage."

"This is a second date, right? What's his name again? Trent?"

"It's Terry."

Marley makes a face. "Right. Can we rename him Trent? It's so much cooler."

"No, we can't rename him." I smooth my hands over my hips. This dress is great for highlighting curves, but the chest exposure is extreme for me. I lean forward at the waist, which only makes it worse. "I should wear a camisole."

"Do not ruin that dress with a cami. Unless you want to send the message that you're not interested in sleeping with him."

"There's no rule that says I have to make that kind of decision by date two."

"Honestly? You're twenty-seven, Ri. Don't waste your time on someone who doesn't make you tingle when you look at him. If you're not interested in getting horizontal with this guy, why go out with him? Especially with a name like Terry."

Typically I would agree, but I need a distraction from the dreams I keep having about a certain hot suit. Plus, Terry seems safe. "Terry isn't a terrible name."

"You're only saying that because the last guy you matched with was named Eugene." She rolls onto her back and moans, "Oh, Terrrrry, right there, that's it, Teeerrrrry."

"Is that necessary?" I retie the wrap in an attempt to achieve more coverage.

"I'm demonstrating how unsexy his name will sound when you're moaning it later tonight."

"I'm not sleeping with him tonight, so you can give it up."

"The fact that you don't *want* to sleep with him is a problem."

"I didn't say I don't want to, just that I'm not going to." I don't think I want to sleep with him.

She crosses her legs and props her chin on her fist.

"Maybe you should cancel and we can go dancing or something. You can borrow one of my dresses and pick up some supersexy hot guy and hump each other on the dance floor to loud music."

"It's too late to cancel. And I hate nightclubs. Drunk, sweaty guys are not my thing. Besides, Terry and I have a lot in common."

"Loving numbers and chocolate martinis doesn't scream compatibility. Also, I don't think men should love chocolate martinis, it seems wrong. Like guys who drink Shirley Temples." Marley rolls off the bed and bats my hands away, adjusting the dress so I'm showing more instead of less of my lady lumps. "Maybe you have too much in common. Maybe you should be looking for someone who's less . . . numbery."

"*Numbery* isn't even a word, and we're a nine-out-of-ten match according to the compatibility test." The whole nine-out-of-ten thing has me fascinated.

Terry is an accountant, which means he loves numbers the same way I do. The consistency and the variables turn me on. Terry doesn't seem to have that effect on me, and while that should technically deter me, I actually find it reassuring. Lack of sexual chemistry means I'm less likely to lose my head over him.

Marley sighs. "Are there any sparks? Do you need to bring spare underwear with you when you're on a date? Do you want dinner to be over so he can be your dessert? If no is the answer to any of these questions, then this date is pointless."

"Relationships are not just about sex, Mar."

She pushes me out of the bedroom and into the bathroom, forcing me to sit while she retrieves the hair dryer. "If there isn't any chemistry, you're friends."

I ignore the chemistry bit. "We're going to Fresco's for

dinner tonight." It was his idea, not mine. Maybe the romantic setting will help with the lack of sparks.

She pauses with a brush in her hand. "Really? That's swanky. So he must be feeling you. Now the most important question is: Who's paying?"

"I didn't ask. I'll have to wait and see." Last time we went Dutch. It was just coffee. He's really upping his game.

My sister sighs dramatically. "Seriously? If he doesn't pay and he doesn't make an attempt for a real goodnight kiss, you have to cut him loose."

The idea of his tongue in my mouth makes me shudder, but I keep quiet. Marley does my hair and makeup. I'm not the best at putting it on myself, but she's a pro.

She forces me to wear a pair of wedges that are two inches higher than I'm used to, because they make my legs look longer. I don't need any help in that area. I'm five eight, my legs are already pretty damn long. It's a short walk, though, so I should be fine. I make sure I have my wallet, phone, lip gloss, and mace tucked away in my purse, and I'm ready for this date. Which I'm still not excited about.

"I'll text in an hour to see if you need saving," Marley says as I head for the door. "And if you're not coming home tonight, make sure you let me know. And text me an address so I can call the cops if you stop responding to messages."

"You're getting ahead of yourself."

"I'm being positive."

By the time I get to the restaurant, my feet already hurt, but dinner is a sit-down event, so I'll be able to get some relief from these ridiculous shoes.

I spot Terry as I approach the front entrance of the restaurant. He's sitting on a bench, head bent over his phone. He hasn't noticed me yet, so I take the opportunity to give him a full assessment with a "Marley lens." We have very different criteria for what we consider to be viably datable, but even I can admit that Terry is a little . . . lacking.

Marley has a propensity for dating surfer boys and beach volleyball players. Bleach-blond hair, rock-hard abs, and a killer smile are pretty much all she requires. Conversation isn't a top priority. Marley doesn't do serious. Neither do I, but casual isn't my strong suit either, which puts me in a bit of a predicament.

Terry is dressed in a pair of beige pants and a short-sleeve button-down. Both are wrinkled, which I find odd. His shoes are brown and he's wearing sports socks. They should be white, but it appears he's washed them with something red, because they have a slight pink hue. In fact, his shirt might also have the same slight pinkish hue.

Terry's profile states he's six one, but I think that's an exaggeration. He's maybe six feet at best. He's also incredibly lean. So much so that I imagine if I put on a pair of his boxers, there's a good chance they would fit me just fine. Not that there would ever be a reason for me to put his boxers on, but for the sake of waist-size comparison.

His brown hair is parted to the side, and I note the hint of recession at his crown. I'm not so vain that he needs to have a full head of hair forever, but I think his profile said he's thirty-one. I imagine in ten years he'll have a horseshoe.

Like the rest of him, his face is narrow. He has a straight nose and brown eyes. I assess my bodily reaction to his physical appearance. Nothing. No tingles. No zingy zaps anywhere. Which is perfect, because it ensures that I won't make any hormonally charged decisions.

I take a deep breath, check my dress—dear Lord this cleavage is insane—and cross the last few feet to stand in front of him.

He looks up when my shadow crosses his phone. He does a full-body scan, eyes moving down to start at my shoes and he works his way slowly up. His gaze gets caught at my chest.

"Rian. Wow." He pushes to a stand, eyes still fixed below my neck for a few more seconds before he finally makes eye contact. His cheeks flush pink, and he jams his hands in his pockets. I think there's a grease stain on the front of his pants, but I don't want to look too closely since it's near his crotch. "You look"—he gestures to my dress—"incredible."

"You look . . . great." My voice is all squeaky. If he knew me well enough, he'd know I'm lying. How great can one look in pants that are a size too big with a stain on the front and a wrinkled shirt? Also, he's sweating. His forehead and upper lip are dotted with perspiration. I don't remember him being this gross last time.

He glances down and then back at me, the flush in his cheeks deepening. He laughs a little and tugs on the collar of his shirt. "I came straight from work. I had a bit of an issue and didn't want to be late."

"Is everything okay?"

"Oh yeah. Fine. Just, uh, problems after a lunch meeting. Everything's fine." He pulls a tissue from his pocket and dabs at his upper lip. "We should go in." He motions me forward, holding the door open like a gentleman. With these heels on, he's almost exactly the same height as I am. Definitely not even six feet, then.

"Would you prefer to sit inside or on the patio?"

"Either is fine with me." My skin pebbles at the blast of air conditioning as I enter the restaurant.

He runs his knuckle along the back of my arm, and my first instinct is to step away from his touch, which isn't a great sign. It's one thing not to have heaps of immediate chemistry, but such an adverse reaction is way bad. "Maybe the patio will be better? It's warmer out there."

I glance at his glistening forehead. "Sure. As long as you're okay with that."

"Oh yeah. Totally okay with outside." His eyes drop and bounce back up. Maybe the camisole would've been advisable after all.

The hostess leads us to a lovely little table on the outdoor patio, away from most of the other patrons. There are a couple of business meetings taking place, and one or two other couples, but we have a bit of privacy, at least until the rest of the dinner crowd shows up.

The view is spectacular, beautiful sandy beach leading to the ocean, quaint houses dot the coastline, and in the distance, the Mission Mansion rises against the bright blue sky, its once stately splendor diminished by the lack of upkeep. I take the seat facing away from it, so I don't fixate on it.

We're still a long way from sunset, but a few clouds streak the sky, and in a couple of hours the view will be devastatingly romantic. At least it could be without sweaty, disheveled Terry sitting across from me.

I ask how his day was and he launches into an animated monologue about an account he's dealing with. I order a glass of white wine and he orders ginger ale—Terry doesn't drink—and I attempt to listen. He drones on and on about the subtle nuances of an accounting mistake made by one of the rival firms in Long Island. I'd like to say it's riveting, but he even makes numbers sound boring.

As the patio continues to fill with dinner patrons my mind wanders, and I start thinking about Pierce, who I haven't heard from since I cut the check at Starbucks. I want to be glad that he hasn't messaged or called since then—that means that he got the hint that I'm not interested.

But, I begin comparing the two men, which is completely unfair. That's like comparing an old, withered potato with a perfectly curved, ripe banana.

Movement to my right catches my eye. I glance over in time to see a tall, leggy blonde who looks like a much more proportional, but incredibly beautiful version of a Barbie doll, being led to the table across from us. She has a to-die-for body, wrapped in a pale-blue sundress, and her face is angelic. A man follows a few steps behind, head bowed as he scans his phone. He's wearing khakis and a crisp white polo, paired with white deck shoes.

I have never seen that combination look so damn good on the male form before. He's built as hell, the sleeves pulling tight around his biceps and the rear view is magical. I finally make my way up to his face.

A face I recognize. *Pierce.*

Sonofabitch. I can't believe he kept pushing for a date and he has a damn girlfriend. A supermodel girlfriend. I bet they have supermodel-y sex in front of mirrors so they can enjoy the view of themselves.

I get trapped in the forest green of his eyes for a moment. They really are a piercing shade. His name is rather apt. One side of his mouth quirks up. He's caught me checking him out. Of course he knows how hot he is. And now I've boosted his horrible ego with my blatant appreciation, while I'm on a date with someone else. I'm a terrible person.

I realize I'm still staring and that appreciation shifts into a leer of disgust. I can't believe he's dating someone so beautiful and has been flirting with me behind her back up until two days ago. What a jerkface. His gaze shifts to my date and his brow lifts as he takes a seat across from Barbie's real-life sister. I have a disturbingly perfect view of both of them.

"Do you know him?"

Shoot. That's my date. I turn my attention back to Terry, keeping my voice low. "I've done business with him before." It's not a total lie.

"Oh." He nods slowly, eyes darting over to the blonde. "Do you want to say hello?"

I wave a hand around and take a gulp of my wine. "Oh no, he's a lying a-hole." I raise my voice and try to focus on my date instead of drilling holes in the side of Pierce's face with my laser-beam eyes. "So tell me about your plans for the weekend."

"Oh, well, I've got this conference next week in New York, so I'm leaving on Sunday morning. On Saturday I usually take my grandmother lawn bowling."

I reach out and put my hand over Terry's, but immediately withdraw because it's clammy. "That's so sweet that you do that with her."

"Have you ever gone lawn bowling?" He's talking to my cleavage.

Despite my irritation, which I'm unsure I have a right to, considering the dress I'm wearing, I bat my lashes, playing up the sexy angle, especially since Pierce is sitting to the right of me with his model girlfriend. "No. I can't say that I have."

"It's actually a lot of fun. People think it's just for seniors, but it's not. I've been playing since I was ten. I won the regional tournament last year. I have a trophy and a plaque and everything."

"Oh wow, that's great." I can't believe I'm on a date with a man who lawn bowls with his grandmother because he likes it. And he thinks he's a hotshot because he beat a bunch of geriatrics in a tournament.

"Maybe you'd like to come with me?"

I catch myself as I recoil and try to recover, plastering a smile on my face. "You mean this weekend?"

He fidgets with his straw and shrugs, then wipes his lip sweat again. His perspiration problem has amplified while we've been sitting here, in the shade. I watch as a bead trickles down his temple and lands on the tablecloth.

Ew.

To make matters worse, his eyes keep darting around, but always seem to end up below my neck, and he's doing this weird swallowing thing. "If you're not busy," he says on a croak.

I give him my sad face. "I'd really love to, but I have to work this weekend." This is true. We have two houses to show not far from here, on the beach. We're also planning to canvas a few of the elderly owners who might be looking to sell while the market is hot since we're almost at the point where we can purchase one of our own properties to flip.

"Maybe another time, then. Um, if you'll excuse me for a second, I need to use the restroom." He shoves his chair back, nearly tipping it over. He also almost takes out a server carrying a tray of drinks when he bursts through the door.

A snort comes from my left. I glance over to find Pierce coughing into a napkin. I throw a glare his way and covertly scratch my temple with my middle finger.

Marley was right, I should've cancelled this date while I had the chance.

CHAPTER 5

GLOBES OF GOODNESS

PIERCE

"Okay, what's the story?" My sister, who's in town on business for the weekend, kicks my shin with her pointy-toed shoes, eyes shifting to the table across the patio.

I hiss in pain. "What the hell, Amalie?"

"Did you sleep with that woman?" She tilts her head in Rian's direction, devious smile turning up the corner of her mouth.

I rub my shin. "Stop staring, and no, I didn't sleep with her." I know it's Rian and not her sister based on the mole above her lip. Also, that dress she's wearing highlights all of her incredible assets. I'd like her in my bed. But not for sleeping.

"Did you *try* to sleep with her? Did she reject you? Is that why she's glaring? She's stunning. What's she doing with that guy? He's so awkward." She flips her hair over her shoulder and makes an attempt at subtlety as we watch the guy nearly trip over his own feet and knock over a server with a full tray on his way to the bathroom. At least that's where I assume he's disappearing to. Maybe to puke out his nerves.

"Maybe he's a nice guy. You ever consider that?" Even if he is a nice guy, he's way out of his league with this one.

"I'd be more inclined to believe that's a pity date. Or maybe some weird setup. Maybe she owed someone a favor."

"Why do you even care?" I glance over at Rian, now sitting alone at her table. I almost feel bad for the poor guy. He doesn't look like he has the balls to manage her. I won't be the least bit surprised if he had to go to the bathroom to deal with a woody. I'm halfway there and I'm not sitting across from her, getting the full impact of that dress's neckline.

I thought she looked great in workout gear, but it had nothing on this dress she's wearing tonight. The hot-pink fabric conforms to every luscious curve, and the deep V highlights the globes of goodness underneath.

"Because that little eye contact thing between the two of you could set an entire forest on fire. There is zero chemistry between that woman and that guy, but the two of you, zing!" Amalie snaps her fingers a few times, drawing several people's attention. She bites her lip and sinks down in her seat, lowering her voice, likely so she doesn't attract any more unnecessary attention with her enthusiasm. "You two might as well be shooting lust rays at each other. And that dress is gorgeous. I wonder where she got it. Lex would love it."

Lex, otherwise known as Lexington Mills, son to Harrison Mills, the owner of one of the most renowned hotel chains in the world, is my sister's fiancé. He bravely asked her to marry him a month ago.

Amalie glances down at the classy, sophisticated dress

she's wearing and frowns. "I don't know that I have enough boob to fill that out the way she does, though."

"I'm your brother, don't talk to me about your—" I make a few random gestures in the direction of her upper body.

"You're so uptight sometimes." She leans in closer and lowers her voice. "So give me the scoop. I want to know why that woman keeps trying to kill-fuck you with her molten-lava stare."

In low tones, I give her the abridged version of the parking lot hit-and-run, the grocery store, and our coffee date. I leave out the fact that I relentlessly antagonized her for a date, until I found out she's seeing someone. That this guy is a better option than me is almost offensive.

"Oh my God. There are two of her?"

"They don't look exactly the same, but pretty close."

"Wow. Too bad this one has a boyfriend. Or whatever he is." She raises a finger, eyes lighting up. "But if they look almost the same, maybe her sister's a viable dating option."

"Her sister is the one who hit my car and drove off. Why would I be interested in her?"

"Hmm." Amalie taps her lip. "Good point. Well, based on the complete lack of fireworks between those two, *and* the way she keeps looking at you, I'd say you might have a chance with her."

I lean back in my chair and drag my eyes away from Rian, who is, in fact, glaring at me. Although, to be fair, I've been checking her out rather shamelessly since we sat down. "She's looking at me like she wants to punch me in the dick, and she's on a date."

"There's a fine line between hate and lust. And that date is clearly not an even match. What do you want to bet she's one of those gorgeous women who doesn't actually realize how beautiful she is, so she dates down?"

"Maybe she's dating him because he drives a nicer car than she does."

"Doubtful." Amalie flips through the menu. "Oooh, I think I want lobster tonight. I'm buying, by the way."

"Oh, hell no. There's no way you're paying. I invited you out for dinner; I'm paying, little sister."

Amalie sets down her menu and bats her lashes. "It's not up for debate, Pierce. I just got a promotion and a raise, it's my treat."

I can give her that. I'm not used to letting her, or any other woman I take out, foot the bill. It annoyed the hell out of me that Rian tacked the four seventy-five onto the check for the paint repair, which is crazy since she haggled me down 20 percent. It's not as if I need to cash the check, anyway. "Fine, you can pay. How's Lex handling that?" I sip my craft brew, enjoying the hoppy, bitter flavor.

"My promotion?"

"Yeah. You'll be working more hours, won't you?"

"I'll actually be putting in fewer hours. And I have two days a week where I can work from home, so it's a good transition."

"Didn't he want you to come work for the Mills Hotels?"

She twists a lock of hair around her finger. "He would set up a desk beside his in his office if he could, but I really enjoy what I'm doing right now. I love him, but I don't know how productive I'd be working in the same office. We'll see what happens in the future. I need some time to be engaged before I go switching jobs again."

Prior to her current job, she worked for her ex-husband's family—in the magazine division of their massive media corporation. It's understandable that she's a little sketchy about working with her fiancé's family.

"How are things with you and Dad?" She looks like she wants to hide behind her menu for asking.

I shrug. "They are what they are. As far as the firm is concerned, I'm just taking a few months off."

She bites her lip. "Mom says he'll get over it."

"Eventually. In a decade or so, I'm sure he will." I fucked up recently. In a very big way. The fact that my sister is actually speaking to me is a miracle. I feel horrible about the error I made and how it's affecting her.

Her nose wrinkles. "Have you seen the dolls? The ones that company came out with?"

"Unfortunately, yes." I'd like to bleach my brain and erase the visual forever.

My father is the creator of Amalie Dolls. They're those horrible plastic dolls with the strange blinking eyes that little girls like to play with. But they're not regular dolls, they have a chip and now, with modern technology, an app. You can program them to interact. It's so weird what sells, and for almost twenty years they've been incredibly popular.

The basis for them had been my sister, obviously. Over time, as Amalie grew up, the line grew with her, morphing into something far more expansive than a single blond, blue-eyed doll in the image of my sister. There are Amalie Dolls of every ethnicity, hair color, eye color, and skin tone. You name it, it exists.

Earlier this year, my father decided he wanted to broaden the market and make "life-sized" Amalie Dolls. In all honesty, the move was a bid to keep the Amalie Doll trend alive. For the past several years, despite the continued attempts at expansion and new developments, sales have been slowly, if not steadily, falling.

I work as a partner in the law firm my father hired to manage his business. After college, I went to law school, because that's what my father wanted me to do, never mind that I had zero interest in law. I specialized in patents, because again, that's what my father felt would be best for my future with the company. I'm very detail oriented. Most of the time. Except when I was pushing the paperwork on this one through, I was a little distracted. It was right at the same time my brother, Lawson, decided we needed to jump on buying the house I'm currently renovating. He's a fly-by-the-seat-of-his-pants guy, so it was all very last minute. I'd pulled a couple very late nights, so I was light on sleep and prone to making mistakes. Usually they aren't quite this big, though.

While I'm good at my job, I didn't have to put in a lot of years or time to earn my partnership in the firm. When your family drops millions into legal counsel, there's incentive to make them happy, and me being a partner made my father happy. It also means that I'm responsible for his account and not a whole lot else. Nepotism at its finest.

So I should be able to manage the few accounts I handle. I should've paid more attention to the wording in the patent, but because I missed one crucial detail, things went sideways. A porn company found a loophole in the patent, and the life-sized dolls took a very different, very X-rated turn. Hence the reason I have some time off while that mess gets sorted.

"You have to admit, the dolls were a genius move on their part." Her eyes light up with mischief. "I might get one for Lex before they're pulled from the shelves."

I'm sure my face must reflect my horror. "Dad would lose his mothereffing mind if you did that. You can't support the company that turned a children's toy into a blow-up sex doll."

Amalie rolls her eyes, as if I'm an idiot for even suggesting this. "You make it sound so much worse than it is. Besides, how would he find out if I bought one? It's not like he has access to my credit card statements."

"I don't know how you can be okay with dolls that look like you being used for personal pleasure." The thought actually makes me nauseous.

"They don't really look like me. They're just blond-haired and blue-eyed blow-up dolls."

She's wrong about that. Those dolls look eerily like my sister, which is why I was so disturbed when I discovered what had happened with the patent. Wording is always paramount.

"Anyway, enough about that. How are things going with Lawson? Is he driving you crazy yet?"

I laugh at that. "He's a hard one to rein in sometimes, but so far it's been fun." Particularly the renovation part.

Amalie smiles. "Good, I'm glad to hear that. He needs somewhere to focus all that energy, doesn't he?"

"He sure does." My younger brother has lots of ideas and not a lot of direction. Like me, he works for our father, except on the marketing side of things. Mostly it's him posting pictures of the damn dolls on social media, and coming up with ways to push the app.

In his spare time, which he seems to have a lot of, he's been dabbling in the real estate market for the past few years, specifically in the Hamptons, where he lives year round. Since going on hiatus, I've taken on a more active role in the renovation side of his venture, where I'm able to foster the more practical aspect of my detail-oriented skill set.

Hands-on has always been where I excel the most. Back in high school I loved reading blueprints and seeing how things fit together. Unfortunately, that wasn't an approved career path. Not when my father had worked so hard to take us from lower middle class to elite. When Amalie was born, we lived in a tiny three-bedroom house. By the time she was six, we lived in a mansion.

"We're supposed to sell a property I've been working on this weekend." I'm actually pretty excited to see what it will go for.

"Will you reinvest in another one?"

"That's the plan."

Amalie tilts her head a little. "You really like this, don't you?"

"Yeah. It doesn't even feel like work." At first the time off from the firm felt like a punishment, but then I started working with my brother, getting my hands dirty, but in a good way. "As much as I don't like that Dad's still pissed at me, I think my screwup might not be the worst thing in the world."

"Have you thought any more about talking to Dad about this?"

I have discussed my unhappiness with my career path more times than I can count with Amalie. "I don't think now is a good time."

"It'll never be a good time. You can't spend your life doing something you hate."

"I can't really afford to do what I'm doing if I lose my trust or my shares in the company, though, so I can't quit either." Jesus. We're such spoiled brats.

Amalie frowns. "Dad wouldn't pull your trust or take your shares."

"He's threatened it before."

"When you were screwing around in college, being a frat boy. This is different. I'm not working for the family business and I still have my trust and my shares," she says with a raised eyebrow.

"You're the reason the company exists in the first place. It's different for you. Anyway, we'll have to see how things go this summer, and if this can be more than a hobby. For now it's a good break if nothing else." The server delivers our appetizers, saving me from further discussion on this subject. I spear a few leaves of lettuce. Amalie has calamari and it smells fantastic. My salad smells like garlic. "Can we share?"

"Having healthy-choice remorse?"

"Not if you're willing to let me steal a few of those."

She pushes a few to the edge of her plate, specifically the ones that look like tiny octopi. "These ones always freak me out. You can have them."

"So generous." I steal her fork out of her hand and eat the ones she's already speared.

"Hey!"

I hear an indelicate snort from my left and glance over. Rian is still alone. Maybe her date isn't coming back. I revel in the joy of that possibility as I take another moment to appreciate her. She has a nice neck, long, slender, and her hair is pulled up away from her face, highlighting her cheekbones and the delicate line of her jaw. When I reach her face, I find her glaring at me.

Man, she looks pissed off. Maybe because I keep staring.

She slaps her napkin on the table and pushes her chair back with a loud scrape. She smooths her dress out, squares her shoulders, and takes four long strides, stopping in front of our table.

My grin widens as she gets right up in my personal space, one fist propped on her curvy hip. Her height puts her chest close to eye level—okay, I still have to look up a bit—but I'm forced to lean back in my chair to make eye contact.

"Hi again," I offer by way of greeting.

"You!" She points a shaking finger at me.

I glance at my sister, who has set her silverware down to watch whatever is about to go down. Her smile is almost a smirk. It's an expression we share since our mouths are the same.

Rian turns her attention to my sister and takes a deep breath, plastering on a strained, but somewhat piteous smile. "I'm so sorry to interrupt your dinner, but I feel it's only right to warn you that your date is an a-hole."

I'm not sure if she's censored because we're at a restaurant, but I think it's pretty cute.

Amalie's grin widens, showing off her perfect, white-toothed smile. Her nose crinkles, and she directs her next statement at me. "I love her already."

Rian's brow furrows, her confusion obvious as Amalie turns back to her.

"He really can be an asshole, but I assure you, he can also be very sweet. When he feels like it."

"I find that hard to believe, considering he's been messaging me all week until about two days ago asking me on a date, and he's been eyeing all the women in this restaurant," she says with faltering accusation. "Which is . . . ridiculous since you're absolutely gorgeous. Like a Barbie doll. And I mean that as a compliment—"

"Untrue," I cut in. I like how defensive she is of a woman she doesn't even know, although she's wrong about me eyeing every woman in the restaurant. I'm solely focused on her.

Her angry gaze cuts to me. "Are you serious? What the heck is wrong with you? She could be a model and your eyes are all over the place. And you've been asking me out relentlessly!" She snaps her fingers in my face. "You are unbelievable! I mean, I know this dress is a bit"—Rian makes flailing motions and then tries to hide some of her cleavage—"but that's not an excuse!"

"Oh, you have every right to show those off." Amalie nods her appreciation, which I echo silently.

I bark out a laugh. "You're not helping here, sister."

Rian's head whips around, her mouth opens and then clamps shut with a click of her teeth. She blinks a few times. Her cheeks flare red. "Sister?" It's a tiny, mortified whisper.

"Mmm. You don't see the family resemblance." I gesture between Amalie and me. Really, it's only our smiles that are similar. "Rian, meet Amalie, my baby sister. Amalie, meet Rian. Her twin ruined the paint job on my Tesla and fled the scene a couple of weeks ago. I mistook Rian for her last week and said a few things that may have painted me in an assholish light."

"Shocking," Amalie deadpans. She extends a hand to Rian. "If it makes you feel any better, Pierce treats his car like it's his girlfriend, since he doesn't have a real one."

A hint of a smile appears as Rian takes Amalie's offered palm. "That's outrageous. He seems like such a catch."

Amalie's grin grows wider and she turns to me. "I really, *really* love her." Still holding Rian's hand in hers, she asks, "Are you single?"

Rian's eyes go wide. "I'm on a date. And I like men. A lot."

Amalie throws her head back, laughing. "I like men too. A lot." She lifts her ring-clad hand and wiggles her fingers, the diamond-wrapped one glinting in the sun. "I'm not asking for me." She inclines her head in my direction in the least stealthy head nod ever.

"I already have a date." She gestures behind her.

Amalie frowns at the empty table. "Hmm. That's a complication. I suppose Pierce is someone to consider in the future if this current date doesn't work out." She releases Rian's hand.

"Uh, right."

"Rian?" Shit. Her date is finally back.

All three of us turn to find him standing behind her. I have a moment to better assess him. I guess he might be okay looking, in an I-work-in-a-cubicle-with-no-sun-ever kind of way. His pallor is pasty white, and he appears to be sweating. Why is she dating this guy?

"Oh, Terry! I, um . . . you're back! I was just saying hello." She motions to us, her cheeks flushing again.

He gives us a nod of acknowledgment, then his eyes roll up and he blows out a breath. "I, uh . . . I'm not feeling very well. I probably should've cancelled. I went for Mexican at lunch with some colleagues and my digestive system is sensitive—" His explanation is interrupted by a loud gurgle.

Rian takes a cautious step back. "Oh, that's . . . unfortunate."

"I'm so sorry. I was really looking forward to our date. And your dress is . . . wow. But with pants this light, there really is no margin for error. I should've worn brown or black. Even dark gray would've been okay since I had the enchiladas. I need to go. Now. I have to . . . I'll call you?" And with that, Terry turns tail and basically sprints back the way he came, one hand over his mouth, the other on his ass.

Rian stares at his retreating form with a cross between incredulity and possibly relief, although it's hard to tell.

"I think it would be in your best interest not to answer should he have the balls to call you again. Any man who can't handle Mexican food should be on a no-date list," Amalie says.

"Yeah." Rian expels a breath and looks at her empty table. "Well, uh, I guess I should be on my way, then."

"Or you could join us?" Amalie suggests.

She's almost as persistent as I am.

Rian raises her hands like she's been subjected to electroshock treatment. "Oh no! No, thank you. I should go.

I've embarrassed myself more than enough for one day."
She takes a step back. "It was nice meeting you, Amalie.
I apologize for . . ." She gestures to me as she continues to
back away. "Anyway . . ." She grabs for her purse. "Bye!"

I watch the sway of her ass as she rushes for the door.
She avoids touching the handle, using her hip to push it
open.

Amalie claps her hands. "Well, that was fun!"

"I'm glad you're entertained."

"I seriously think you need to ask her out."

"She's already said no." Several times. I nab one of the
mini octopi from her plate and pop it in my mouth.

"So ask again."

"Annoy her into dating me, then?"

Amalie sets down her fork, her expression turning serious. "Whatever works. Come on, Pierce. I haven't met a
girlfriend since you and Stacey ended things, and this one
seems like fun."

"Stacey was the one who ended things when she decided to screw someone else behind my back."

"She's a ladder-climbing bitch and you're better off
without her. But that was a long time ago, Pierce. You need
to put yourself back out there. Not every woman is out for
your bank account or your ability to slingshot their career."

"I know that, Amie. I'm not sure if you noticed, but she
thinks I'm an asshole. And just because you haven't met a
girlfriend doesn't mean I haven't dated. Besides, it's not
like I'd want to bring anyone to a family dinner."

"Mom and Dad have been a lot better over the past
couple of years."

She's right. They have. I love my parents, but their relationship is tumultuous at the best of times. At the worst
it's downright embarrassing. "I never know if they're going
to start some kind of bickering match at a family get-

together. I don't want to be subjected to that kind of drama, let alone bringing anyone else into it."

She sighs. "Fine. I'll give you that, but you haven't introduced anyone to *me*. There hasn't even been a mention of a girlfriend in forever."

"I don't want to be tied down."

"You don't have to be into BDSM to be in a relationship." Her grin drops when I don't laugh. "Seriously, Pierce. You're such a good guy. It'd be a shame not to share that with someone else because you got burned once, don't you think? I mean, look what happened to me, and I'm willing to get on the horsc and ride again."

"Such a bad analogy."

"You know what I mean."

I appreciate her concern, but I don't want to get into this with her. Not right now, if ever. I'd met Stacey in my last year of law school. She was smart, fun, great in bed, gorgeous. I'd proposed after graduation. She'd said yes.

I'd made partner fairly quickly after that. But when I started to reconsider my passion for law, Stacey had been quick to shoot down my suggestion that I walk away from this career to try another. And then my mother got sick. Her battle with cancer combined with my uncertainty as to the future of my career was enough to push Stacey into someone else's arms. Someone who could propel her career forward faster than me. I haven't been in a serious relationship since.

People could only let you down if you allowed them to. So I didn't.

CHAPTER 6

BEACH HOUSE SIXTY-NINE

RIAN

"I told you that dress was perfect!" Marley thinks this whole thing is hilarious. She's far more interested in Pierce being at the same restaurant than the rather abrupt end to my date. I still haven't told her about him asking me out. Relentlessly.

"My boobs were like a homing beacon." I dig my spoon into the half-pint of toasted coconut ice cream. I stopped at the convenience store down the street from our duplex on the way home and stocked up on snack foods since I missed out on dinner.

"That's crazy that he was at the same restaurant as you! What are the chances?" She bites into a giant carrot with an obnoxious crunch.

"Slim to none."

"I can't believe you called him out. Well, okay, I can totally believe it, because it's definitely something you'd do, but damn, I would've paid good money to see that go down."

I sink into my chair and shovel more ice cream into my

mouth. Now that I'm home and I've had time to reflect on my actions, I'm highly embarrassed by them. This is why I'm the paper-and-numbers girl and Marley is the one who deals with the public, because I do humiliating things. Granted, he *was* staring at my chest, and has been pestering me for a date, which would've been very rude if he had a girlfriend.

His sister seems nice, though.

One of our phones buzzes on the coffee table. Marley is quicker than me and nabs them both, rolling her eye when the screen on mine lights up.

"For the love of all that is good and holy, do not message him back." She tosses it to me.

Terry has left four new ones. He's been pretty desperate to reschedule the date. He's thrown out three options for the week after he comes back from his conference.

I refuse to acknowledge that I'm disappointed it's not Pierce. I don't bother to check the messages. Pierce's sister is right, any guy who can't handle Mexican food should be on a no-date list.

"Maybe you'll meet some hottie on the beach this weekend." Marley flips through channels, looking for decent brain candy. At my quizzical expression, she elaborates. "Angelica and Lauren rented a beach house for the weekend, remember?"

"Oh, right, it totally slipped my mind, to be honest." Angelica, better known as Gel, and Lauren used to live down the street from us. They've been roommates forever and moved to New York City a few years ago, so we don't get to see them very often anymore. They're obviously doing well if they can afford to rent a Hamptons beach house for a weekend getaway.

"It's on the calendar in the kitchen. Have you packed a bag yet?"

"What?" I think I'm slipping into an ice cream coma.

"They invited us to stay the weekend, or did you forget about that too?"

"Why would we stay with them when we live near the beach?"

"We don't live that close, and because it's fun and convenient. It's supposed to be ridiculously warm this weekend, bikini weather even. If we stay with them, we can get our drink on and have some fun with friends we rarely get to see."

"But we have the open house on Saturday afternoon, and then the bungalow on Sunday," I remind her. We're holding back on listing the second house until Sunday morning on the request of the sellers. They want the other property on the beach to sell first, hoping to entice buyers their way. Nothing stays on the market long in the Hamptons, so we anticipate it will sell during the open house. On the up side, we'll have a gauge with which to price the bungalow. The better the price point, the better our commission and the happier the sellers are.

"They're not scheduled until the afternoon, and we'll be close since Gel and Lauren rented a place in Hampton Bays. We can have fun tomorrow night, and then when the open house is over on Saturday, we can get our party on again."

"I don't know, Mar." My sister loves to get her drink on, especially when she's with Gel and Lauren.

"Oh, come on. We can have a girl's night out. We'll go to a fun bar on the beach. You can wear one of my dresses and hook up with some hot guy named Trent, who buys you drinks instead of making you pay for your own like Terry."

I don't actually like it when guys buy my drinks. It's as if they think because they spent ten dollars on me, it automatically means they can get handsy. "You know how I feel about the bar scene."

"You need to let loose, and we haven't seen Gel and Lauren in forever. Plus, we can troll the beach for potential properties. I was talking to another agent yesterday and there might be a couple of places coming up for sale, something about people being concerned about zoning laws or whatever. Consider it a multipurpose work-vacation."

She has a point. Staying on the beach has some definite advantages. Not the least of which is the opportunity to canvas desirable properties and their owners.

"It's supposed to be a gorgeous weekend. We can work on our tans. Check out hot guys playing beach volleyball."

Always with the volleyball players. "Okay. Fine. But no getting superhammered tomorrow night. We need to be functional for the open house on Saturday. Based on the market, this property should go for over asking and that check I cut for the Tesla paint job won't hurt so much."

Marley's tongue peeks out and her eyes light up. "Has he texted you again?"

"No. And I can't imagine he will after tonight." I should be thankful, not disappointed. I grab my empty ice cream container and head for the kitchen. "What time will Gel and Lauren get to the beach?"

"Gel said noon and we can meet them there any time after that. I already have the address and everything."

We've been working our butts off lately, and it would be nice to enjoy the beach and not just show the view to other people.

The following day, Marley's ready to hit the beach at 12:01, having already packed my bag for me first thing this morning. I check the contents and toss in some jeans, a T-shirt, and extra underwear.

We take the Acura—I'm driving because I don't trust Marley for obvious reasons. She keeps changing the radio station, blasting music, and singing off-key; she also doesn't know any of the lyrics.

I turn it down so I can speak without yelling. "Have you heard from Gel and Lauren? Are they at the beach house already?"

"Gel texted while you were in the shower and said they were leaving soon."

"Should you check in with them? It would be kind of weird for us to show up before them."

"Sure. I can do that." Marley shimmies to the music as we make the short trip from our duplex off the beach to the rental.

"Hey! How's it going? We're on our way and superexcited to see you," Marley says into the phone. There's a pause, and then she turns the music all the way down. "Oh no. That's not good. Is Noodles going to be okay?"

"What's going on?" I turn right onto the street that leads not only to some of the oldest beachfront properties, but also the Mission Mansion. It's farther down the beach, and in one of the more exclusive areas, but the sprawling eight-thousand-square-foot mansion is hard to miss since it's the biggest home in the immediate area.

Marley holds up a finger, *uh-huhing* and *mmming* a bunch of times before she says, "Okay, keep in touch." She ends the call as I pull into the driveway of a gorgeous beach house, a big, bold, black 69 fixed to the front door. I shift the car into park and wait for her to explain what's going on.

"They're not going to be here until tomorrow at the earliest," she says.

"What happened?"

"Noodles ate a pound of butter."

"Oh God." Noodles is Gel's labradoodle. She's the sweetest dog, but she eats everything. Including socks. "Is she going to be okay?"

"Yeah, but she has wicked diarrhea, so they have to stay put until she's done destroying their lawn. They said they'll check back with us tomorrow, but they might not be here until Sunday, depending."

I'm surprised at my disappointment. Not just because I don't get to see Gel and Lauren, but also because I'd been looking forward to a weekend on the beach. I put the car in reverse.

"What're you doing?"

"Going home."

"Park the damn car, Rian."

I take my foot off the gas and hit the brake. "We can't stay if Gel and Lauren aren't here."

"We sure can! We have the code. She's forwarding the email from the rental company. As far as anyone knows, we're Gel and Lauren."

I consider this for a moment. Possibly so many moments that Marley feels she needs additional justification.

"They rented the place for the weekend. Why let it go to waste because their dog ate a pound of butter? Gel said she wants us to enjoy it if they can't. It's too late to cancel and they can't get their deposit back."

She has a point. I shift back into park and Marley lets out a whoop of excitement. "We're gonna have so much fun!"

I cut the engine and step out into in the warm sunshine. We're having such great weather for May, and I'm looking forward to spending some time on the beach soaking up the sun—with my laptop, but still.

The two-story clapboard house is a sight to behold and the craftsmanship is stunning. Marley keys in the code while I lug our bags up the front walk. The interior is as breathtaking as the exterior.

While the outside retains that classic Hamptons style, the interior is modern and fresh. Granite countertops and a massive open floor plan including a wall of windows facing the beach make this a desirable piece of property.

Marley lets out a low whistle. "Can you even imagine how much we'd get for this if we could convince the owner to sell?"

"I was thinking the exact same thing." There must be some kind of brochure around here somewhere with their information.

I leave our bags at the entrance and cross through the massive kitchen, stopping at a wrapped basket that contains two bottles of wine—one white and one red, as well as antipasto and crackers. Whoever rents this place out pays very close attention to the fine details. There's even a bowl of fruit and a list of all the amenities nearby. It seems like whoever the owner is, they go the extra mile to make the renters feel comfortable.

I hold up the personalized, handwritten note wishing Gel, Lauren, and Noodles a pleasant stay. "I wonder if we'll meet the owner or if he or she has someone who manages this place for them."

A set of sliding doors lead to a gorgeous cedar deck that smells new, a fabulous hot tub set to the right. This place is amazing. I'm so glad Marley convinced me to stay, because this is so much better than a weekend in our duplex, driving back and forth to the beach for open houses.

The crash of waves on the beach, kids laughing, and the low strains of music coming from somewhere close by are suddenly drowned out by the sound of a lawn mower revving to life. A few seconds later the mower appears from under the deck. Then the person pushing it comes into view.

Sweet mother of all things delicious.

The man pushing the mower is dressed only in a baseball cap, a pair of cargo shorts, and bright-green running shoes. His bare, tanned back is covered in a sheen of sweat that glistens in the sun. The glistening isn't the only notable thing about this man. It's the broad shoulders and tapered waist, along with the flex and shift of muscles in his back and arms as he pushes that mower across the lawn.

I've never considered lawn mowing to be a sexy activity until this very moment.

I want to call out to Marley so she too can get a look at our lawn boy, but I don't want to alert him to my presence. I hope he has to spend the entire weekend tending the gardens. The flowers are already in full bloom. They must need a lot of watering. I envision this man, standing with a hose in his hand, spraying those lovely rose bushes, turning the water on himself when he gets too hot, letting it run down his back in sweet, sweet rivers . . . God, it's hot out here.

When he reaches the edge of the lawn, he pivots with the mower. His ball cap is pulled low, obstructing my view of his face.

But that chest. So broad. So defined. And there's an actual six-pack. Not a pretend six-pack, or a four-pack, or the kind where the guy is obviously flexing to achieve definition, but a real one. And just from pushing a lawn mower. It's not even uphill.

I'll be so disappointed if his face isn't awesome.

I take a few steps backward until I hit the sliding glass door. I knock on the window until Marley finally appears. "What's up?"

"Check out our lawn boy."

Marley follows my head jerk. "Whoa."

"Right? I wonder if he comes with the house. He can mow my lawn any time he wants." I say this rather loudly so I can be heard over the lawn mower.

Except as I'm yelling, the mower cuts out, which means everyone within a five-mile radius can hear me, including the lawn boy. I try to move Marley in front of me so I can hide behind her and disappear back into the house, but she bars the way.

At the same time, lawn boy pinches the brim of his hat between his thumb and finger, lifting it as he tilts his head up. He's about thirty feet away from us, but based on his smirk, he definitely heard the *mow my lawn* comment. Awesome. Maybe I can blame it on Marley. My cheeks heat; not because the sun is shining on my face, but because I'm embarrassed to have been caught saying something so highly inappropriate. I take in the rest of his face. Oh man, it's not disappointing in the least. He's smokin'. And wait . . .

I squint and frown, wondering if this in an optical illusion. Or maybe I'm developing an obsession. The more I look at him, I swear, lawn boy is Pierce. The same Pierce whose car Marley hit. The Pierce who I embarrassed myself in front of last night. Yup, that Pierce. I give my head a slight shake and blink a few times.

Lawn boy cocks his head to the side, his brow furrowing in an expression that likely matches mine.

"Is that . . . ?" Marley doesn't finish the question as lawn boy abandons his mower and heads for the stairs.

I'm mesmerized by the flex and pull of muscles in his shoulders as he grabs hold of the railing and takes the steps at a jog. When he reaches the top of the stairs, I'm hit with the full force of his hotness. I'm also now 100 percent sure lawn boy is Pierce, which is . . . confusing. How does someone who maintains lawns afford to drive a Tesla and wear Tom Ford suits?

If his chest was impressive at a distance, it's magnificent close-up. I take in the wall of lightly tanned, toned muscle. Even his nipples are nice, which is an odd thing to notice. I allow my gaze to travel lower, over the defined ridges of his abs, past his navel, down that sweet treasure trail to where his shorts hang low on his hips, revealing the deep, cut V that leads to the magic handle behind his fly.

I'm staring at his crotch, and possibly about to start drooling based on my sudden need to swallow several times in succession, and he's now standing in front of me. Also, Marley is elbowing me in the side.

"Huh?" I lift my stubborn gaze back to Pierce's face.

He's smirking. Of course. His tongue peeks out of the corner of his mouth, and he drags a sweaty forearm across his forehead. "You're stalking *me* now?"

I snap my jaw closed and cross my arms over my chest, in case my erect nipples are visible through my shirt. "What? No. Of course not."

His smile slips, the cockiness replaced by confusion as he looks from me to Marley and back again. "What're you doing here?"

"I could ask you the same thing." We've been running into each other a lot lately. This is getting weird.

"I own this place; it's a rental."

"So you're not the lawn boy?" Sometimes I suck at words.

CHAPTER 7

BEACH BABES

PIERCE

Rian's eyes go wide, and the very pink hue to her cheeks deepens further.

I laugh, not just at her expression, but at her choice of words. From the few interactions we've had, she doesn't seem like she holds back much. "Lawn boy? That's not very politically correct."

"Maintenance man, you know what I meant," she mutters, eyes dropping. They land on my chest and slide lower before shifting to the side.

"So now you know why I'm here. The mystery remains as to why the two of you are."

"Our friends rented this place for the weekend." Marley gestures behind her. "They invited us to join them. You can call to confirm that if you don't believe me."

"Mar." Rian elbows her sister in the side.

"They actually called yesterday about additional guests. Interesting that it happens to be you two." I can only imagine what my sister will have to say about this. She was all over me about Rian last night. Something about it being kismet. I'm sure she'd consider this proof that we're meant to be. But if I'm being honest, I kept asking her out prior to discovering she was seeing someone because I find her attractive beyond the surface. Antagonizing her gave me a thrill I haven't felt in a while. Based on how she's looking at me, I think it's probably mutual. Today's outfit consists of a pair of cutoff jean shorts and a gauzy shirt, which gives me a fantastic view of her hot-pink bikini top. And that firecracker personality of hers is another check mark.

"Maybe we should go." Rian shifts uncomfortably. "This is . . . weird."

"Why? Because of the car? Or because you told my sister I'm an asshole?"

Rian blows out a breath, eyes trained on my chest as she says, "I thought you were checking me out while you were on a date."

I'm fighting a losing battle against a grin as she continues to justify her actions. "In that case, it was very kind of you to issue a warning about my wandering eye. Although that problem didn't seem to be isolated to *me* then, and it certainly doesn't seem that way now either."

Rian's gaze shifts up to mine, her *oh shit* expression priceless. I'd like to snap a picture of her face and add it on her phone contact, although I have a feeling she might not appreciate that.

"Well, I guess this settles it then. I'm going to go put my stuff in a bedroom, and you two can let this sexual tension fester some more." Marley turns around and struts back into the beach house, leaving me alone with Rian.

She's right about the tension. It's starting to make my boxers tight.

"You have to admit, it's interesting the way we keep running into each other lately."

Rian adjusts her shirt, which has slipped off her shoulder,

and fiddles with the end of her hair. "And every single one of those interactions has been embarrassing for me."

"I would say entertaining rather than embarrassing. Now, why don't we start fresh, and this time I'll try not to come off as a complete asshole, and we can pretend I haven't asked you out and you haven't said no half a dozen times, or accused me of trying to blackmail you into having sex with me." I grin as I hold out my hand. "I'm Pierce."

Rian bites her bottom lip, fighting her own smile. She slips her palm into mine. It's warm and soft, but her grip is firm. "Hi, I'm Rian with an *i* instead of a *y*."

"Hi, Rian with an *i*, why don't I take you on a tour of the house?"

She chuckles and ducks her head. Her hand is still clasped in mine. Maybe my sister is right—maybe I'm not alone in my appreciation of this woman and her sassy, give-no-fucks attitude. I already know she likes what she sees, the *mow her lawn* comment is proof of that.

I open the door and motion her inside. "When do you expect Gel and Lauren to arrive?"

"They might not be here until tomorrow. Their dog ate something he shouldn't have; they're waiting for the aftermath to pass before they put him in a car."

"Oh no, that's no good. Will Noodles be okay?" One of the prime features of this rental is that it's pet friendly.

She glances over her shoulder, looking a little surprised. "I think so. It's not the first time he's done it. It's just unfortunate it happened right before their vacation."

"I'd hate for them to miss the weekend, especially with the weather being what it is." I give her a tour of the kitchen, showing her where to find everything.

"The finishes in here are gorgeous. Who did all the work?"

"I did a lot of it myself."

Rian runs her fingertips across the countertop. "Wow. That's . . . impressive."

"I'm a handy asshole." I give her another wink, which causes her to flush again.

"Sorry about that," she mutters.

I lean in, getting into her personal space until she takes a cautious step back. "I'm just having fun with you. You're wound up pretty tight, aren't you?" Stepping around her, I motion for her to follow me. "Come on, I'll show you where the bedrooms are."

Her sister has commandeered the master suite, which I'm sure will only last until their friends arrive.

I open the door to the second bedroom. "You'll probably want dibs on this."

Her arm brushes mine as she steps inside. The room is spacious and light. The pale walls and white furniture are meant to echo the light, beachy feel of the house. "Who decorated this?" She runs her hand over the comforter and looks at the ceiling. Pushing up on the balls of her feet, she stretches to touch a crystal dangling from the chandelier. "The details are incredible."

I shove my hands in my pockets, reveling a little at the compliment. "I did, with the help of Amalie."

"Your sister." Her finger trails along the footboard of the bed. "She seems like fun."

"She used to get herself into all kinds of trouble when she was a teenager."

"Really? But she looks so sweet."

"That's how she managed to get away with so much." I follow Rian through the room. "There's a private bath through here."

She presses her palm against my shoulder, peeking in behind me to take a look. I tense at the unexpected contact and the shot of warmth that follows.

"Sorry." She takes a quick step back, hitting her elbow on the edge of the dresser. "Ow!" She sucks in a breath, rubbing the spot.

"Are you always this jumpy?"

And she's immediately on the defensive, again. "No. Sometimes. Not always. Just around people."

"All people?"

"No, just cocky, self-assured, shirtless ones."

I chuckle and head for the door. "Why don't I show you how to work the hot tub and the barbeque, and then I'll leave you to it?"

"Oh. Yeah. That'd be great."

The barbeque is pretty straightforward, as is the hot tub. Rian gets a kick out of the rules posted on the privacy deck. "Who would eat in a hot tub?"

"You'd be surprised." I pull the cover back over. "You wouldn't believe the things I've found in there."

"Do I want to know?"

"Probably not. Just because I post rules, it doesn't mean people follow them. I've found a lot more than leftover chicken wings in there."

Rian makes a face. "Like condoms?"

"Among other things."

She makes a gagging sound. "Maybe I'll skip the hot tub while I'm here."

"It's cleaned between rentals."

"Every time?"

"Every time."

"So why bother with the rules if you know they're going to get broken."

"Because if they break them, and I find out, I get to keep their cleaning deposit."

"Ah. Now it makes sense."

"Anyway. I should finish up the lawn so you can enjoy

your afternoon. I'm down the beach if you need anything."
I motion in the direction of my brother's beach house. It's
closer to the rundown mansion at the crest of the beach.

"Right." Her eyes dart down and then come back up.
"Okay, great. Thanks."

I turn to leave.

"Pierce?"

"Yeah."

"Thanks for being so nice about this, especially after
the car stuff." She gestures to the beach house.

"Like I said, it's just a car. And as long as you don't
throw any parties, we'll be fine." I leave her to settle in and
get back to work.

Fifteen minutes later the two of them head down the
path to the beach, towels and bags under their arms. Rian
gives me a wave, rushing to keep up with her sister. They
both have plastic cups with lids and straws.

I take my time on the lawn. Using the WeedWacker on
the perimeter, being extra thorough since it allows me a
great view of the beach and Rian. My patience is worth it.
Her cover-up lasts all of two minutes.

Sweet fucking Christ. That body is something else. Her
hot-pink bikini—it must be her favorite color—has ties on
either hip, holding the tiny triangles of fabric together.

Where her sister is all straight lines and long limbs,
Rian is lush and curvy. The two of them seem oblivious
to the attention they're drawing as they spray each other
down with sunscreen.

It doesn't take long for the volleyball players to invite
them to join in. Marley doesn't take much to convince, but
Rian stays put. She stretches out on her towel, facing the
beach house, and flips open a laptop. I go back to my weed
whacking.

After I'm done with the lawn I don't have any more

reasons to stick around, so I grudgingly head back to my brother's place. I find Lawson reclined in a lounger. Beside him sit Amalie Dolls in their own tiny beach chairs, wearing bathing suits and hats. A bottle of kid's sunscreen—a product endorsement—is positioned on the small table between them. I'm sure if I check our social media feeds, there will be a series of images posted with those damn dolls, probably talking about sun safety.

It's crazy what sells dolls.

"I don't know why you don't hire someone to mow the lawn. I'm sure there's some kid who would do it for twenty bucks." Lawson stretches his arms over his head and yawns.

I poke him in the stomach, hard. "Maybe you should mow a few lawns instead of drinking all those beers, brother. You're getting soft." That's untrue, but for a guy who likes to dress like a hippie and pretend he gives zero fucks about anything, he spends a lot of time in front of a mirror.

Lawson bats my hand away. "Fuck off. My abs are steel."

I head inside for a minute and grab the binoculars. Trip, my dog—whose full name is Tripod, because of his three-legged status—comes back outside with me. I need to take him for a run soon or he's going to go stir-crazy. He might only have three legs, but it doesn't slow him down. Plus, it'll give me a reason to stop at the rental again.

"You creeping on the hotties?" Lawson asks as I drop into the chair next to him.

"I'm keeping an eye on our properties." I scan the beach. Rian's bikini isn't difficult to spot.

She's lying on her stomach, pen poised between her lips, feet crossed over each other, legs swinging.

"You mean, you're keeping an eye on those girls renting out sixty-nine. Are they hot?" He grins like a perv.

"So you know that girl who hit my car in the grocery store parking lot?"

"How the hell could I forget? You bitched about it enough."

"Did I mention she's a twin?"

"No. You did not. Are they hot?" He takes off his sunglasses. "I wonder what a threesome with twins would be like. Do you think it gets confusing?"

"You're disgusting."

"Oh, come on. I bet you've thought about it, though, right? I mean, how could you not? Two hot girls who look the same, taking turns riding you. A threesome with twins is going on my bucket list."

I give my brother a look. "You do get how messed up that is, right? That's considered incest."

"They'd be doing me, not each other. So it's fine."

"I think you need to stop subscribing to porn sites."

"I only watch the free stuff. Anyway, back to the twins you're not going to have a threesome with, which is really too bad." After a few seconds of silence, he makes a go-on motion with his hands and folds them under his chin.

"They're the ones staying in beach house sixty-nine."

"No fucking way!" He grabs for the binoculars. "Gimme those. Dude, if you're not gonna try and get in there, I sure as hell am."

"There's not a chance in hell either one of them would sleep with you." At least I hope not. Especially since I'd like to be the one to get Rian into a bed eventually.

Lawson punches me in the side and nabs the binoculars, but I get him in a headlock. He loses his hold on them and they hit the deck, bounce once, and then slide through the three-inch gap between the glass panel and the bottom of the deck, landing on the ground ten feet below us.

"You dumbass! Now how am I supposed to check them

out?" He makes no move to find out if the binoculars sur-
vived. I'm pretty sure they're broken based on the fall.

"You're not. We don't have time for you to cross twins
off your bucket list this weekend. We've got an open house
tomorrow."

"Yeah, about that. I think we might want to reconsider
selling." He settles back in his chair.

"What? I put weeks into getting that place ready. What's
the point of holding onto it?" More than that, the financial
gain from selling is far more substantial upfront than rental
fees. I'm not currently pulling in a salary while I'm off. I
have money in my bank account, lots actually, but part of
the benefit of flipping the house is having more capital on
hand to make new purchases.

Lawson lifts his sunglasses and gives me his *chill out*
look. "Just hear me out before you shit a pile of bricks. I
know originally we were planning to flip, but what if we
could capitalize on the summer rental market?"

"We already have sixty-nine as a rental." Law and his
grand schemes. He always has one going.

"So what's one more to take care of, just for the summer? It's prime rental time. People want to be on the beach
in the Hamptons. It's a smart move."

"I don't know, Law. Aren't you kind of screwing the
agent out of a commission?"

"No. I actually got some insider info that the Franklin house is going up for sale this weekend and it's right
down the beach from sixty-nine. It's a smart buy. The
Franklin place is in decent shape; all we'd need to do is
some minor renos to make it palatable for renters. Then
we bank all the money we make this summer. So if the
agent can get us in to see the Franklin house first, they'd
still get the commission."

"Is that possible?"

He shrugs. "I'll call and see what she can do."

I wait for him to pick up his phone, but he just sits there. "Don't you think you should do that now?"

"It's not a rush."

"The open house is tomorrow. And we want to know if it's a rumor or if it's actually true that the property is coming up for sale."

"Oh, it's true. I stopped by the Franklins' yesterday. Their granddaughter was over. We had a nice little chat." He grins and wags his eyebrows.

"Christ, Law, where's your damn moral compass?"

"Calm your tits, her granddaughter is twenty-three. She thinks I'm supersweet. Gave me all the details and made me promise not to say a word."

I shake my head and push up out of the chair. "You should probably still call, especially if you want to get in there first and make an offer." I leave him to it, annoyed at the abrupt change in plans. Working with Lawson is a lot like riding on a roller coaster. I'm willing to put up with it because I see the potential benefits of real estate and rentals. I've been working for my dad for five years and I like it less and less. Working with Lawson might not be easy, but I actually enjoy the renovation side of this, and the rental part hasn't been difficult so far, so I can see the allure.

As much as I enjoy what I'm doing, I don't like the idea of letting my father down, not when he's worked so hard to give us this life. I don't want to appear ungrateful for all I have, but I don't want to spend the rest of my life doing something I hate either.

CHAPTER 8

JUST BEACHY

RIAN

At five thirty Marley decides she's had enough of the volleyball boys, and we head back to the beach house.

She grabs my arm as she stumbles up the steps and flops down on the couch once we're inside. "Oh wow, it's so much cooler in here."

"You should put on some after-sun lotion." Neither of us is particularly fair, but she's been out there for hours and I doubt she thought to reapply. I cross through to my bedroom and root around in my overnight bag for the aloe lotion. By the time I return, she's relocated to her bed and she's already passed out. I adjust her position so she's on her side and put a garbage can beside her in case she can't make it to the bathroom. I didn't monitor her consumption, but she's had far more to drink than me.

While she's napping, I take a quick shower, throw on a pair of jeans and a loose shirt, and pull my hair up in a messy bun. An hour later she's still fast asleep and my stomach is rumbling. I don't want to wake her on the off chance she'll get up ready to party.

Instead, I head down the beach toward the restaurants so I can grab us some food.

There are some nice restaurants along the beach, many of which boast a lovely view of the Mission Mansion in the distance. We're still quite a ways off financially from being able to buy it if it went on the market, but we're closer now than we've ever been to the one part of our past that I'd love to have back.

I glance at the patio to my left. Couples sit across from each other, hands clasped, wine glasses full, appetizers waiting to be shared, bodies angled toward each other as they engage in private conversation. It's intimate and romantic, something I haven't had in such a long time. It's then I realize I'm back at the scene of my horrendous date with Terry and am once again staring at Pierce. Unless I had far too much sun. In which case, I'm having a hallucination and he's not actually here.

"Hey." He lifts a hand in greeting, a small questioning smile on his full lips. He's dressed casually in a pair of jeans and a crisp white golf shirt. I'm grateful he's fully clothed this time.

It means my mouth works slightly more efficiently. "I'm really not stalking you, despite how this looks." Or maybe my mouth is still a problem.

"That's rather unfortunate. I'm actually quite fond of the idea of you stalking me." He slips the papers in front of him into a leather messenger bag. "Where's your sister?"

"Sleeping off the booze she drank this afternoon."

"Ah." He nods in understanding. The server drops off a glass of wine and a plate of calamari, the delicious aroma wafts over me, making my mouth water and my stomach rumble.

I take a step back. "I should let you eat."

"Or you could join me this time." Pierce pushes out the chair to his right. "The calamari here is fantastic."

"Oh, uh. Thanks, but—" I take another step back, flustered.

"You don't like calamari?"

"I like calamari, but I—"

"Still don't want to have dinner with me?" he asks, head tilted, fingers tapping on the table.

"I was going to pick up some takeout and bring it back to the house."

"I thought you said Marley was sleeping off her drinks."

"She is. I'm not really dressed appropriately for this place, though." I adjust my shirt, drawing attention to my distressed jeans with the strategic tears all the way up my thighs.

"You look perfectly appropriate. Come keep me company." He taps the chair to his right again, eyebrow raised in challenge. As if this is some kind of dare.

The car situation is sorted out so there's no chance of blackmail, and he's been nice about us staying in his rental despite Marley and the hit-and-run. I don't want to be rude. I can order takeout and sit with him while I wait. It's not like this is going to turn into a date.

Pierce stands and pulls out the chair kitty-corner to him. He tucks me into the table before taking his seat again. Moving the calamari between us, he hands me a set of silverware and beckons the server over.

"What would you like to drink? My sister usually gets the sauvignon blanc with the calamari."

"That would be perfect, thank you." I try to recall what the cost per glass is from the last time I was here.

"We'll take a bottle, please," Pierce tells the server who sets a menu on the table and leaves us alone.

He props an elbow on the table and leans in. "You got

a little sun today." I startle when he skims my cheek, and once again, the connection between our eyes and the point of physical contact create a current that steals my breath.

I'm caught, trapped, unable to break eye contact.

The server returns with the wine, snapping the spell. I still haven't looked at the menu, so I ask for a few more minutes. I have to wonder how long we sat there, staring at each other, or if our server is just very fast.

Pierce takes a sip of his wine and I do the same, flipping open the menu so I have somewhere else to look that isn't him.

"Did you play football in college?" I blurt the question before I can really consider what I'm asking. It's a weird lead-in.

"Not college, but I played in high school. Why?"

I lift a shoulder. "You look like the kind of guy who would play. Were you a quarterback?"

"I played offensive line. Think you got me all figured out?" He stabs a piece of calamari with his fork and pops it into his mouth.

I roll my eyes. "No. You just have that look."

"What look?"

"The jock look. Like you played all the sports and were probably good at them without even having to work at it."

He laughs. "Well, that's untrue. I didn't love playing football, but my father wanted me on the school team so I endured it for a few years. I'm better at golf. What about you? Did you play sports in high school?" He leans back in his chair. "Wait. Let me guess. You were a cheerleader."

"I don't think I fit the cheerleader profile."

"Oh? And what would that be?" He nudges the plate of calamari closer to me, encouraging me to try some.

"Friendly, chipper." I unfold my napkin and spread it

across my lap. I cross one leg over the other, my foot brushing Pierce's shin.

"You don't consider yourself friendly?"

"What did you call me before?" I tap my lip. "Prickly."

"I like your prickly."

"You're kind of intense, huh?"

He hitches a shoulder and smiles. "So are you."

I shove another piece of his calamari in my mouth and browse the menu so I'm ready to order when the server comes back. This place is expensive and not what I would've chosen had I not run into Pierce. I settle on pasta—a smart and cost-effective choice.

"So is Amalie your only sibling?" I ask once I've placed my order.

"I have a younger brother. What about you?"

"It's just me and Marley. So you're the oldest of three?"

"I am. Let me guess, you muscled your way in front of your sister so you could be the first born."

"Ah." I hold up a finger. "That's where you're wrong. She was first out of the gate. I was behind her by three minutes. She took her sweet old time getting out, so she was born at eleven fifty-eight and I was born at twelve oh one, so technically we don't even have the same birthday."

"So you were prickly right from your first breath, then," he says with a smile.

"Seems that way."

"Tell me about the date you were on the other night."

Oh, no way. That was mortifying the first time around; I don't need to relive it. "There's not much to tell. You saw how it ended."

"I assume he's tried to reschedule, though."

"How would you know that?"

Pierce crosses one leg over the other, posture deceptively relaxed, but his eyes are sharp. "He's not an idiot. He knows he's dating up with you."

I'm sure my confusion is obvious. What does that even mean? "Dating up?"

"As in, he's aware that you're out of his league and that he's lucky to have had an opportunity to go out with you at all. Especially with a name like Terry."

"What's with everyone ragging on his name? My name is Rian. I sure don't have a right to make fun of anyone else's name." I take another sip of my wine, mostly to keep my mouth and hands busy. Pierce does that chuckle thing. I fight the urge to look at him, and lose. "What're you laughing about?"

"I think your name suits you perfectly, and I think Terry's name suits him perfectly, but I don't think you and Terry suit each other at all, so I'm curious as to how you met and how many times you've been out."

"What is this? Some kind of dating inquisition?"

"Like I said, I'm curious. Especially since you'll go out with him and not me."

"Well, I'm here now, aren't I?"

"Only by chance." He props his chin on his clasped hands, giving me his full attention. It's unnerving. "So back to this Terry guy. I want to know how he managed to get you to willingly go out with him, yet I have to pretty much blackmail you into it."

"If you must know, I met him through a dating site," I mutter into my glass.

"Excuse me?"

I glance up to find him staring at me with disbelief.

"Don't give me that look. Lots of people use online dating sites. It helps weed out the undesirables, and it's a lot better than the kind of guys I'd find in the bar."

"Based on what I witnessed the other day, I'm not so sure the site you're using is doing a very good job at the weeding part, or the matching you up with someone appropriate."

"Oh? How would you know what's appropriate for me?"

He lifts a casual shoulder. "I'm calling it how I see it. Terry isn't a good match for you. Even my sister agrees."

"Well, you're wrong about that. Terry and I are a nine out of ten on the compatibility scale."

He arches a brow. "Is that so?"

"It is so." Why do I enjoy this tension so much? I avoid guys like Pierce for a reason. I might be attracted to him, but I'm well aware nothing good can come from dating someone like him. Especially if he ever found out about my past and my scandalous family history. The last guy I told couldn't ditch me fast enough. His excuse? He couldn't associate with someone who came from a family of thieves. Those were quite literally the words that came out of his jerk mouth.

"And how exactly does one determine a nine out of ten level of compatibility?"

"There's a test."

"Of course there is." He pulls out his phone. "Which site would I find the test on?" He starts thumb typing. "Is it e-Love Forever, or The Right Fish, or oh, what about this one, LoversRUs?"

"It's none of those." I shrink down in my seat, my face heating under his scrutiny. "It's a paid site. Those are better."

"Ah yes, that makes sense. So Match4Life then?"

I purse my lips and glare.

"Perfect." He pulls his wallet out of his back pocket and flips it open, slipping out a black Amex.

"What're you doing?"

"Setting up an account so I can take the test."

"But why?"

"So I can see how compatible we are, of course."

"Oh, of course." I don't know him well enough to be able to tell if he's making fun of me.

We're both silent as he fills in the credit card information. Next he completes his general profile. My curiosity piques when he gets to the questionnaire portion of the test. I don't know what I want more, for the test to come back determining we're incompatible, or the opposite.

"Height, six two," he mumbles, "Am looking for, hmm . . ." He scrolls through the options. "What did you put down here? Hang out? Is that like playing video games in Terry's basement apartment in his mother's house?"

"Haha. He has a condo, and he doesn't live with his mother."

"So he says. Have you been to his place?"

"No! Absolutely not!"

He chuckles. "Good to know. So just dating then, or did you go with long-term?"

I hold my glass with both hands to keep from biting my fingernails. I feel far too exposed with this line of questioning. "I put dating."

He quirks a brow but says nothing as he clicks boxes and makes selections.

"You should put athletic for body type," I say, to be helpful.

"What did you put?"

"Average."

Pierce's gaze roams over me in a slow sweep. "There's nothing average about you, Rian. Terry is average. You are spectacular. Too bad that's not a category."

I watch as he types in his profession, a little surprised by his response.

"You're a lawyer?"

"I am."

"But you own rental property? Are you a real estate lawyer?" My mouth is suddenly dry, and I try to tamp down on the panic. I don't go by my given last name. It's unlikely he'd be able to connect me to my father and the shitstorm he caused almost a decade ago, and Pierce doesn't look old enough for that to be relevant. But still, it's another potential red flag. In the past, when people have found out who our family is, it can be painfully embarrassing. Career-wise it could be damaging.

He laughs. "No. I'm a patent lawyer."

That's a relief. "Here in the Hamptons?" I wasn't aware there was much to patent around here, except maybe boob jobs and collagen injections.

"No, I work out of Manhattan most of the time. It's not a particularly riveting job. Mostly it's a lot of paperwork and attention to small details. The rental properties are a hobby."

"How do you manage a hobby in the Hamptons when you work out of Manhattan? That seems like a long commute."

"I'm, uh, taking the summer off, so I'll be back to boring patents in Manhattan soon enough. But I like working with my hands, so for now it fits."

"If patents are boring, why are you going back after the summer?" I press.

Pierce rubs the blue-black nail with the pad of his thumb. "Obligation and financial security are the two primary reasons."

"Ah, but if those two factors weren't in the way, what would you do?"

"I'd create and fix things. As a kid, I was always taking stuff apart and figuring out how to put it back together, or making things out of other people's junk. Drove my dad nuts, but I loved it. Still do, I suppose."

I glance at his hands; the ones that did all the work on the rental. They're nice hands, despite the nicks and scabs and the one black nail, or maybe that's what makes them nice. "Well, you're good with them."

"You don't know the half of it." He winks, and I roll my eyes.

"You're getting distracted." I tap the edge of his phone.

"Right. Well, I think it's almost pointless to finish. I already know what the outcome is going to be."

"You think so?"

"Most definitely. The test will determine, without a doubt, that you and I are meant to be, and all this denying me the opportunity to take you on a real date is futile." He focuses on the test again. "Describe my personality in one word?" He scrolls through the list. "Hipster? Princess? I'm at a loss here since they don't have asshole as an option. Any suggestions?"

"Hmm, that's tough." I spin the stem of the glass. "What about professional, or athletic? Those fit."

"Professional sounds too stuffy, like I sit behind a desk all day and tell people what to do."

"Is that accurate?"

"Not currently, no. And athletic has other implications. I don't want people to think all I want to do is go for runs and pump iron and look at my own reflection." Pierce clicks *animal lover.*

"Do you have a lot of pets?"

"I have a rescue dog."

"That's sweet."

"That's me, sweet as pie." He flashes a grin and moves on to intent. "Wow. So there's a category for looking for marriage, huh? That must be for the superserious online daters. Don't want to give any mixed messages, I guess. Is that what you picked?"

I shoot him a dirty look. "I put dating, but nothing serious."

"Really? I would've pegged you more for a relationship kind of woman, not the casual hookup kind."

"Guess you pegged me wrong." He's not wrong, actually. As much as I might like a boyfriend, I have some trouble staying in a relationship once I'm in one. Being open and honest with a background like mine proves difficult. The last serious relationship I had went up in a ball of flames when I stupidly trusted the guy enough to tell him things I obviously shouldn't have. Hence, I want to date, but not get to the point where I have to share. Besides by putting "dating, but nothing serious," I think it casts a wider net, even if I only date one guy at a time.

He moves on to the question about his longest relationship. I'm surprised when he scrolls to *over three years*. That's a long time to be with one person. My longest relationship was almost two years, but that was in high school. Since then I haven't made it past seven months. I wonder what happened to end his, and who initiated the breakup. I decide it was probably him. I imagine she wanted to settle down and he wasn't ready to commit.

I avert my gaze when he moves on to income. Based on his credit card, it has to be pretty significant. You can't get a black Amex without a hefty bank account. When he finishes the survey portion, he moves on to the description. "I feel like I'm writing my Miss America Pageant speech." He types away for several minutes before he finally hits submit. "Now what?"

"You can check for matches." I don't know why I'm suddenly so nervous.

"I don't want to check for matches. All I want to see is how compatible this site thinks we are."

"Then I guess you pull up my profile."

"Which is what?"

"JustBeachy90."

"You didn't use your name?"

"Are you kidding? Never use your real name on a dating profile unless you want some creep to knock on your door in the middle of the night."

"Is that from personal experience?"

"No. I've heard some horror stories."

"Right, okay." He pulls up my profile and frowns.

"What?"

"That can't be right." He turns his phone toward me. "Is this you?"

I chuckle, but part of me is disappointed. We have a two out of ten. "Yup. That's me. Guess we're about as incompatible as two people can get."

"You must've filled out the questionnaire incorrectly, then." Pierce slips his phone into his pocket. "If you'd done it right, we'd be a ten out of ten, and Terry would be a one at best."

"You're unreal, you know that?"

"I'm just saying . . . you and me? There's something here. But you and Terry? Not even a little bit of anything." He's so relaxed and confident it's infuriating. And a turn-on, but mostly infuriating.

"Chemistry and compatibility aren't the same thing," I argue.

"Ah! So you admit we have chemistry."

"I'll admit that you're attractive, although I'm sure you're already highly aware of that."

He ignores the semi-compliment. "You know what your issue is? You're going about this all backwards."

"How so?" If nothing else, I'm entertained by his persistence and his ridiculous arguments.

"Physical attraction is half the battle, you have to have chemistry before you worry about compatibility."

"Maybe in the short-term, if you're looking for random hookups. But if you want a relationship to last, then you need to be compatible, or it's doomed to fail."

"Are you speaking from experience?"

I shrug. "People either grow together or they grow apart. It's a lot easier to grow together if you've got more than orgasms to get you through the tough times."

He regards me with curious intensity. "Well, you said you weren't looking for anything serious, so the whole compatibility thing shouldn't be your top priority anyway."

I'm relieved when our food arrives and the tension is interrupted. I hate that he has a point. I'm terrible at meaningless sex, unable to separate attraction from emotional connection. But at the same time, I don't want to let anyone get too close. It's a conundrum.

I arrange my utensils beside my plate and smooth my napkin over my lap. I'm actually starving, not having eaten since before noon, apart from a few of Pierce's calamari, so I have to make a conscious effort not to start shoveling food into my mouth. Instead, I carefully twist the noodles on my fork before taking a bite. It's delicious. Probably the best food I've eaten in years, to be honest. Maybe since my grandmother passed away and my father took off with almost all the money and left Marley and me with a ton of debt.

I glance at Pierce, intending to ask him how his steak is, but he isn't eating his dinner. Instead, he's staring at me. "What?" I set my silverware down and dab at my mouth with my napkin. It comes away clean.

"You have nice etiquette."

"Uh, thanks?"

"My mother would approve."

I hold up a hand. "Whoa. Slow your roll, big man. This isn't even a real date, and you're already talking about introducing me to your mother?"

"I made no mention of introducing you to my mother. I just said she'd approve. Not even remotely the same thing."

"Okay. Good. Just making sure. Am I going to be able to eat this without you staring at me the whole time?"

"I'll try to minimize my visual observations."

"Thanks."

"Anything for you, Rian."

I pop another forkful of noodles in my mouth and give him the eyebrow, to which he responds with a wide grin. Despite my reservations, I think I might actually like him.

We eat our respective meals in relative quiet, me trying not to inhale mine, Pierce apparently enjoying the heck out of his steak based on the speed with which it disappears.

I don't want to admit it, but under the cocky front, he might be a nice a guy, and I'm a little sad that he's only a two in the compatibility department. I also don't want to acknowledge that he's right about there being something between us. Some kind of frenetic energy that seems to heighten all my senses and put me on alert—in my pants.

"Rian?" Pierce dips his head and snaps his fingers. "You still with me?"

"Yeah. Yes. I'm here." I sit up straight and lean back, so he's not quite in my personal space anymore. "We should get the bill. I should head back."

I need some distance from this man, especially after

consuming half a bottle of wine. I check my phone, but there are no messages from my sister, so I assume she's still sleeping.

Pierce signals the server and asks for the bill. I should've stopped at one glass of wine and it probably would've halved my portion.

When the server arrives with the bill, Pierce already has his credit card out.

"I would like to pay for half of that." I hold out my card but he covers my hand with his.

Pierce addresses the server, "It's fine. Thank you. I have it." He turns his smile on me. "Please let me."

I don't want to start an argument in front of the server, so I wait until he's gone before I pull out my wallet.

"What're you doing?"

"I'm giving you cash for my part of the bill."

"I've already got it."

"Yes, but we've established that this isn't a date. And I owe $112 of the $274 bill, and I'd like to pay my portion."

Pierce frowns. I don't know how it's possible, but his serious face is as attractive as his non-serious face. "You didn't even see the bill."

"I don't need to see the bill to know what I owe."

It takes Pierce a moment to understand. "You did that in your head."

"It's simple math."

"What's the square root of pi rounded to the sixth decimal place?"

I roll my eyes. "That's too easy."

"I only know what it is rounded to the second decimal place because that's what they taught us in school. How about the square root of 700,051?"

"How many decimal points do you want?"

"Two?"

"836.69."

Pierce sits back in his chair with his jaw hanging open. "You're a genius."

"I'm just good at remembering numbers. It's mental math, that's all." Internally, I berate myself for showing off. I used to catch so much heat in high school. Teachers thought I was cheating on tests, and sometimes they hated it when I was right and they were wrong.

And that very skill set is what took us from the top and sunk us all the way to the bottom all those years ago, when I unknowingly helped my father swindle countless families out of their hard-earned money to pad his bank account.

Pierce bites his knuckle and leans forward, forcing me out of my head. "Do you have any idea how sexy that is?"

"You think it's sexy that I can do math in my head?"

"Yes. You're gorgeous, outspoken, and intelligent. It's a hard-on-inducing trifecta."

CHAPTER 9

SEAWEED ATTACK

PIERCE

Okay, so maybe I should've left out the hard-on-inducing part, but seriously, smart, gorgeous, with a spicy personality. She's everything I want in a woman. I'd like to think eventually I would've met her without the little grocery store incident, but I'm actually thankful now for the scratched paint.

Rian seems to give in regarding the dinner bill, slipping her wallet back into her purse with a frown. I make a small adjustment in my pants before I pick up the bag of Rian's leftovers and stand. I use the manners my mother instilled in me and pull out her chair. "I'll walk you back."

"You don't need to do that. I've taken up most of your evening. You've been more than generous." She motions to the bag of food. As if I'd let her pay for dinner when I invited her to eat with me. "And it's just a few minutes down the beach."

"Would it make a difference if I tell you it's as much for me as it is for you?"

"Why? To ensure my sister isn't throwing a kegger?"

"Well, that's one reason, but mostly it's because I like you, and I'll take as many extra minutes with you as you're willing to permit me."

She blinks a few times, possibly taken off guard by my frankness. "I really never know what I'm going to get with you."

"I'm pretty transparent most of the time." That's not entirely true. But in this circumstance, with this woman, in this particular situation, I'm definitely transparent.

I shoulder my messenger bag and motion for Rian to go first. The sun is about to drop below the horizon, the sky streaked with wisps of clouds that hold onto the colors, deep orange shifting to stunning shades of pink and purple.

"It's so pretty here at night." Rian's gaze sweeps over the shoreline and holds down the beach.

"Would you like to go for a walk?" I point in the direction of Mission Mansion rather than the beach house.

"Oh, no. I should check on Marley. We can head back."

I'm a little disappointed. Dinner conversation was easy when she finally let her guard down.

I'd offer to take her to my place for a drink, but Lawson already has his own friend over and I have my doubts they're doing much in the way of talking, hence the reason I was out eating dinner alone.

Rian slips her shoes off as we make our away across the white sand to the shoreline. The water laps at her feet, and she stares out across the horizon, captivated by the sliver of sun sinking into the water. The waning light reflects in her hair and on her face. Her cheeks are pink from too much sun, but the golden glow frames her face.

"God, the view is gorgeous," she murmurs.

"It really is." I tuck a loose tendril of hair behind her ear and bite the inside of my cheek to stop from laughing when she looks my way and rolls her eyes.

"Please hold your cheesy lines."

"You really are beautiful."

"You can stop now." Her cheeks flush further, and she moves deeper into the surf.

Dusk has settled, sending a gray cast over the beach and darkening the water. Rian stumbles and then shrieks. She flails, her vigor creating a wide splash radius that manages to reach me. "Something's touching me!"

It's too dark to see what it is, so I drop the bags on the beach and rush to remove my shoes.

"Ow! Oh my God! I don't know what that is! What if it's a shark? I stepped on something slimy and it's moving!"

I laugh. She's standing in less than a foot of water. There's no way it's a shark, at least not one that could actually do any damage. It's more likely something harmless, or a jellyfish at the very worst.

She launches herself at me as soon as I'm close enough. She's not all that graceful about it, and her aim is off, so I have to rush to catch her before she falls face-first into the shallow water. She scales me, wrapping her legs around my waist while slapping at her ankle. Her chosen position isn't a great one, my right arm is pinned to my side—by her crotch.

She's a lot stronger than she looks, considering the way she's hanging off me. The side of her face is pressed against my chest as she reaches around to pull at whatever has her so tangled up. She sets me off balance as she continues to kick and flail, causing us to both go down.

I spin so I'm the one who lands on my back in about six inches of water. She drops onto my chest with a grunt. "I got it!" she yells, victorious, thrusting her arm in the air.

I check out the offending attacker. "Some lethal seaweed you got there, huh?"

She glances at the green slippery leaves in her hand and frowns, then looks down at me, still half lying in the water. My pants and shirt are soaked through the back. Her jeans are wet, and her shirt is splotchy with water.

She cringes and bites her lip, one hand planted on my chest. "I'm so sorry."

"You know, if you wanted to get your hands on me, all you had to do was ask. You didn't need to pretend you were being eaten by the plankton."

"That wasn't . . . I didn't mean to . . ." She doesn't make a move to get up, despite the way the tide rushes in rhythmic sweeps every few seconds, covering her calves and licking at my elbows.

Now that I have her this close and unguarded, I'm fully prepared to take advantage of the situation. I sit up in a rush, upsetting her balance once again. She grabs my shoulders as I bring a knee up to prevent her from toppling backward, and wind an arm around her waist.

We're face-to-face. Her eyes lock on mine, full lips parted. I want to know what they feel like. I want to find out if she kisses like she's fighting or submitting. Or maybe both.

I brush her cheek with mine, breathing her in, mouths close but not touching She stills. I wonder what's going through her head in that suspended moment. Whatever the conflict, she must resign herself because the hand on my chest slides into the wet hair at the nape of my neck and she turns in instead of away, nipping at my bottom lip.

First kisses are powerful. This imperfect situation has all the right components. Romantic with a setting sun backdrop and a beach—not ideal that I'm mostly soaking wet, but definitely memorable.

Her lips part in expectation, but I don't claim her mouth. Not yet. Instead, I sweep my lips along the edge of her jaw. She shivers, fingers flexing against the back of my neck, nails biting in as she tips her head back, exposing the long, gentle line of her throat. I run my nose down the expanse and press my lips against the sensitive space where her neck meets her shoulder.

Threading my fingers through the long silky strands, I cup the back of her head so I can adjust the angle. I nibble along her throat until my lips are almost at her ear and suck on the sensitive skin there, smiling at her soft gasp.

"Rian."

She makes a sound, more of a moan than anything, really.

"I'd like to kiss that pretty mouth of yours."

I get another moan, this one lower, and she attempts to turn toward me.

I duck my head, lips moving along her collarbone and up the other side of her throat. Then I follow the edge of her jaw, slow, soft brushes interspersed with light nibbles the closer I get to her chin.

She must realize I'm not rushing this, because she stops trying to twist her head toward my mouth. Instead, she readjusts her position, settling her weight on my thighs, edging closer until her chest meets mine. One hand stays against the nape of my neck, while the other begins to wander, sliding down my bicep. I feel a slight squeeze before it drifts along my forearm to where my hand rests on the dip in her waist.

Her pinkie slips under mine, possibly in a subtle attempt to encourage me to touch more of her. While that's definitely something I want to do—eventually—I also don't want her attention divided.

I want her wanting.

Drawing out the anticipation heightens the experience,

it's a sensual torment, a sensory override. I need her focus on my mouth, on where it is and where she wants it to be.

When I finally get to her chin, I bite, not hard, but enough that she sucks in a breath. I tip her head down and flick my tongue out, skimming her top lip. Her hand tightens on the back of my neck again and I loosen my fingers in her hair. As soon as I do, our mouths connect like two meteors colliding.

Any thought I had of finessing my way through this disappears when Rian sucks my bottom lip between hers, dragging her teeth across the skin. She presses her body against me, legs spreading wider in the sand as she shifts forward.

I'm achingly hard. I've been halfway there since dinner. And suddenly I have friction to complement the hardness. She runs an aggressive palm up my arm and over my shoulder, fingers back in my hair. She angles her head to the side, opening wider, tongue searching for mine.

I wonder what sex with this woman would be like. Definitely not soft, she's too much of a battle in the middle of a storm. When I finally stroke inside the warm softness of her mouth, she groans and tries to bite my tongue.

She clambers up when I retract, both hands on my shoulders in an attempt to push me back. So I grip her waist and flip her over. She sucks in a shocked gasp when she finds herself on her back in the sand and the surf.

"What the heck!" She pushes on my chest with one hand, the other arm hooks around my neck, as if she's fighting to force me back up but keep me close at the same time. "I'm soaked!"

"Oh yeah?" I settle between her thighs, and she stops pushing away as soon as she feels me there.

"That wasn't very nice." A tremor runs through her.

"The part where I saved you from the dangerous sea-weed, or the part where you dragged me into the water? Or are you referring to me kissing you? Because I thought that was very, very nice, actually." I glance up when I hear voices in the distance. I didn't realize we'd already made it back to beach house sixty-nine. It's only a hundred feet away, to the right.

"The part where you made me as wet as you are."

She rolls her eyes as soon as the grin starts to form on my lips. I dip down and brush them over hers again. Her knees press hard against my hips, arms tightening around my neck.

Those voices grow steadily louder.

"Hold on." I push up until I'm on my knees. She keeps her grip on my neck, but she doesn't react quickly enough to keep her legs around my waist.

"I hear people," she whispers.

I unhook her arms, turn around and crouch down. "Hop on."

"What?"

"Hop on. I'll carry you back." There's a moment of hesitation before she climbs up and links her ankles at my waist. I nab the takeout, my messenger bag—which thankfully didn't get wet—and our shoes, and jog across the beach.

It's mostly dark inside the house, apart from the light on the second-story deck and a faint glow coming from the kitchen.

"Do you think your sister locked the sliding door?" I ask when we reach the stairs to the deck.

"Unlikely, and I know I didn't," she replies, her expression chagrined.

"It's a pretty safe beach and there's an alarm system in

the house. I'll show you how to arm it." I'd forgotten earlier, too preoccupied with her unexpected appearance.

She's right, the door is unlocked. The air conditioning hits us when we step inside and Rian shivers.

I survey the living room, tidy apart from the rumpled blanket on the couch. "Where's your sister?"

"She was sleeping when I left, and she wouldn't go anywhere without letting me know." She meets my questioning gaze with a hot one of her own, despite the fact that her teeth are chattering.

"We should get you out of those wet clothes."

"What about your wet clothes?" Her grin turns saucy.

"We should get me out of them too, I suppose." I hadn't planned on taking this much further than a kiss, but my hard-on seems to have other plans.

"Come on." I grab her hand, dropping the takeout and my messenger bag on the kitchen counter before I lead her down the hall to the laundry room. My logic: While our clothes dry, Rian and I can get to know each other better—with our hands and mouths.

Typically I enjoy working my way up to sex with a woman. I don't get a thrill out of one-night stands. I like prolonged anticipation, drawing it out over several dates. A long kiss good night, a message that I enjoyed myself, a call to set up another date, maybe rounding second and third base after a nice romantic dinner, and then eventually, they're the ones begging me to get naked. This isn't ego talking, and it isn't a game—it's human reaction to delayed gratification and attraction. Rian is proving to be a challenge, because all I can think about is getting my mouth on hers again and my hands on her skin. Forget prolonging anticipation.

As soon as we pass through the door, she closes it without turning on a light.

Rian slips a hand under my shirt. "My God, there are so many ridges under here. Where's the light?"

I slap the wall a couple of times until we're both blinded.

Rian glances around and frowns. "This isn't my bedroom."

"You thought I was going to take you straight to your bedroom?"

Her cheeks flush. "Uh . . . I guess?"

"What did you think I meant when I said we should get you out of those wet clothes?"

"That you want to have sex with me."

That is a definite want. Maybe even broaching need at this point. "I couldn't just be worried about the way your teeth are chattering?" I pinch her chin between my thumb and finger to stop it from trembling. "And your lips are turning blue."

"Possible. But considering you're rocking a killer hard-on, I'm going to say this isn't just about being chivalrous."

I glance down at the front of my pants. She has a point. I'm definitely hard and it's very obvious. "It's partly about chivalry."

"Right. So dry clothes. I'll help you out of your wet ones, then." She resumes her mission to pull my shirt over my head. She's quite a bit shorter than I am, despite being a tall girl, so I drop to my knees on the mat in front of the washing machine so she can get it over my head.

"So helpful," she murmurs.

"Just making it easier for you, being chivalrous, as it were."

She drops my shirt on the floor, her lip caught between her teeth as she runs her fingers through my hair. When she reaches the nape of my neck, she drags her nails gently over my shoulders. "Even your muscles have muscles. It's like the big ones are having sex with each other and making new little ones under there."

I chuckle. "Should I take that as a compliment?"

"Definitely. Your body is a masterpiece."

"So is yours, and I'm looking forward to getting my hands on every single inch of it if you're interested." I grab the shirt from the floor, lean to the right and flick the dryer door open so I can toss it inside.

I settle my palms on her hips. "You help me and I help you?"

"Sounds very equitable."

I slip my hands under her shirt, fingertips dragging along her sides as the fabric rises over her stomach and I stand. Rian's eyes are on mine as she lifts her arms for me, and I draw her shirt over her head.

Her bra is exactly what I'd expect from her, bright green with white polka dots. I trace the edge that dips into the valley. "I like this a lot."

"My cleavage or the bra?"

"Both."

She steps up and flicks the button on my pants. Then motions to her waist. "Your turn."

I slip one finger into the waistband of her jeans, and I flick the button open. She whimpers, then I drop my hand. "Your turn."

She lowers my zipper with the same slow deliberation. "Oh." She bites her lip.

I'm wearing pale boxers. My pants are soaked. The fabric underneath is transparent and conforms to the contours of my erection. I reach between her hands, still gripping my pants, and pull her zipper down, then fold back one side of the fabric. Her panties are black satin.

"I wasn't planning to show this stuff off tonight." She motions to her bra and her panties.

"Would they match if that was part of your plan?"

She shrugs. "Maybe? I guess it depends on how much effort I feel like putting in."

"Did they match when you went out with Terry?"

"No. And don't bring him up again, especially not when I'm about to take your pants off." Her tongue peeks out as she pushes my pants over my hips.

Rian dips a single finger into the waistband of my boxers. I grab her wrist before she can get in there and fold her arm behind her—gently, of course. I walk her backward until her butt hits the washing machine and I'm pressed against her. I plant a palm on either side of her and drop my head until my mouth is at her ear. "It's not your turn."

Like mine, her wet jeans stick to her panties, almost taking them along for the ride.

I'm not ready for her to be naked, yet. This slow fore-play is far too much fun. I adjust the panties so they're no longer at risk of coming down with her jeans.

Inch by slow inch, I shimmy her jeans over her hips until they finally fall to the floor. My palm glides down the outside of her leg, and I sweep along the crease at the back of her knee, down her calf to her ankle, encouraging her to lift one foot, then the other so I can rid her of the denim.

While I'm crouched in front of her again, I grab my own jeans, retrieve my phone and wallet from the pocket, toss our pants into the dryer and shut the door.

Rian bites her lip. "Shouldn't we dry everything?"

Rising again, I pause to kiss her stomach, just below her naval. "If I take off your panties and you take off my box-ers, I'm going to have an awfully hard time not getting inside you."

"And here I thought that was the point of getting na-ked."

Grabbing her by the waist, I move over and set her on top of the dryer. Rian parts her legs, making room for me. I reach around to pick a setting and the dryer rumbles to life under her. Twisting her long hair around my hand, I kiss a path up her neck.

I pause at the corner of her mouth. "Rian?"

"Mmm?" Her fingertips glide over my chest, nails circling my nipples.

I lean back, taking in her parted lips, and hooded, glazed eyes. "What do you want to do while we wait for our clothes to dry?"

"Uhhh . . ." Her brow furrows.

"There are board games in the living room." I'm playing with her, although I'd like to give her an out if she feels like she needs one.

"You think I want to hang out in my underwear and play board games with you?"

"It could be fun."

"No, thanks." She claps a palm against the back of my neck and pulls my mouth to hers, biting my lip.

"What do you have against board games?"

"Nothing." She tries to slip her tongue inside my mouth, but I have her hair wrapped around my hand, which means I can prevent her from going after my mouth.

"What do you want right now?"

She makes a noise in the back of her throat. The kind I associate with annoyance. "Your lips on mine. Your tongue in my mouth. Your hands on my body. The big old hard-on you're sporting rubbing up against me."

"That's quite a list."

"I thought I'd lay it all out for you. Give you the details you say you're so fond of."

I brush my lips over hers, unhurried despite the way her legs tighten around my waist. I keep my hands in mostly

PG areas. Rian juts her chest out, trying to press it against mine. I mash my erection against the warm steel of the dryer. It prevents Rian from getting her hands on it, and Lord knows she keeps trying.

"Will you stop torturing me and touch me already!" She groans as I kiss her neck.

"I am touching you." I run my hands up her calves and slip my fingers behind her knees, kneading there while I kiss a path along her collarbone.

"Nowhere good," she mutters.

"You don't think so?" I twist her palm up and press my lips to her wrist. "You don't like this?" I brush softly along the path of veins in her forearm until I reach the crook of her arm, then I bite gently. "Or this?"

"Seriously, what the heck did you do? Take a course in erogenous zone stimulation? I have some pretty big ones that need attention, namely the two you couldn't stop staring at the first time I met you and one between my legs." The hand on my shoulder moves down my chest again. I catch it before she can get to my boxers.

I nab her other wrist and pin them behind her back with one hand—not hard, just firmly, so I can cup her chin in my other hand.

"What're you doing?" She's snappy, eyes glazed with confusion.

"Will you stop fighting me for one goddamn second and enjoy the fact that my main priority isn't to stick my dick in you so I can get off?"

Some of the fight dies. "You don't want to stick your dick in me?"

"Of course I do. It's not my number one priority . . . yet."

"Yet? So it is a priority, you're just getting off on torturing me first?"

"I'm getting off on how worked up you are. That's not the same thing." I drag a single finger from her chin down her throat, between her breasts, and over her stomach, stopping when I reach black satin. I'm pretty sure she growls.

I still have her arms pinned behind her back. I drop my head at the same time as I move my other hand to her upper thigh, pressing my thumb into the junction, where the seam of her panties meets her skin. Running my nose along the edge of her bra, I ease my thumb inside her panties.

Rian sucks in a needy breath and her toes curl against my thighs.

I skim close to her clit, not making contact.

"Just touch me!"

I meet her vicious, angry gaze. "How long do you think it'll take for me to make you come with you this worked up?"

She arches an angry, horny eyebrow. "Who says you'll even be able to?"

CHAPTER 10

THE ORGASMATOR

RIAN

Ever say something to someone and realize you've set yourself up to be bested? I'm pretty sure that's exactly what I've done based on the downright evil glint in Pierce's gloriously sultry eyes. Also, his smile is both the sexiest and scariest thing I think I've ever seen.

I have no idea how I managed to get myself into this situation. My hands are currently pinned behind my back while a dryer rumbles under my butt. My mostly bare butt, thanks to my thong. I mean, what in the ever-loving frack am I doing? I don't have sex with someone I've only been out to dinner with once, and not even on an actual planned date.

But here I am. And here he is, looking damn well amazing in only boxers, so I guess I'm going to go with it.

I should've known better than to trust someone this hot, with that evil Prince Charming smile. I have a feeling this man is going to take me on a ride I'm never going to forget.

His thumb rubs back and forth along the edge of my

panties. It's simultaneously too much and not enough. My entire body is ready to explode and he's skirting the detonator. I need him to press my button and put me out of my misery.

And then his thumb slips out from under the fabric. So of course, I struggle against his hold on my wrists, which are still pinned behind my back. Why am I letting this man get away with this? Why is this so hot?

"Stop fighting." His mouth hovers over mine, tongue flicking out to touch my top lip before he sucks the bottom one between his teeth. At the same time, he grazes my lust button—but he does it over my stupid panties.

It doesn't seem to matter that there's a layer of wet satin dampening the contact. I jolt at the sensation. I also groan. Loudly.

"Does that feel good?"

"No. It felt awful. There's too much fucking fabric in the way." Here's the thing about me: I don't usually swear much. I'm pretty polite in the general sense of the word, but apparently when orgasms are withheld from me, I get a little bitchy. And sarcastic.

Pierce has the audacity to laugh. And then he goes and does it again. This time when I moan, it's his name, and it comes out sounding somewhere between an angry growl and a whiny sob. It's embarrassing—at least until he pushes my panties to the side and makes direct thumb-to-clit contact.

Pierce finally releases my wrists. I'm about to grab hold of his shoulders for balance, but the welcome pressure between my thighs disappears.

"Lift your ass," Pierce orders. Really, it's the kind of firm, authoritative demand I expect from an officer of the law. So, of course I comply. I'm a law-abiding girl, after all. Unlike my hit-and-run sister.

My panties are yanked down my legs. He drags me to the edge of the dryer, slides his palms up my inner thighs, and drops to his knees.

"I have ocean vagina." Any further protest dies when Pierce suctions himself to said vagina and he starts to swirl his tongue. And then it's all I can do to hold onto his shoulders and enjoy every second of the ride. And ride I do.

I basically use his tongue as my personal massager until I come, and then come again. The second time I have to bite the palm of my hand to stop from screaming his name. I'm still breathing like I've been playing chicken with a freight train when he pushes back up to a stand.

"Please tell me you're going to sex me now." I'm grateful that it sounds more like a demand than a plea.

"Only because you're so polite." Pierce grabs his wallet from the top of the washing machine and retrieves a condom.

I make myself useful by removing my bra, then push his boxers over his hips. His erection springs free. It's pretty damn big. Not scary-porno big, but it's definitely in proportion with the rest of him, and it's so . . . veiny. I have a feeling the aerodynamic qualities are going to be a serious advantage in the orgasm territory.

He flicks the condom to me and I fumble to catch it. "Wrap me up, baby."

With his eyes on mine, he slides a finger inside me, pumping a couple of times before he adds a second one. It's smart. He's big. A little warm-up down there is well-advised. It makes it difficult to focus, but I position the condom at the tip and grip the shaft. I smile when he groans as I roll it over the head and down the shaft.

I'm superready for some hot sex and whatever dirtiness he wants to throw my way. He doesn't shove his way in there, though. Instead, he runs the head up and down, around and around, teasing. After a dozen infuriatingly slow passes, the head disappears inside.

I put my hand on his chest to prevent him from going any farther. "Go slow," I tell him. "I want to watch this happen."

His eyes snap up to mine, hot and needy, and his jaw tics. A smirk curves up the corner of his mouth. "You really have no idea how perfect you are. And don't worry, I want to watch me stretch you with my cock too."

I clench at his words. "That was way dirtier than anything I would've said."

"I can dial that back if you'd prefer."

"No, thanks. I think I like it."

Our gazes dart back down at the same time. I clamp a hand on the back of his neck and he does the same to me—except he's far more gentle about it. We watch as he disappears inch by gloriously slow inch. I am stretched with a capital S. Maybe even all caps. Shouty ones. It looks so hot.

"Fuuuuuck." It's a drawn-out groan through clenched teeth. "You feel incredible."

"Thanks, so do you."

He laughs a little. "I can't wait to feel you come on me."

"Pretty sure you're not going to have any trouble making that happen." Not based on the way everything is tightening below the waist already.

Pierce shifts his hips back and then forward again, the tiniest little bit, the most miniscule of movements. I don't think it can be effective at all, until he starts the same back-and-forth motion and combines it with gentle, but firm, circles on my lust button. It doesn't take long before the tightness in the pit of my stomach radiates outward and I come again. Harder than before. It's insanity. I can't stop moaning my appreciation through my orgasm.

Pierce lets out a triumphant groan. "Keep coming, baby. I love it."

I've never been with someone who talks this much during sex. I figured it would be distracting, but it's actually quite encouraging. I'm being praised for having an orgasm when it's him doing all the work.

Pierce kisses me as I come down from the epic high. "Hold on, baby." He brings my arms up behind his neck and hooks the backs of my knees into the crook of his elbows, pulling me right to the edge of the dryer. "You ready to come some more?" He winks, gives me a dirty grin, and then the real sexathon begins. All I can do—quite literally—is hold on for the ride. He manages to pound two more orgasms out of me before he comes himself.

I'm a ragdoll by the time he pulls out. I'm not even sure if my legs know what their purpose is anymore. I would like to have sex with this man for the rest of my living days. Maybe not daily, though. Every other day would probably be safer. I won't even need boot camp if I had him on a regular basis.

"Holy crap balls." I loosen my grip on the back of his neck. My fingers are cramped from holding on so tight, and a line of crescent-shaped marks decorate his skin. "That was—"

"Spectacular?" Pierce rolls the condom off, ties it at the end, and tosses it in the trash in the corner.

So much damn ego. I don what I hope is a bored expression and lift a shoulder. "I was going to say it was okay."

He grins, tongue caught between his teeth. He runs his palms up the outside of my thighs. "I think you're my new favorite person."

I laugh. "So you have a thing for women who minimize your sexual prowess?"

"I have a thing for women with nice boobs." He cups the right one and slides a hand into my hair. Tilting my head to the side, he kisses me, slow and sweet, discordant to the dirty sex we had.

The dryer buzzes under me, and I jump at the sound. "Wow. That's some good timing."

Pierce backs off and helps me down. My tailbone is a little sore from the pounding I took on the top of a metal surface, but I'm more sated than I've ever been in my entire life, so I'll take the bruise. I could sleep for ten hours after that.

I brace myself on his chest, testing out my legs. So far they're holding my weight, although they're definitely wobbly.

"You okay there?"

"I'm good, just relearning how to use my legs after being turned into a sex pretzel." I move to the side while Pierce retrieves our warm, dry clothes.

I stumble a bit as I shove a foot into the leghole of my panties. Pierce's warm palms settle on my hips. "Need some help getting dressed?"

"I can manage, but thanks." I lean against the washing machine for stability. Pierce takes it upon himself to fasten the clasp on my bra. I wouldn't have bothered with it at all, but he seemed intent on being helpful in some way. He drops a kiss at the top of my spine as he adjusts the straps, then hands me my shirt before he puts his own on.

Once we're both dressed in mostly fresh, but oceany-smelling clothes—ones I'll be out of as soon as he leaves—we stand facing each other.

He stuffs his phone in his pocket and gives me one of those grins accompanied by a head tilt, as if he's waiting for me to make the next move. I don't know what the next move is.

This isn't something I make a habit of doing. In fact I've *never* done something like this. I don't pick up random guys and sleep with them in laundry rooms. I go on dates. I suss a guy out and make sure he's not some crazed psychopath before I sleep with him—and I rarely ever get to that point. Marley is the one who has one-night stands. All of this is on fast-forward for me. And he's too hot for his own good or mine. This was such a bad idea. Panic over what I've done sets in.

"I have to be up early tomorrow," I blurt.

The smile on Pierce's face grows wider. "Is that you asking me to leave?"

"Uh . . ." The answer to that is yes, but now I feel like a jerk. He was very attentive. I came a lot. It still doesn't make inviting him to spend the night a good idea. "I mean, you don't *have* to go. We could have a drink or something?"

It doesn't come out sounding very confident, or certain.

"But you'd prefer I leave." He's not asking.

I blow out a breath. "I, uh, don't usually do this." I run a palm down my face, covering my mortified expression. "That sounds so horribly cliché."

Pierce chuckles, low and deep. I find myself barricaded by his arms, one hand planted on either side of me, body close but not touching as he leans in. The tip of his nose brushes mine. "What part of this don't you usually do, Rian? The dinner part of the evening? The romantic walk on the beach? The hot sex? The kicking a guy out after you get what you want from him?"

Why does he have to be so intense? And why is he calling me out like this? "Well, the dinner part was kind of accidental, wasn't it? And the beach part wasn't really as romantic as it was embarrassing for me. And if you must know, usually I have sex in a bed, not a laundry room, and there are typically several dates before the nudity happens. And I'm not kicking you out, I'm just saying I need to be up early." I don't want him to go, which I think could be a problem. I might actually like him. But he's exactly what I avoid. There is a reason I go out with the Terrys of the world. I need to think, and him being here doesn't help me do that.

"If you have to be up early, why ask if I want to stay for a drink?"

"Are you always like this?"

"Like what?"

"So pushy and confrontational."

"You think I'm being confrontational?"

"Is it possible for you to answer a question directly?" He's right up in my space again, his face only inches from mine. His lips are close. I'd like to shut him up by kissing him. But I'm not sure that's smart. I worry that I'll end up naked again—definitely by choice and not coercion.

"I like you."

"That's not an answer to any of the questions I asked."

"I'm too busy staring at your mouth to remember what the questions were." He kisses me again before I can protest. It's another minute or two of tongues slow dancing before he finally disconnects. Embarrassingly, I follow his lips, trying to keep them glued to mine.

"I actually have to get back to my place. My dog, Trip, needs to be let out and I can't trust my brother to do that, so you don't need to worry about inviting me to stay for drinks, or a sleepover, or whatever."

I huff a quiet laugh. Of course he's been playing with me. He doesn't want to spend the night; he just wanted the invitation.

"I'll be around tomorrow afternoon. Will you?"

"I should be." I try to sound nonchalant instead of eager.
I'm not sure I'm successful.

"Great. I'll see you on the beach, then?"

"Sure."

When he moves out of my personal space, I finally feel
like I can breathe again. I follow him out of the laundry
room and down the hall. I stop short when Marley comes
into view, a forkful of pasta halfway to her mouth.

Her eyebrow is raised as her gaze moves from Pierce
to me. She drops the fork in the Styrofoam container and
props a fist on her hip. "I *so* called this."

Dear Embarrassment,
I'm breaking up with you. Forever.
No love,
Rian

CHAPTER 11

EMBARRASSMENT FOREVER

RIAN

"Okay, well, thanks for checking on the dryer. Sorry that you had to come here so late!" I say, very loudly.

Marley snorts and Pierce barks out a laugh.

"I'll see myself out then. Enjoy the leftovers." He nods to Marley before turning to me. "I hope the dryer keeps doing its job."

I follow him to the patio door. My palms are sweaty and my face is surely the shade of a beet. He turns as he steps out onto the deck. "So this is how you're playing it?"

"I panicked. I told you, this isn't how I usually do things."

"That makes two of us. I don't usually get kicked out, especially not before the post-coital snuggles."

What does it say about me that I'm kicking out the man I've had the best sex of my life with less than fifteen minutes after the act is over? I'm having regrets all over the place. And he's a snuggler? I thought all men hated after-sex snuggles. I avoid commenting on that, though. "You said you had to check on your dog. I figured you wanted an invitation to stay to stroke your already enormous ego, but then you'd already have a reason to say you had to leave anyway."

"I was trying to make you feel better about this." He motions between us.

I bring my fingers to my lips and start to bite my nail, but realize it makes me look anxious—which I am—and they're dirty from being in the sand not that long ago. Plus, they smell like sex, so I drop them and clasp them in front of me instead.

"Look at you." He moves in.

My feet stay where they are, but the rest of my body angles away. "What're you doing?"

"Trying to kiss you goodnight before I leave. Unless you've changed your mind and decided you want me to stay."

I purse my lips, and he gives me that damn smile again. So cocky. So knowing.

"It's all right. I get it. You have an early morning, and there's no way you'll be able to keep your hands to yourself if I'm in bed with you."

"You are such an—"

Before I can finish the sentence, his palm curves around the side of my neck, thumb caressing the edge of my jaw, and he tips my chin up. It all happens in less than a second. And then his lips are on mine, tongue sweeping out, aggressive for a few strokes before he disengages, throwing me completely off-kilter. "Don't worry. Next time we'll get to cuddle."

I push on his chest. "Who said there's going to be a next time?"

"Trust me, hotness, there'll be a next time. See you tomorrow." He backs away and gives me a final departing wave, then disappears down the stairs.

"Oh my God. That man is unbelievable."

"I should've put money on that."

I turn around, trying to come up with some witty retort, but I've got nothing. She totally called it, and I made Pierce do the walk of shame. Well, it was more swagger than walk, but still, he's gone and he was totally right, about everything. How stupid am I?

"Whatever's going on between the two of you is like pheromone chemical warfare."

"What does that even mean?"

"Being in the same vicinity as the two of you is like . . ." She struggles to find the right words. ". . . like tripping on ecstasy while shooting opiates."

"You've never done either of those things." At least I don't think she has. She better not have or we have issues.

"Well, the way you two are when you're near each other is exactly what I imagine it would be like." She stuffs another forkful of noodles in her mouth.

I make a huge show of stretching and yawning. "Well, I'm going to bed. See you in the morning!"

"Whoa, wait a damn second, you need to explain what happened here. Based on what I overheard, you got the boning of your life and from the look of things, you made him leave. I want some details."

"If you overheard, you don't need details. We have an early morning. I need sleep and him staying would prevent that. Plus, he needs to take care of his dog."

"This is such bull. What was he saying about seeing you tomorrow? Are you setting up a date for boning round two?"

"I'm not going to sleep with him again." I'm totally going to sleep with him again if the opportunity arises. I already know it. That was too good not to repeat. The cuddling I don't know about, though—it leads to talking and talking changes things. It blurs lines and pushes boundaries. It makes it difficult to stay on the right side of casual.

"Should I remind you now that you said you weren't going to sleep with him in the first place?"

"Well, I mean it this time." I don't mean it at all.

"A hundred buck says you do."

"I'm not making bets with you about this."

"Because you know you'll lose."

"I'm going to bed and you should do the same." I walk down the hall, ending the conversation.

The next morning my alarm goes off at seven forty-five. Because our job often requires us to be out of the house late in the day, and into the evening, I'm not much of an early riser, but it's a showing day and it's making me nervous. Most of the time I'm not involved in the showing part, so nerves aren't an issue. However, when we have multiple showings in one weekend, which we've been doing more of lately, I've become part of the whole process.

And this time I'll be front and center. As we get closer to having our own Hamptons beach house to flip, which will hopefully be soon, I need to assess what people are looking for and take note.

I pass by Marley's room on the way to the kitchen to make coffee. She's still asleep. I leave her where she is while I brew the coffee, aware if I wake her before it's ready, she'll be a complete bear.

Muscles I didn't know I have ache. I eat a banana while I wait, hoping the potassium will keep them all from seizing. Sitting on the stool is uncomfortable on account of the sex last night. I'd grab a cushion from the other side of the room if it didn't entail standing or walking. Dear Lord, that man knows how to use foreplay as a weapon.

I shake my head and focus on the information for the

house we're selling, reviewing all the important details. I'm halfway through the pot of coffee when Marley comes storming out of her bedroom, a rumpled, angry mess. "Motherhumper! That bastard!"

"What's wrong?"

"That shady sonofabitch." She viciously punches buttons on her phone. "He thinks he can get away with a stunt like this, he's got another thing coming." She paces the length of the kitchen. She has to push her wild, knotted hair out of the way to get the phone to her ear. "You can't pull a house off the market less than six hours before I'm supposed to show it." She stops pacing and props a fist on her hip. "Where'd you hear that and what does it have to do with anything?" She makes her angry, pursed-lips face. "That doesn't absolve you—I can't—do you know what a pain in the ass this is going to be? How many phone calls I'm going to get? Fine, yes. We'll be there in an hour. You better make this worth my while."

She ends the call, tosses her phone on the table, and throws her hands up in the air. "Stupid wishy-washy men."

"Can you please explain what's going on? What just happened?"

"The open house today is cancelled. The seller is taking the house off the market."

"What? We need that sale." Without it, it will delay our own flip.

"I know." She runs her hand through her hair, but it gets caught in the knots. "Fuck a duck!" she yells and then struggles to free her fingers from the mess.

"He said he has a solution, but won't say what it is over the phone. I don't know if this guy is hosing us or not, but we need to get over there and deal with it." She whirls around and stomps down the hall muttering, "Face-humping cock-smack. I hate every penis on this planet."

I hope this guy really does have a workable solution, otherwise Marley may castrate him. She may be the more face friendly of the two of us, but if she feels like she's being screwed over, she's a heck of a lot pricklier than me.

I head to my own room to shower and get dressed. As the numbers-and-paperwork girl I lean toward a more businesslike appearance at these things, but since it's a beach house, Marley thought it might be better to go the sundress route. So I picked out a cream sundress and a pair of strappy sandals in a floral print for a burst of color.

Marley appears twenty minutes later fresh-faced in a bold coral dress with white heels and a giant necklace that looks like it weights fifty pounds and draws a lot of attention to her chest area. I'm certain this is purposeful.

"I have the contracts. You have everything else?"

I pat the messenger bag hanging from my shoulder. "Sure do."

"Let's go. This jerkoff better not screw us out of our commission or he's going to be short a set of balls when I'm done with him."

I grab the keys from the counter before she can—there's no way I'm letting her drive, not when she's in this bad of a mood.

I put the address in my phone. We could walk there in ten minutes based on the GPS coordinates, but we're both wearing heels, so no thanks to that. Also, my thighs are killing me. "Wait, I thought we were selling 105 today."

"We were. The seller lives down the beach. We're going there." She mutters profanity under her breath. The drive to the house is short, and we pass the bungalow we're supposed to put on the market tomorrow, but we won't have as good a gauge on asking price now. I signal right and pull into the driveway of a gorgeous two-story beachfront house with a beautifully manicured lawn and stunning gardens.

I have a strange sense of déjà vu as Marley wobbles unsteadily down the beautiful cobbled walkway. Maybe the seller wants to move into 105 and unload this place instead. I can only imagine what we'd get for this one, even though both properties on either side are a little rundown and out of date. This place is closer to the Mission Mansion, so it's incredibly desirable.

Marley hits the doorbell and a soft chime tinkles from inside the house. When it doesn't open two seconds later, she jabs it again.

I bat her hand away. "Don't be antagonistic. We might be able to persuade him to change his mind."

Marley gives me the side-eye, takes a deep breath, and nods. "Put your game face on," she says as a shadow appears in the doorway and the lock turns.

A wide smile spreads across Marley's face as the door swings open. Standing in the foyer is a surfer hippie. Well, maybe a wanna-be surf hippie. His shoulder-length, dark blond hair is pulled back in a ponytail, and his semi-overgrown beard is supposed to scream *I don't care*, but it's too clean around the edges for that. He's wearing a pair of what looks like pajama pants and a button-down white shirt. Except it's completely unbuttoned. He has a nipple ring. I'm 100 percent certain the necklace he's wearing is woven out of hemp, and if someone asked him, he wrestled the shark who belongs to the tooth dangling from it. If I had to guess, he's likely a fan of freeballing.

Marley steps into the foyer and leans forward, kissing him on his scruffy cheek with a loud *mwah*. "Lawson! It's so lovely to see you again."

He returns the embrace and the kiss on the cheek. "You

sure about that? You sounded less than impressed not long ago."

"Well, what did you expect when you cancel a showing with only hours' notice and tell me you're taking the house off the market?" She's still smiling, but there's both warning and bite in her tone.

"Don't you worry, sunshine. I'm going to make it up to you twice over. I promise." His gaze shifts over to me and his eyes go wide. "Uh. Am I seeing this right?"

Marley laughs and motions me inside. "This is my sister, Rian."

He extends a hand. I'm surprised to see the nails are trimmed and cleaned. Actually, they look manicured. And I think his eyebrows might be shaped. What's up with this guy?

His smile is suddenly a smirk, as I slip my hand into his. Then he blatantly peruses me. Like it's the most obvious once-over ever. "Rian? That's a unique name. I didn't realize you and Marley were twins."

"Fraternal, but yes. And it's nice to meet you too, Lawson." It's a very non-surfer hippie name.

"Come on in and sit down, we can talk about my plan, and hopefully I can thaw those frosty auras the two of you are throwing off."

Auras?

As we pass through the foyer and down the hall, I notice a doll by a closet door. There's a tiny little hook beside it, and it looks like it's hanging up a jacket. Weird.

"Lawson is the owner of this house, and 105."

"We own a couple more, but yeah, that's right." He nods and calls out, "Hey, bro, the Realtors are here!"

"Coming!"

The hairs on the back of my neck stand on end and goose bumps rise along my arms. I know that voice.

I've heard the word *coming* in that exact deep baritone. It's been growled in my ear along with other words to form phrases such as *Are you coming?* It's been taunted against my lips: *I can feel you coming again* and *Ah, fuck, I'm coming.* Flashes of last night strobe behind my lids with every rapid blink. Now that I'm no longer coming like a porn star on ecstasy, I'm wholly embarrassed by my horribly wanton display. This cannot be happening right now.

The thump of shoes hitting the stairs tells me it is, indeed, happening.

"Oh no." I take a step back, toward the door in preparation to escape what will surely be a very awkward, embarrassing situation, but it's too late.

Last night's orgasm provider appears, and dear sweet Lord in heaven, he looks absolutely edible. His hair is perfectly styled, not a single strand out of place—which wasn't how it looked last night when he left. I'd had my hands in it a lot, particularly when he'd gotten on his knees for me. I need to return that favor. Next time maybe . . . wait. No. We're representing them as agents. This is bad, on so many levels. There should not be a next time. No matter how much my vagina wants there to be one. Or the rest of me.

My face must be the same shade as a stop sign, and there's absolutely nothing I can do to avoid this epic train wreck. Pierce does not seem like the kind of guy to let something like this slide. Beyond the embarrassment, I recognize that this whole thing seems rather suspect.

"Oh shit," Marley mutters.

I'm outside of Pierce's line of view, hidden somewhat behind Marley and a pillar. He rolls the sleeve of his crisp white dress shirt—his is actually buttoned and he's wearing a tie, it's hot pink—and turns his attention away from his brother, who's busy grinning like a fool, in our direction.

That tie is like a flare signal, and I have to wonder if I've been set up by this guy, and what the damn purpose is if that's the case.

He stops short as his gaze lands on Marley and then moves farther to the right, to me.

His tongue sweeps out to wet his bottom lip. If I thought Lawson's perusal was blatant, it's got nothing on Pierce's. I feel as if I'm being undressed when his gaze moves over me.

His delectable mouth curves up at the corners, one side tipping higher. "This is a surprise."

"Yes. It is that." I nod slowly in agreement, uncertain as to whether or not his is as authentic as mine.

"So you two know each other?" Lawson is bouncing on his toes, still smiling.

"We sure do." Pierce's grin widens.

When will the embarrassment end with this man?

CHAPTER 12

FATES ALIGN

PIERCE

Normally I don't buy into the idea of fate or kismet, or any of that other bullshit. But even I can recognize how unreal this continued running into each other has become. Inside of a few weeks, I've gone from a couple of chance meetings to these highly unlikely collisions.

Rian looks like a deer caught in headlights. A very beautiful, somewhat angry deer, with wide, panicked eyes. She's wearing a very conservative, ultrafeminine dress that's probably meant to make her blend into the background. She's highly unsuccessful. Especially in contrast with her sister's overly loud, extra beachy outfit. The absence of color puts the focus on her face. Her sandy brown hair falls in loose waves around her shoulders, curling at the ends. I had my hands in that hair last night. It's soft, and it smelled like the ocean and some citrusy, fresh shampoo.

She takes a halting step away from me, and her hand flutters up to her throat. The same throat my lips were on, the one my palm was curved around. Her tongue darts out, wetting her bottom lip on a quick exhale.

It's obvious she wants to bolt, and I suppose I can understand why. Our rather unconventional introduction seems to be pushing far outside the realm of anything considered normal.

"I'm so confused," Rian says. "What's happening right now? Is this some kind of prank?" She looks to her sister. "Are you responsible for this?"

Marley shakes her head. "I'm as stunned as you are."

Rian rubs her temples. "So let me get this straight. You two are brothers and you own this place together?"

"No, this is my place, but Pierce is crashing here for the summer," Lawson replies with a smile. "However, we co-own the property we've taken off the market."

"What about the place we're currently staying, sixty-nine? Do you both own that too?" Marley asks.

"Correct."

"May I please use your bathroom?" The color has drained from Rian's face, which concerns me.

I point down the hall. "There's a powder room around the corner."

"Thanks." Rian grabs Marley by the wrist and hauls her away.

They both disappear inside and the door slams shut, followed by the low whir of the ceiling fan.

"So that's your hot fuck from last night, huh?"

I'd like to slap the grin off Lawson's face. "Keep your voice down, asshole."

"Calm your tits. They're not listening to us." He motions to the closed bathroom door, which does little to muffle the high-pitched, yet hushed tones coming from the other side. "This is a very interesting turn of events."

"It sure is."

"Marley's the one who hit your car, right?"

"Yeah."

Lawson strokes his beard. "You know, we could make this work to our advantage."

"Whatever you're scheming, you can stop now."

He splays his hands on the counter. "Just hear me out. We could get them to lower their commission on the other property, and if you're sleeping with the twin, I bet we'll get great insider information. You rock starred that shit last night, right? Or wait, did you pull a fuck and chuck? Is that why she's freaking out? Did you bail in the middle of the night or something?"

"I didn't pull a fuck and chuck." I don't tell him that she was the one who kicked me out.

"Huh, well, she seems pretty sketched out about you being here. Why's that?"

I shrug. "I don't know her well enough to answer that question."

"I'm gonna go try and listen through the wall." He moves around the island, toward the bedroom connected to the bathroom.

I follow along behind him. There's no way I'm letting him eavesdrop, so I knock on the bathroom door. "Everything okay in there?"

Lawson gives me his what-the-fuck look to which I arch a brow. The door swings open and Marley steps out of the bathroom. Rian's hand shoots out and she grabs me by my tie, pulling me into the small space. She throws the lock, leans against the door, and crosses her arms over her chest.

The panic is gone. In its place is wary mistrust. "You need to explain this."

"Okay." I lean against the vanity and mirror her pose. "What exactly would you like me to explain?"

"Did you know?"

"Know what?" I'm antagonizing her. I know exactly what she's asking me: Did I know she was connected to our property, and that she was supposed to sell our flip?

She uncrosses her arms and stalks over, jabbing her finger into my chest. "Don't play with me, Pierce."

Her eyes are fiery, hot with unwarranted and misplaced anger, but behind that wicked front is hunger and longing, and a little bit of fear. I get it. I feel it echoing around in my cells. Pushing this woman's buttons turns me on in ways that defy logic and rationality. "I enjoyed playing with you last night."

Her jaw clenches and she exhales through her nose. Her cheeks heat, a burst of pink against her creamy, peachy skin.

"Did you enjoy being played with?" I nod, more to myself than her. "I think you did."

"You are unbelievable. Did you convince your brother to take the house off the market? Is this because I didn't invite you to stay the night?"

I bark out a laugh. "Seriously? You think my ego is that easily bruised?" I lean down so I'm only inches away from her face. Close enough to see the green flecks in her amber eyes. Close enough to watch her pupils dilate and feel the warmth of her breath pass over my lips. "I know why you sent me home, and it has nothing to do with not wanting me in your bed all night long."

She blinks a few times as if she's been slapped. Her expression shutters. Oh yes, I'm familiar with this kind of emotional guarding. I do it all the time. But there's something different about her, about this connection we share. I'm not willing to back down entirely, but I'll back off for now. I straighten, giving her the space she seems to need.

"To answer your question, no, I didn't know. I'm as

shocked to see you this morning as you are to see me. I thought you were an accountant."

"I never said I was an accountant, just that I'm good with numbers." Rian paces the small space. "How is this even happening?"

"Maybe it's kismet." I grin at her incredulous expression and lift a shoulder in a slight shrug. "You have to admit, it's pretty wild."

"It's crazypants is what it is." She stops her pacing and props her hand on her hips. "Okay, so here's how this is going to go: What happened between us last night isn't going to have any bearing on the deal we're making today." She purses her lips and points a finger in my face. "And just because I came more than once, doesn't negate the fact that you and your brother are pulling a house off the market hours before an open house."

"I can get on board with that. Does this mean that once this deal is done, we're going to celebrate with more orgasms?" I wink.

"You're incorrigible." She flips the lock on the door. Before she can open it, I flatten my palm against it and lean in, crowding her. She tenses. "What're you doing?"

That's a good question. I'm not actually sure. I'm being an asshole again, maybe because that seems to be the version of me she responds to the best, which begs the question, what the hell happened to make her so jaded and angry? So I antagonize her, just to see how far I can push. "You sure you're calm enough to be rational out there?"

"I'm perfectly calm," she says to the door. The tremor in her voice gives away her lie.

"You're sure about that?"

"Yes."

"As long as you're sure."

"I'm sure."

I duck down and whisper in her ear, "Say that when you're looking at me."

She spins, hair whipping me in the face. We're nose to nose. Her expression in no way reflects her rigid stance. She's the picture of serenity as her eyes meet mine and stay locked there in the gentlest of challenges. They say *go ahead and fuck with me; see who wins*. They say *keep pushing my buttons*.

"I'm perfectly calm. Are you?" Her voice is jazz-club smoky.

"Not even a little bit."

Her brow furrows in confusion.

"I need to tell you something." I'm too close for her to be comfortable, but I don't want to leave the bubble of her space. I feel that same pull, the one I felt when I confronted her in the grocery store. The same pull that had me messaging and calling her the week that followed. The very feeling that was missing when I watched her sister scratch my car.

"What's that?" Her voice is all breathy and soft.

"I really love this dress on you."

She smooths her hands over her hips. "Oh."

"I thought you should know."

We stare at each other for what seems like forever, both of us leaning closer until the tips of our noses touch. We jump at the rapping on the other side of the door. "You two coming out anytime in the next millennium?" It's her sister.

I push away and Rian shakes her head, but she's still smiling as she puts her hand on the doorknob and twists. Looking over her shoulder, she says, "Business is still business."

CHAPTER 13

NEGOTIATIONS:
ROUND TWO

RIAN

I clap my hands together and feign calm. I am not calm. I am not okay. This whole thing could blow up in my face and I would really like to keep my face. It's the only one I've got. "Let's get down to business."

"I think you did that last night," Marley quips.

She and Lawson snicker, Pierce coughs from my right. I glare first at her, then at Pierce, who both quickly school their expressions. Lawson's smile is wide and his teeth are blindingly white against his tanned skin. "Oh come on, you have to admit that was funny. We're doing business, you got the business from my brother last night."

"Can it, Law," Pierce mutters. "And will you please button your shirt?"

"I don't like being confined by fabric."

Pierce shakes his head. "You're a pain in my ass, you know that?"

"Sure do. All right." Lawson slaps a palm on the table. "While you two were having a lover's quarrel and some super quiet sex in the bathroom—"

"We were not having sex in the bathroom," I snap.

"Whatever, it's cool either way. Just as long as there aren't any messes to clean up, we're golden." He gives me the thumbs-up. "So this is how it's going down. I received some intel that our neighbor two doors down are putting their bungalow on the market tomorrow. I want to get in there and put an offer on it before it goes public." He points to Marley. "And I need you to work your magic to make that happen."

"Who told you they were putting it up for sale?" Marley glances at me, a hint of potential accusation in her eyes.

I try to use facial expressions to indicate that I in no way divulged that information to Pierce last night. I was far too busy having orgasms to talk about what houses might be for sale on the beach. Besides, he didn't even know what I do for a living until now, and I didn't realize he wasn't just a landlord.

"I might've had a conversation with their granddaughter the other day. So I'm thinking, since you owe my brother some money for damaging his car, you can get us in to see it first and give us a break on the commission. Drop it by a percent or something."

"No. Absolutely not," I cut in. "First of all, I've already given Pierce a check for the paint and that has nothing to do with the sale of the house. So no discount for anything."

"How about half a percent?"

"Still no."

"My brother could've called the police, but he didn't," Lawson says with an arched brow.

"And you're breaking a contractual agreement by taking your house off the market, so don't throw out baseless threats in a bid to cheat us out of money we'll earn by getting you a good deal on the house."

"Fuck, you're hot," Pierce says.

All three of us look at him. I'm sure my face is red again. And for the love of all things Coco Pebbles, my nipples have perked right up. So stupid. This guy is way too smooth, too good with his words and his hands and his magnificent man hammer. He's too intense. It's bad. Intense equals dangerous. This kind of lust dulls all the other senses, whitewashes reason, makes a person do thoughtless, senseless things; like having sex with a relative stranger on a dryer after one dinner date. And it wasn't even a *real* date.

Pierce taps the counter. "I said that out loud, huh?"

"You sure did. Good job holding your cards close, dude." Lawson shifts his attention back to me and clears his throat. "Okay. No cut on commission. Can't blame me for trying."

"Okay." Marley smiles, no longer pissed off at the situation. "Now that that's settled, you want me to see if I can get you in to see the property before it hits the open market?"

"Exactly. You think you can make that happen?" Lawson sips a seaweed green shake. It coats his mustache and makes it look like he sneezed all over his upper lip until he licks it away.

"Let me make a few calls."

Of course Marley can make it happen. She's the agent on the house Lawson is talking about. All she has to do is call the owner and set up a walk-through. All I need to do is draw up the paperwork. And we'll make full commission on the sale, which could put us in an excellent position financially. It means we might finally be able to finance our own flip.

I don't like how much it seems like a setup on both sides. It feels . . . dishonest not to let them know that we're the selling agents.

But I know Marley, and she isn't going to tell him we're the selling agents until she absolutely has to. Not when he's pulled his house from the market in the eleventh hour. She slips her phone out of her purse and crosses through the living room. Flipping the latch on the sliding glass door, she steps out on the deck, leaving me alone with Pierce and Lawson.

"So, kind of ironic that you're the lawyer and he's the one with the piercings, huh?" I gesture between them and wish my mouth and brain would work in tandem instead of independently of each other at times like these.

"Right?" Lawson grins. "And I even have the junk jewelry. Guess you already know my brother here is too straight an arrow to decorate his dick."

It's on the tip of my tongue to tell Lawson it actually curves a little to the right and is fantastic without any decorations, but luckily Pierce speaks before I do.

"Really? Was that a necessary share?"

Lawson inclines his head in my direction. "She's the one who brought it up."

Pierce sighs. "If we're going to look at a house, you need to change out of your hippie gear and dress like a real human."

"I'm not changing, and I've already been in that house. I know what it looks like. I want it. We just need to know what we have to offer to get it."

"Do you mind if I talk to my brother alone for a moment?" Pierce asks me with a tight smile.

"Oh! No, not at all. I'll just step outside." I'm glad for the reprieve. I join my sister on the deck. Now that I'm thinking with my brain and not my sex parts, I realize I should've followed her in the first place, then maybe I wouldn't know about Lawson's peen piercing. Those two men couldn't be any more opposite.

Marley's heels lie on the deck, while she paces the length in bare feet. She gives me some kind of eyebrow wag with a little thumbs-up, then she inclines her head to the right.

I glance over and do a double take. Beyond the loungers that are set up facing the beach with a perfect view of the volleyball nets in front of our rental, and the side table with what appears to be a set of broken binoculars, lies a dog. Apparently, Pierce really does have one.

Trip—I think that's his name—lifts his head when he sees me and pops up, running around in a circle before he trots his lopsided way over. He only has three legs. I'm instantly in love with this dog, and a little bit more enamored with Pierce. Trip seems to be completely oblivious to the fact that he's missing a leg.

I rub that space under his chest that makes so many dogs happy, and his tail thumps on the boards.

That's when I realize it wasn't the dog Marley was pointing out, but the set of dolls perched in lounge chairs, tiny glasses with little umbrellas in them poised in their plastic hands. Huh. Odd. Maybe one of them has a kid. Oh God. What if I slept with a single dad? What if he wants me to be his baby mamma?

I can barely handle doing my own laundry and cleaning up after myself and my sister, let alone a little child. It'd be one thing to mess up my own offspring, but I don't want to be responsible for messing up someone else's.

"Actually, we're in the area. We could arrange to meet in say, twenty minutes? They're very keen to move quickly. Yes. Definitely. We'll see you then." Marley ends the call and does a little hip shimmy, then looks over her shoulder to make sure we're not being watched from the other side of the sliding glass door. "It's on. We need to make sure they give their best offer up front. They were planning to follow the listing for their place as a gauge, but I said if we start at $799K, that we should get a little over $800K for it with so few on the market and what other comparable properties have gone for."

"Does this feel dodgy to you?"

"Does what feel dodgy?"

"Don't you think we should tell them we're representing the sellers too? What if they think we held off on putting up the property until tomorrow to scam them?" My fingers are at my mouth and I'm at risk of biting my nails.

Marley's confused expression shifts to understanding. She takes my hand in hers and squeezes. "We didn't do anything wrong, Rian. You're not scamming them. We're going to make a legitimate sale like we always do, no messing with numbers, no playing odds or people."

I take a deep breath. "It's just . . . he's a lawyer and he's in real estate. What if he knows people who knew Dad? He could figure out who we're connected to and then no one would want to buy from us."

"Take a breath, Rian," she says softly. "We're completely ethical here. Is it crazy that you've slept with this guy and now we're potentially selling them a house? Sure, but it has nothing to do with what happened with Dad. You need to stop owning that; you were a kid and you had no idea what he was doing."

I exhale my panic on a nod. Logically, I know she's right, but all of these pieces coming together make me anxious, as does the fact that I've slept with a relative stranger—and would like to do it again, despite current circumstances. Beyond that, being so close to affording our own flip makes me as antsy as it does excited. And maybe it has something to do with being so close to the Mission Mansion this weekend, where so much of our history is tied up. As much as I want to be close to it, I still get nervous. We've done our best to distance ourselves from our family's scandalous past, but if it ever came out, our careers in real estate could come to a grinding halt. Who would want to buy houses from a couple of girls whose family is responsible for stealing millions of dollars through real estate fraud? It doesn't matter that *we* weren't responsible, a sullied name taints the generations that follow.

"Do you think we should reconsider giving them a break on commission since we'll be getting all of it?" I fight to keep my fingers from migrating to my mouth.

"Let's see what they offer first." Marley motions to the dolls, probably to distract me. "What the hell do you think this is about?"

"Maybe one of them has a kid?"

"Yeah. I thought that too, but those dolls are too perfect. Like they've never been played with, and there was one in the hallway. It's odd, right?"

"Yeah. Definitely odd." It would be my luck to hook up with someone who's extraordinarily awesome at sex and also a serious weirdo. I'd like to say this doll thing will deter me from hooking up with Pierce again, but I don't think that's true.

I'm mostly calm and rational once we go back inside and inform them that we've secured a walk-through. While Lawson has been inside the yet-to-be advertised house, Pierce has not, so we make the ridiculously short drive down the beach to the property in question. Pierce decides I need to be the one who shows him around, leaving Marley and Lawson to talk offers.

"This is one of the bedrooms." I Vanna White the room and step aside to let him go first. It's outdated, but at least it's just bad paint and no wallpaper. Sometimes that stuff is a nightmare to get off, especially if it's circa the seventies. I have no idea what kind of glue they used back then, but it sure was made to last.

The rose-and-doily décor is awful, and for most Hamptons buyers, it would be an absolute turnoff. They want move-in ready summer homes, not properties they need to sink time and money into before they're visually palatable. If Marley and I had the capital ready, we would've already put an offer in on this one, but we only have enough to purchase, not enough to cover the cost of a renovation without making things tight. This sale will change that, though.

"I messaged you this morning and you haven't responded yet." Pierce brushes by me.

Even that simple, innocent contact makes all my special parts zing. The presence of a bed doesn't help either. "It's rude for me to check messages when I'm with a prospective buyer."

"Even if you've slept with that prospective buyer? The same prospective buyer who's messaging you?" He takes a look in the closet. "This is small, but workable."

"You can probably give yourself a tour; you don't need me." I turn to walk away, but he grabs my hand and threads his fingers through mine.

"What're you doing?"

"Keeping you from running away." Pierce tugs me forward and brings our twined hands to his lips, biting my knuckle. I clench my jaw and try my hardest not to make any noises of pleasure, or do anything else to encourage him to continue. "Where do you feel that?"

"Pardon?"

He bites my knuckle again. "Where does the sensation resonate the most?"

"Where your lips just were." That's untrue. That's where it starts, but it's as if the sensation pushes through my veins and ends right in the sweet spot between my thighs. Which I clench, lest I give in to the urge to wrap myself around him and front hump him.

"I don't believe you."

Why does it feel like he's burrowing his way into my head when all he's doing is touching me? "Why ask the question if you're not going to trust I'm being truthful with the answer?"

His lips turn up against the back of my hand. "Why're you still so prickly with me, Rian?"

I try to pull my hand away, but he tightens his grip. "Why do you ask so many uncomfortable questions?"

"I didn't realize I was making you uncomfortable."

I scoff. "Yeah, right. I don't buy that for a second. You get a kick out of antagonizing me. You like to have control over these interactions we have so you pose uncomfortable questions and use intimacy to unnerve me."

"Are you psychoanalyzing me, or yourself?"

Probably a bit of both. "This thing you're doing, this game you're playing with me, you're too good at it. How often do you do this?"

"Do what exactly?"

"This whole seduction routine."

He almost looks hurt. "You think this is a routine?"

"Isn't it?" It's bad that I don't want it to be, that I want this connection we have, these strange coincidental meetings to be fate throwing us together, even if it is a colossally bad idea.

"Why are you so hell-bent on villainizing me?"

That's a good question. One I can't answer honestly because it's tied up too much with a past I can't share. I think I like him. No, there's no thinking. I *know* I like him, and the chemistry between us is unreal. It makes me feel vulnerable, and vulnerability is a weakness. Besides, he's just so perfect, *too* perfect—he has all the right components—physical, sexual, and I bet if I got to know him better, I'd probably like every side of him—which is terrifying, because he can't know every side of me and still like me. "Why do you keep coming after me? I haven't even been nice to you."

He's still kissing my knuckles, lips sweeping back and forth. "You were nice to me last night, before you kicked me out, anyway."

"You're not going to let that go, are you?"

He flips my hand over and kisses the inside of my wrist. "Probably not. Can I tell you something else? Something important?"

He looks so earnest. Please don't let him be a baby daddy. "Sure?"

"My intention last night wasn't to get you naked."

I roll my eyes. "Oh, come on."

"I'm serious. I usually like to take things a little slower. I mean, I'm certainly glad I had the opportunity to get my hands on you, and I won't lie and tell you I wouldn't love to have that opportunity again, but I had no expectation that would happen last night."

"You could've said no."

He laughs. "No, I couldn't have."

"Because I'm so irresistible?"

"Yes. You're smart and sassy and sexy, and right now all I want is for you to bite my lip like you did last night, and I'm a little obsessed with knowing what color your panties are."

I stare dumbly at his gorgeous, sincere expression. If I end up sleeping with him again, I won't be able to kick him out. I won't want to.

"Help a guy out here. Say something, Rian."

I grab his tie with the hand that isn't still twined with

his and drag his mouth down to mine. And I do exactly what he wants. I bite his lip. Well, it's more of a nibble.

"Thank fuck. I thought I was going to lose my ever-loving mind."

Fingers still laced, he folds my arm behind my back—I think this is his thing—his other hand slides into the hair at the nape of my neck, twisting through the strands to anchor there. I suck his bottom lip, dragging my teeth across the sensitive skin.

Pierce makes a low, rough sound in the back of his throat and a shiver forces its way down my spine, goose bumps exploding on my skin.

He angles my head to one side and slants his mouth over mine, tongue pushing past my lips, hot and aggressive. Our chests and hips meet, his hardness pressing against my stomach.

It's like I can taste the pheromones in the air, and it only serves to fuel the lust. Our tongues dance and twirl, battle and stroke, teeth nip and bite.

Pierce rolls his hips. "I want to fucking *consume* you," he groans into my mouth.

I get what he means. I would seriously rip his clothes off and ride him on the horrible floral print comforter, get as much of him inside me, have as much of his skin touching mine as I could, *if* I wasn't suddenly conscious of the fact that my sister and his brother are upstairs, talking numbers.

The numbers I usually deal with.

I grasp his chin in my free hand and push his face away. It's the only way I'll be able to end this kiss. We're both panting. I tip my head back even as he tries to bring our mouths together again. And I want him to. The desire is visceral, a shimmer in the air, a heat in my veins, and a fire in his eyes.

That is what wanting someone is.

This is the pinnacle of desperate attraction. This is the chemical reaction that ignites and burns until there's nothing left but ash.

This insatiable craving is why people ignore a two out of ten on a compatibility test.

"Enough," I whisper. My voice comes out a smoky rasp, but there's command in it and he yields.

He nods his head once, eyes darting to my lips, the longing making his lids heavy. "Never. But okay . . . for now."

He releases my hand and he takes a step back as he smooths out my hair. "Sorry. That was . . . I . . ."

"You're fine." I'm not sure I am, though. My whole body feels like it's been lit up and I'm on overdrive.

He glances down to where his very impressive erection pushes against the fly of his dress pants. "Well, that's questionable." He turns around, his broad back shifting as he rearranges things—I can see his reflection in the mirror across the room, though. His eyes roll up as he moves things around and his lip curls.

I don't think I've ever had this effect on another person before.

The power is intoxicating.

His eyes meet mine in the reflection and his grimace turns into a grin, which matches mine. "Now who's enjoying whose discomfort?"

I raise my hand, finger and thumb half an inch apart. "Me. But just a little."

"Not interested in helping me resolve it, then?"

I shake my head. "I'm going to show you the rest of house now, and you're not going to antagonize me into kissing you again."

He nods his agreement.

"Great." I put a little extra sway in my hips. "And Pierce?"

"Yeah?" He follows me out of the bedroom.

"Mint green."

"What?"

"You said you wanted to know what color my panties are. They're mint green."

He grabs the top of the doorjamb and heaves a deep sigh. "Patterned or solid color?"

"Solid."

"Cotton, satin, lace, or a combination?"

"Lace."

"Thong?" He sounds hopeful.

"Cheekies."

"Ah fuck." He bites his lip. "Wanna give me a peek?"

I laugh. "Nope."

"Never hurts to ask."

CHAPTER 14

DANCING IN THE SAND

RIAN

It isn't until after I've given Pierce the tour that Marley informs them we're the selling agents. She was right, my paranoia was unfounded, but then, she wasn't the one to inadvertently help our father swindle millions of dollars out of unsuspecting families. Surprisingly, they don't try to negotiate the commission down.

Pierce refuses to put in an offer without having a private conversation with his brother. Lawson is ridiculously keen on buying the property, ready to throw out whatever figure is necessary. Pierce wants to make sure the minor renovations needed can be done in a time-sensitive manner so they can capitalize on potential summer revenue. It's smart. Pierce is smart. Logical where his brother seems impulsive.

We leave them to discuss it with the expectation that they'll call before four in the afternoon with an offer, otherwise we're going through with the open house the following day. Marley and I lounge on the deck, anxiously watching the minutes tick by as we wait.

Pierce calls at 3:39. Not Lawson. Pierce. And he calls my phone, not Marley's.

"You still haven't answered my text messages from this morning," he says by way of greeting.

"Is this a social call or a business call?"

"Both."

"It can't be both. It has to be one or the other."

"Why can't it be both?"

"You have twenty minutes until your window of opportunity closes."

"To get into your panties tonight?"

"Do you ever stop?"

"Not really."

"I'm talking about putting an offer in on the house. Your time is running out. We can't do social until we're done doing business, and social doesn't include getting into my panties, FYI." Such a lie. Although it won't be the mint-green ones I was wearing earlier, those are already in the laundry pile, courtesy of the effects of that kiss we shared.

"Okay. Let's clear up the business first. We can talk about your panties later. We're putting in an offer."

"If you're putting in an offer, you should be talking to Marley, not me."

"I don't want to talk to Marley. I want to talk to you."

I sigh and put the phone on speaker, dropping it on the table between our loungers. "I draw up papers. Marley presents offers. You have to deal with both of us."

"You know what would make this even easier?"

"If you dealt with Marley?"

"If we came over there and discussed it in person." I roll my eyes at Marley, but before I can respond, Pierce says, "We'll be there in less than ten."

"You only have nineteen minutes left to make an offer. You better get your rear in gear."

"Get the paperwork started."

"Don't tell me wh—"

The call cuts out.

I huff, annoyed. "It better be a good offer."

Pierce and Lawson come sauntering up the stairs to the deck like they own the place—which they do—a few minutes later. Lawson is wearing board shorts and the same open, button-down shirt as before. Pierce is no longer wearing a dress shirt and tie. Now he's sporting a pair of board shorts and he has a T-shirt slung over his shoulder, Trip on his heels.

"Let's make a deal, ladies." Lawson pulls up two deck chairs.

Pierce gives me a slow perusal. "I was expecting the pink bikini, but I think I might like this one even better."

I'm wearing my yellow polka-dot bikini. It's superfun and has a cute little tie right between my boobs, which is where Pierce's gaze snags as he takes a seat beside his brother. Trip sits in front of Pierce, tongue lolling and tail wagging. He's so freaking adorable. The dog, not the man. The man is gorgeous. And he knows it, based on the way he flexes his abs when I accidentally caress them with my eyes.

"Bottom line, gentlemen." Marley slaps the arms of her chair, apparently unfazed by everyone's half-dressed state, including her own. "You need to put your best offer on the table. If they don't like it, they're going to hold an open house tomorrow and you'll be out of luck."

Lawson slaps the arm of his chair. I can't tell if he's making fun of Marley or they have the same mannerisms. "We'll go ten over asking."

"This place will go into a bidding war. It's the only house for sale on this end of the beach since you're not selling yours anymore, and there's nothing comparable in

Hamptons Bay," Marley counters. "Everyone who was expecting to come to your open house will now be at theirs. But if ten over is your best, Rian will prepare the paperwork."

I'm already typing away on my laptop, pulling up the documents—which are set to go apart from the dollar amount because I *knew* they were going to put in an offer, it was just a matter of how close they planned to cut it.

"We'll go $819K, so twenty over asking."

"Whoa, what? This is a bungalow, Lawson." Pierce's head whips around, as if this is news to him.

Lawson gives him a look. "Best offer, bro. Get with the program. We've got three minutes to make a move."

"Fine, $819K, but you're cutting into my reno budget with this." Pierce looks annoyed. "Next time you don't get to waffle until the eleventh hour."

"I'll call the seller. Hopefully your offer will offset your down-to-the-wire timing," Marley grabs her phone.

"It's on you if we don't get this," Pierce mutters to his brother.

I stand with my laptop propped on my hip, grateful for the opportunity to go inside and throw on a sundress so I can feel more business than beach babe. "I'll get the paperwork together."

The seller—the Franklins—pick up on the fourth ring, at 3:58 p.m. Talk about cutting it close. I prepare the paperwork and have Pierce and Lawson sign the documents so we can present the offer.

We spend the next two hours with the sellers. We priced it high and they've been offered well over asking, so the Franklins are thrilled.

By seven thirty the only thing we have left to do is make sure the financing is secure. We have to wait until Monday when the banks are open since Lawson and Pierce put in a cash offer, which speaks to their capital if they can fork over more than three quarters of a million in cash without lopping off body parts.

"We're totally going out and getting hammered to-night!" Marley says as soon as she hangs up with Lawson, the proud new owner of a seriously outdated house in need of about forty thousand dollars in upgrades and renovations. I know. I did the math when we talked about putting it on the market and whether we could afford to buy it from the seller.

On the upside, the commission on this place puts us in the market for a flip once that money is in our account.

Marley's right to want to celebrate. This is exactly what we've been working all these years for. We're finally out of the crapper and on our way up. Not Mission Mansion up yet, but maybe one day. It's a dream that feels far out of reach, but this is a step closer.

I jump into the shower and let Marley do my hair and makeup while we polish off the bottle of white wine left for Gel and Lauren, who are still uncertain as to whether or not they'll be able to make the trip tomorrow since Noodles isn't 100 percent symptom free. I even let Marley pick out my dress—it's supertight with a plunging neckline and an ultrashort hem.

"I don't know about this. I feel like I'm going to struggle to keep all my assets covered." Every time I pull on the hem to cover more leg, I reveal more cleavage.

"Which is why it's perfect." Marley tosses me a pair of electric-purple heels. The dress is lawn green. I like bright colors, but this is a lot, and not enough at the same time.

"These are a bit much, aren't they?" Does electric purple go with lawn green? I don't know. I feel like I should be in a nineties' music video.

"Nope. Put them on." I'm already tipsy enough that I'm

starting to think this outfit is a great idea and that my butt looks fantastic.

I stuff my identification, credit card, lipstick, and phone into my tiny clutch.

As soon as I close my purse my phone vibrates. I've already messaged Pierce, letting him know that Marley and I are going out to celebrate. If I happen to run into him, I'm not opposed to a little celebration of the orgasm variety.

I'm two drinks and two shots into my night and currently leaning on the railing on the perimeter of the dance floor, keeping an eye on my sister—there are at least two different groups of guys head bopping within a three-foot radius of her. I'm sure they're all playing rock, paper, scissors to see who gets to take her home at the end of the night. It's happened before.

A hand settles on my hip and I turn with the intention of telling whoever it is to back off, but when I look up, I get an eyeful of Pierce's perfect face.

He leans down, cheek brushing mine, lips touching my ear. "You know, it would've been a lot easier to find you if you'd been more specific about where you'd be celebrating tonight."

"There aren't that many bars down here. I was pretty sure you'd be able to figure it out without too much trouble."

Pierce chuckles and laces his fingers with mine. "Come on."

I glance at Marley, who gives me a thumbs-up and then goes back to grinding her butt against some random on the dance floor as Pierce tugs me toward the outdoor patio.

It's a little quieter out here, the music not so throbbingly loud.

Pierce maneuvers us through the impatient crowd until

we're at the bar. He cages me with his arms from behind, his chest pressed against my back, protecting me from the throng of bodies three deep behind us. The bartender seems to know him personally, so we're able to secure drinks quickly—I opt for water this time, aware I'm tipsy and already planning to make questionable decisions where this man is concerned tonight. I don't need every last one of my inhibitions gone.

Drinks in hand, Pierce links our fingers again, leading me through the crowd to a secluded corner on the patio.

He clinks his beer against my water bottle. "Congratulations on the sale."

"Congratulations on the buy." I take a long swig from the bottle, unsure where we're going from here.

He leans against the railing, apparently getting comfortable. "Why didn't you tell me you were in real estate last night?"

"Marley does more of the selling and networking. I'm the numbers girl."

"And why is that?" He tips his head, observing me in a way that makes me nervous.

"She's better with people than I am."

"Says who?" He tucks a strand of hair behind my ear.

I shrug and look away. "It's the way it is with us. She likes the limelight and I like behind the scenes."

"That's interesting, considering the dress you're currently wearing."

I'm suddenly hyperaware of the way Pierce is looking at me; as if I'm something he'd like to devour. A trickle of sweat works its way down my spine, and the cool breeze from the water makes me shiver. "It's Marley's."

"Why am I not surprised? I'm on the fence about whether or not I'd like to thank her for all the attention you're drawing in this. I thought I might have to throw a couple of punches with the way all the guys in there were looking at you."

"No one was looking at me."

"You're adorably oblivious, you know that?" He moves in closer, angling himself so he almost acts as a shield, blocking me from the other people in the bar.

"Oblivious?"

"Yes. Oblivious. You're too busy worrying about what your sister's getting up to to notice all the attention you get."

Marley has always been the brightest star with the biggest personality, and I've always been in the background. Beyond that, after the family scandal a decade ago, it was better to be a wallflower than to stand out, like I am now in this ostentatious dress. "Someone has to take care of her and keep her out of trouble."

"And what about you? Who takes care of you, Rian?" Although the question seems innocent, it's far more loaded than he can understand or imagine.

"We take care of each other." Nerves make my mouth dry.

Pierce leans in closer, fingers skimming my cheek. It's the gentlest caress. "Why are you so guarded?"

"Why do you ask so many personal questions?"

"Because I like you and I'm trying to get to know you."

"You like me because I let you screw me on a dryer." I take another sip of water, my face as hot as the rest of my body.

"I liked you before that." His grin widens. "And I like you more because of that."

I gesture between us. "This isn't a good idea if we're going to be working for you and your brother." Lawson is too hungry for this property for it to be the last he buys.

"Business is business. We can keep it separate. I had a

lot of fun last night." He dips his head and his cold fingers tilt my chin up. "I think you had fun too. I think we could have more fun, together." His lips hover over mine. "What about you? What do you think?"

Flashbacks of last night flicker through my head like a slideshow on fast-forward when his chest meets mine and his thumb sweeps across my bottom lip. We have one more night at the beach house before we have to go back to our apartment and real life. Who knows what will happen after that? Based on our conversations, he's only here temporarily, anyway. I can't deny the sex was awesome, or that I kind of like how much joy he derives from antagonizing me. I could have a summer fling, the kind I should've had years ago, before my life fell apart.

I grace him with what I hope is the same cocky smile he likes to give me. "I'm up for some fun."

"I knew you'd come around."

He kisses me, a quick brushing of lips before he steps back. "Wanna get out of here?"

I find Marley to let her know I'm leaving with Pierce, to which I get a thumbs-up and a *have fun*. And then we're out the doors, heading for the beach.

He crouches when we reach the sand and removes my shoes, carrying them as we walk down the beach. Quickly. I've had a few drinks and it's fairly dark, aside from the moon and the stars and the porch lights from houses. We make it halfway down the beach before he spins me around, crushing my body against his. He takes my face between his palms and tilts my head back as his tongue sweeps inside. I latch onto his forearms, my legs turning watery under the unexpected but welcome kiss. We drop to the sand, mouths fused as I pull him over me.

"We should've left sooner." He grinds his hips against me, his groan desperate, one hand shoved in my hair. The other smoothing down my side and then back up. He breaks the kiss, biting my bottom lip before nibbling his way down my throat. He palms my breast through the fabric, squeezing.

I bite my lip to stifle a moan. I can't believe we're back to making out on the beach. It might be deserted for the most part, but I can both hear and see the bar in the distance.

I'm too consumed to care, though, high on the sale and the buzz of hormones and alcohol. We're both frantic mouths and roaming hands, tugging at fabric, unbuttoning, unzipping, pushing and pulling. Fingers explore, panties are pulled to the side, the tear of foil brings with it tangible relief to the ache between my thighs. Or bodies align and then he's in me, the dark sky lit up with a million stars I can still see as my eyes close and I let sensation take over. We crash into each other like waves at high tide, desperate, chasing a building release.

"I'm gonna come, Rian, and I don't want to go over the edge alone."

"I'm right there with you," I whisper into his ear.

Two thrusts later I come on a moan that he smothers with his mouth. The kiss is as vicious as the orgasm. He follows after me, movements erratic and intense as his own release steals his coordination.

After a few long, suspended moments, he lifts his head from the crook of my neck, thumb stroking along my jaw, eyes fixed on mine. And then he smiles. "We're having a sleepover. We're going to do this all night, and I'm going to cuddle you like a motherfucker after I finishing sexing every last orgasm out of you."

"Okay." I mean, what else can I really say to that?

CHAPTER 15

CUDDLE FUCK

PIERCE

This is not how I meant for tonight to go down. I'd planned to catch up with Rian, have a few drinks, and maybe invite her back to my place for a private celebration for two.

Except I hadn't gotten that far. I blame it on the little green dress. Currently I'm still inside Rian. Still breathing hard, because I fucked her on the beach. And she let me. My cock twitches despite having come less than thirty seconds ago.

I have a system, a routine, a plan I usually follow with women, and she's blowing that all to shreds. I'm usually a lot better at taking things slow, but not with Rian.

"Are you okay?" I ask, guttural and low.

"Yes." It's more raspy whisper than anything.

I scan the beach. Thankfully it's still empty. We're close to my brother's place. Closer than we are to the rental. I fold back on my knees and shift the top of her dress so it covers her breasts. This is the second time I've fucked the hell out of this woman. In two days.

I ease out and adjust her panties—which I never bothered to take off—and her dress into place so she's not flashing the world when she stands. It's only after she's covered that I slip the condom off, tie a knot in it and shove it in my pocket. Gross, yes. But better than leaving it for a bird to choke on and die. Or a toddler to pick up while making sand castles tomorrow.

"Come on, hotness." I take her hands and pull her into a sitting position. As I stand, I bring her with me. The temperature has dropped significantly since the sun disappeared.

Rian shivers and crosses her arms over her chest, head bowed as I pick my shirt up off the ground and shake it out.

"Arms out, baby," I murmur.

She peeks up.

"You're shivering. Let's get you inside and warmed up."

"What about you?"

"I'm the asshole who fucked you on beach in May. I deserve to be cold." She slips her arms into the sleeves. It's huge on her, but at least it's a barrier against the cool breeze coming off the water.

I grab her shoes and tuck her into my side, walking briskly up the beach. She has to jog to keep up, so I pause for a moment, dip down, tuck her knees into the crook of my arm and swing her up.

"What're you doing? I'm too heavy!" Rian protests, but latches her arms around my neck and snuggles right in. If I'd been smart enough to wait until we were back at her place, we could be in a damn bed now.

"Hardly," I scoff.

Clouds have started to roll in, and I have to wonder if we're in for a storm tonight.

I jog toward my brother's beach house. The three thousand square feet of open concept living space feels small with the two of us currently living here together. But once the master bedroom is renovated in the bungalow we purchased, I can always move in there while I finish the rest of the house. My condo in Manhattan is way too far to be a reasonable drive, so I haven't been back in weeks. And I don't really want to.

I have to set Rian down to unlock the door, but I wrap one arm around her, keeping her tight against my chest.

"God, I'm itchy," she mumbles as she reaches down to scratch her calf, while holding onto my arm for balance.

I open the door and usher her inside. Most of the lights are off, apart from a small lamp in the living room. I guide her upstairs to my bedroom, which is also mostly dark, and as far away from my brother's as it can possibly get. I don't flick on a light until I reach my private bathroom.

We both hiss at the sudden brightness. It takes a few seconds for my eyes to adjust, and I cross to the shower, turning on the water.

"What're you doing?" Rian asks.

"Warming you up with a nice hot shower." I turn around and pull my shirt over her head, sand fluttering to the floor around her feet.

She arches a brow. "Are you planning to join me?"

"How're you going to get your back if I'm not in there with you?"

She braces a hand on the vanity and scratches her leg again. "Seriously, why am I so itchy?"

"It's probably the sand." Or the friction from the sand. I turn her around with the intention of unzipping her dress. "Oh shit."

"That doesn't sound good." She meets my slightly horrified gaze in the mirror.

I clear my throat and try to make my eyes look less like they're about to pop out of my head. "You've got a few bites." A few is an understatement. Her shoulders to her mid-back and from mid-thigh to ankle are covered in tiny, angry bites. There have to be more than a hundred.

"What kind of bites? How many is a few?"

"Um, judging from the look of them, I'd say sand fleas."

"Fleas?" Her shriek echoes in the confines of the bathroom. She spins so her back is facing the mirror and cranes her neck to see over her shoulder. Her mouth drops. "Oh my God! *Oh my God.* A *few* bites?"

"It's not that bad." It's actually worse than that bad.

She checks out the back of her legs, which are a mass of tiny, raised red bumps. She reaches behind her, likely with the intention of scratching. I grab her hands and clasp them in mine. "Don't do that. It'll make it worse."

"But I'm so itchy. I need to get out of this dress. What if there are sand fleas stuck under it?" She starts hopping from one foot to the other.

"Let me help you out of it, then you can get into the shower. I have antihistamines and I'll draw a bath. I have salts I use when I have allergic reactions. They're holistic or whatever." I don't know why I'm explaining, other than I feel bad and I want to fix it. I also don't want this to be the last time Rian and I have sex—selfish of me, I know.

I get Rian out of her dress. Thankfully, most of the bites seem isolated to the backs of her legs and her shoulders, although a few managed to get under the fabric. I'll inspect her better when she's done with the shower.

I find the antihistamines, both in pill and cream form—I'm definitely going to take the opportunity to rub it all over her body in penance—then start the bath.

"There's so much sand in my hair," she calls from the shower. "It's like half the beach is in here. God! Are there fleas in my hair? I'm so itchy! I hate you so much right now."

"I promise I'll fix it, hotness," I call back, dumping the oatmeal, Epsom salts, and lavender pouch into the giant Jacuzzi tub.

She sticks her head out of the shower and glares at me. "You do not get to call me pet names, a-hole."

"Is that *my* pet name?" I don't even bother to fight my grin as she shoots me the bird and disappears back into the shower.

The glass is foggy, but I can make out her silhouette, all soft curves and long hair streaming down her back. I fill a glass with water and strip out of my own pants. Gathering our discarded clothes, I drop them in the washing machine and put it on the sanitize cycle.

Now that I'm naked too, I see that I haven't escaped unscathed. My forearms have suffered the same fate as Rian's back and legs, and I have a few scattered bites on my chest. Nothing compared to her, though. I wrap a towel around my waist so I'm not swinging free when she gets out of the shower.

I'm going to have to take excellent care of her if I want to get back in her good graces tonight. I have a few ideas on how to accomplish that. The shower turns off, and she steps out onto the mat, nipples tight, body covered in a flash of goose bumps as the cool air kisses her skin.

I wrap her in a towel and hand her the glass of water. "You should take this."

"What is it?"

"It's an antihistamine."

She inspects it, the name is stamped in the pill, so that must appease her, because she pops it in her mouth and drains the glass of water. She scans the bathroom floor. "Where are my clothes?"

"I put them in the wash. It'll be about thirty minutes before I can put them in the dryer." I motion to the tub.

"I poured us a bath. It should help with the itch until the antihistamine kicks in."

She regards the tub, and then me, skeptically.

"I don't have to join you. Whatever you prefer."

Her gaze moves over me, assessing, considering. She drops her towel. "You can join me."

Stepping up to the tub, I hold out my hand and help her in. She sinks into the water on a groan.

"Where do you want me?" I ask.

"You can go sit in the corner." She motions to the other side of the tub. I get in and spread my legs so they frame hers, running my hands up her shins under the water.

"I'm blaming the dress for this."

Rian snorts. "Nice apology."

I shift, water sloshing over the edge of the tub as I straddle her thighs and brace a forearm on either side of her. I get right in her face, rubbing the end of my nose against hers before I back up far enough that I can see her clearly. "I'm sorry you're so irresistible. I'm sorry I was an asshole. I'm sorry I couldn't wait to until we were here, with access to a comfortable bed, before I got inside you. Is that better?"

She bites her lip and ducks her head. "A little. It doesn't change the fact that I'm still itchy as heck, though."

"Give the bath a few minutes to work its magic." I settle back against my side of the tub. "Tell me how you got into real estate."

Rian's eyes shift away from mine, moving to where she swirls the bubbles on the surface of the water. "When our grandmother passed away, she left us a duplex. Marley and I moved into the upstairs and rented out the main floor. I guess that's when we started to see the value in property."

There's something in her voice, and the tension in her

shoulders that makes me want to push for more. "I'm so sorry she passed. Were you close to your grandmother?"

"Yeah. She was a special woman. Smart, savvy. She would've been a force if she'd been born in this generation."

"Kind of like you, then?"

She laughs. "I don't know about that, but I hope one day I can achieve even half of her success. What about you and your brother? You said this was his hobby, but it seems like he takes it pretty seriously."

I run my fingers absently up and down her shin, under the water. "He's been dabbling for a year or so. I think we'd both like it to be more than a hobby, eventually anyway."

"Well, everyone needs a place to live, and there are always people with money looking to buy beachfront. Most people either don't have the vision or the interest in fixing up a place. You have both. When you have capital and the ability to see the beauty in possibility, you can do well in this industry."

"Wouldn't flipping houses be more lucrative than selling them?"

Rian lifts a shoulder. "If you can buy the right place at the right time for the right price, you'll get the most return on investment, but you still need the capital to do that."

"If you could have one house on this beach, which one would it be?" I ask.

"The Mission Mansion," she replies without hesitation.

"Why the Mission Mansion?" It's gorgeous and eclectic, one of the largest homes on the beach, but it's in need of some serious renovations and repairs. From what I understand, the owners spend most of their summer in Europe, so it's gone mostly unused and ignored for the better part of the last decade, which is sad.

She drags her fingers along the surface of the water, creating ripples. "Marley and I used to spend a lot of time there in the summers when we were teenagers."

"Really? You knew the previous owners?"

She's quiet for a few seconds before she replies, "My grandparents did."

I'm only semi-surprised by this answer. There's something refined about Rian that I can't quite pin down. "It must've been amazing inside."

"It is. Or at least it was." Her smile is wistful, almost sad. "It holds a lot of special memories for me. I'd hate to see it get any more rundown than it already is."

"Do you think it will ever go on the market?" From the little I know about the property, the last time it changed hands was about a decade ago, but I never paid particularly close attention to the place other than to admire it. It's unfortunate that it sits vacant now.

"Maybe one day. It's a pipe dream, anyway. I'll never have the capital for that place." For a moment she looks so forlorn, before she gives me one of her soft, questioning smiles. "What about you? What property are you most interested in?"

"I don't know. I haven't given it much thought. I think the more rundown the better, though. I like fixing broken things."

She mutters something I don't catch.

"What was that?"

"I'm turning into a prune." She rises from the tub, water sluicing down her gorgeous, naked body. "And I'm still itchy."

Fifteen minutes later Rian is facedown on my mattress. No, we're not having sex. I'm atoning for my sins by rubbing Benadryl cream on her bug bites. The sheer number is insane. They cover her shoulders, her calves, and the back of her thighs. I keep running my palms up and down, and then higher, up the back of her legs. She moans when I knead her ass. There are bites there too, so it's an area that needs attention.

"What're you doing?" Her voice is raspy, groggy.

"Trying to keep you comfortable."

"I think you're trying to cop a feel."

"I can do both, can't I? I think they call it multitasking."

She snorts a tired laugh.

My pillow is going to smell like her tomorrow. My whole bed is. And tonight I'm going to bask in the scent of Rian, because she's going nowhere. She's half asleep already, body languid, arms loose at her sides.

When I'm done taking care of the bites, she snuggles into me, tired and spent, I consider that this is moving way too fast. We're like two trains on the same track, heading for each other. A collision is imminent. But I can't find it in me to care.

CHAPTER 16

RELATIONSHIP GOALS

RIAN

I'm floating on a cloud. A warm cloud. A very cozy, warm cloud that smells deliciously of aftershave.

I open my eyes and remember that I'm not in my own bedroom. But then I realize I'm also not in the bedroom of the beach house rental either. It takes about three seconds for all the pieces to fit together. And then memories of last night slam into me; sex on the beach, the sand fleas, the bath, talking, his bed, a rubdown that did not include sex, and then sleep, blissful, blissful sleep.

I'm using Pierce's arm as a pillow. Slowly I turn my head to the right. The sheets hang low on his hips, his hand is under the covers, possibly cradling his junk.

I can't believe I stayed the night. I can't believe he was actually serious about the post-sex cuddling. Or that it appears it lasted through the entire night.

I check the clock on the nightstand. It's already eleven thirty. I haven't slept this late since I was a teenager.

"Morning." Pierce's deep, raspy sleep voice draws my gaze back to him. His one visible eye is barely a slit.

"Hi." My stomach twists a little, uncertain as to how this is going to go.

He smirks, tongue peeking out as he wets his lips. "I cuddled the fuck out of you all night."

I laugh. "That you did."

"You know what that means, don't you?" He wraps his arm around me and pulls me closer. "It means we're dating."

I tip my chin up so I can see his face. His hair is a mess and he has pillow lines on his cheek. "How do you figure?"

"We had a sleepover and we spooned pretty much the entire night. Plus, we had a bath together, and I've taken care of you and all your bug bites, so that totally qualifies as dating behavior."

I settle a palm on his chest and feel the steady thump of his heart. I'm surprisingly not freaked out by this thought. "I suppose that makes logical sense."

His sleep-heavy eyes crinkle at the corners. "So you agree that we're dating?"

"You didn't really give me much of an opportunity to disagree, did you?"

"Since when does that stop you?" His lips meet my temple. "You know what we should do to celebrate this milestone in our relationship?"

"What's that?" I throw my leg over his, fully expecting him to say morning sex.

"We should have Naked Sunday."

"Naked Sunday?"

"Yeah. You know, where we spend the day hanging out naked."

"Is this something you do often?" I imagine spending an entire twenty-four hours sans clothing with Pierce. I can't imagine getting anything accomplished, apart from wearing out my vagina with whatever parts of his body he felt like sticking in there.

"No. I've never actually done it before, but I figured it could be our thing."

"Our thing?"

"Yeah, you know, like the thing we do together, just us. On Sundays. We can make it a weekly standing date from here on." He nods, maybe to himself, like this is the best idea he's ever had.

He's adorably persistent. "Except you don't live alone and as much as I don't mind looking at you naked, I'm not so sure I'm all that comfortable wandering around like this in front of your brother. Also, I have a lot of work to do today since my sister and I sold a house yesterday."

"Hmm. You make a good point about my brother. We'll postpone Naked Sunday, or we can pick an alternate day of the week. Why don't I make you breakfast instead?"

"Oooh, I like breakfast." My stomach growls.

"Awesome." He pats my tummy. "It's settled. I need coffee, how about you?"

"Um, sure?"

Pierce finds some of his sister's clothes in the spare bedroom. Nothing says walk of shame like eating breakfast in last night's dress.

I'm relieved that Lawson doesn't appear to be awake yet. Or if he is, he's not hanging around the kitchen to witness the morning after my beach romp with Pierce. I take a seat at the island, while Pierce makes coffee and then checks the contents of the fridge. "I can make pancakes, waffles, or French toast. Oh, wait. I have cinnamon rolls. I can make cinnamon roll French toast."

"That sounds ridiculously unhealthy."

"We probably burned a thousand calories apiece competing for orgasms on the beach last night. I'm pretty sure unhealthy is acceptable."

"Cinnamon roll French toast it is, then." Pierce has just started cracking eggs when the doorbell rings.

"Who stops by this early on a Sunday morning?" he grumbles.

"It's already noon." I point out.

"Oh. Still. This is our time, and someone is rudely interfering. I'll go tell them to shove off, shall I?"

I can't tell if he's serious or not as he tosses a dishtowel on the island and heads for the door.

"Took you long enough!" The female voice makes me bristle, until I realize it's familiar.

"Uh, not that it isn't nice to see you guys, but what are you doing here?" Pierce runs a hand through his hair and gives me an *I have no idea what's going on* look.

"Law invited us. He said you got the house you were after and that we should come by for lunch." Amalie waltzes into the kitchen, looking fabulously flawless in contrast to my appearance. Her blond hair falls in perfect waves over her shoulders. She's wearing a butter-yellow sundress and has a huge orange beach bag slung over her shoulder. Her nails boast a French manicure. She exudes polish and poise. And I exude last night's sex on the beach.

I'm sure my expression is electroshock-like. I can feel exactly how wide my eyes are and I'm gripping the counter in order to keep me from doing something rash—like bolting.

I glance frantically over her shoulder at Pierce, giving him a *what in the actual heck* look. Because I'm covered in bug bites, wearing her borrowed clothes, after having been screwed six ways from Sunday by her brother.

A wide grin breaks across Amalie's face and she does

jazz hands. "Oh my God!" She turns to her brother. "I was so right!" Then she turns to another man. One I hadn't noticed until now, although I'm not exactly sure how I missed him, considering he looks like a cross between a model, a mobster, and a superhero. "Remember how I told you about that woman who gave Pierce shit at the restaurant? This is her! This is Rian!"

The man in question has dark hair, almost black, and eyes so blue they look like they can't possibly be that color naturally. What is it with these guys and their eyes?

He's as tall as Pierce, and just as broad. Maybe even a little broader. Built like a linebacker. He's wearing a pair of khaki shorts and a T-shirt that shows off a very intricate, colorful full-sleeve tattoo.

His eerily perfect blue eyes dart questioningly to Pierce and settle on me as his eyebrow quirks up. A small smirk pops a dimple in his left cheek, and he lifts a hand in greeting. "Hi, Rian."

"This is my fiancé, Lex." Amalie rests her cheek on his bicep and pats his chest then flits around the island and pulls me into a hug. "I had no idea you were going to be here today! I'm so excited to see you! I told Pierce he should ask you out and here you are." She cocks her head to the side as she takes in my outfit, her teeth catching her bottom lip. "I think I have a shirt exactly like this."

I close my eyes and will myself to sink into the floor, but when I open them, I'm still sitting on the stool and she's put two and two together. "Oh my God!" She claps her hands. "Oh my God! Did you two"—she looks back and forth between us—"Oh! Look at how red your face is! You so did! Are you two dating now? Can we do double dates?" She's back to clapping. "This means you might actually have a plus-one by the time we set a date for the wedding!"

"Amie, baby, you're scaring her," Lex says, but he looks

highly entertained. He turns that panty-incinerating smile on me. "You probably shouldn't give my fiancée your phone number. She's a little obsessed with you, if you couldn't already tell."

"She's not alone," Pierce says from the other side of the kitchen, a warm smile locked firmly in place.

I'm not sure what exactly I've gotten myself into, but I think I might like it.

CHAPTER 17

WHEELING AND DEALING

RIAN

Brunch with Pierce's sister and her ridiculously hot fiancé is an entertaining experience. Amalie is a talker, and I learn about their very interesting beginnings. It's kind of like a soap opera. She was married to Lex's cousin for less than twelve hours before he cheated on her—which is insane, because she's not only gorgeous, but funny and sweet and generally awesome.

I also learn that Pierce can make a mean cinnamon roll French toast. He seems more than happy to have me in his kitchen, wearing his sister's clothes while she regales me with her relationship history.

Eventually my sister calls, giving me the out I don't necessarily need, but want. I excuse myself to the deck to take the call.

"Oh good, you're alive." Her voice full of sarcasm.

"You sound so genuine in your concern," I reply.

Amalie sticks her head out the door. "Would you like another coffee, Rian?"

"I'm good, thanks," I reply.

"Who was that?"

"Pierce's sister."

"Say what now? You're hanging with the family? What's next, are the two of you moving in together?"

"Don't be ridiculous, we're just dating," I mutter, surprised how easy that was to say aloud.

"Dating, huh? What happened to your 'I won't ever date a hot guy again' insanity?"

"He's only here for the summer, so we're having some fun together."

"Uh-huh. You coming back sometime today or should I meet you at home?"

"I'm coming back. Don't leave without me." I don't want Pierce to offer to drive me home. I'm not ready for him to see where I live. Besides, I like his sister, but this is a lot, very, very fast. I mean, brunch with family members is more than I've done in years.

Pierce walks me down to the beach. My dress, shoes, and purse are tucked into a bag that says *sweet* in bold letters on the front. I adjust the strap on my shoulder and face him.

"I'll drop your sister's clothes off before Marley and I go home this afternoon."

"If that works for you, sure." He's still wearing that ridiculous half smirk, as if he can tell I'm suddenly uncomfortable. We have the whole house-financing situation left to deal with and now that I'm dating him, separating business from pleasure seems a bit more challenging.

"I should have all the necessary paperwork for you and Lawson tomorrow."

"Should we schedule a meeting to go over it?"

"Well, Marley typically takes care of that."

His smile grows wider. "You can't avoid me, now that we're dating. You know that, right?"

"I'm not trying to avoid you. I'm just telling you how it usually works. The house deal has nothing to do with us dating." I'm not used to liking someone this much this quickly. I keep reminding myself that Pierce is only here temporarily, and he seems pretty tied to his job in New York even if he'd rather not be, so what we're doing right now is as serious as it's going to get.

"Okay, well, house deal aside, I'm taking you out for dinner this week, so make sure you have some free time." He cups the back of my neck and bends to kiss me. And not chastely. His tongue is in my mouth and our chests meet, his other arm snakes around my waist, keeping me locked against him. He comes back to nip at my bottom lip a couple more times before he finally releases me. "I'll talk to you soon."

In the week that follows, Pierce makes good on his promise to keep business and pleasure separate. Sort of. Okay, not really. Typically Marley deals with the clients throughout the sale, but I'm cc'd into every email, and Pierce calls and messages me about all of the fine details.

Every phone call—which come daily—begins with a question about financing, closing dates, wording in a contract. Once I'm finished patiently explaining something Pierce clearly already knows the answer to, he switches into flirt mode. Both of us have busy schedules this week, so he ends up tagging along with me to my pottery class on Wednesday. It's something I've done since I was a kid, and I took it up again in the past year. It was more fun to have Pierce with me than I thought it would be, especially since I suck at it a lot and have no plans to get better at it. Sometimes practice doesn't make perfect, but in this case I don't mind. Pierce wanted to pretend to be Patrick Swayze in *Ghost*. All he succeeded in doing was making a colossal mess.

After we finished our pottery projects, he gave me a very long, very drawn-out kiss on the middle of the sidewalk and asked me out for dinner the next night. I get what he's doing—withholding sexual gratification in order to secure future dates. It works. I know how worth it those orgasms will be when I eventually get him alone.

I'm meeting him for dinner tonight on the beach since I already have a potential client appointment set up there this afternoon. Marley and I spent all of last Sunday canvassing the older, less well-maintained homes, bringing by cookies and chatting up the owners, looking for potential homes to buy—or sell, depending on the price point and how much work it needs. I happened on Muriel Barber tending her beautiful gardens, and we got to talking about how much work it is to maintain, even with help.

She's a widow, and as much as she loves the place, she's decided she'd like to relocate closer to her son who lives in Texas. Especially since she's about to be a grandmother to twins and she'd like to be around to help.

So today I'm spending a little time with her, making cookies. Which will give me a chance to check out the interior and see if it's within our renovation budget. Marley's doing the same thing at another house on the opposite end of the beach. We're on the same mission: Seek out potential properties and decide whether we can afford to flip or sell, one batch of cookies at a time.

I check my appearance in my compact. Hair pulled up in a neat ponytail. Check. Lip gloss. Check. Reasonably nice outfit good for baking. Check. Baking supplies. Check.

I knock on the door with a big smile plastered on my face and wait. And wait some more. I check my watch. It's after one. We planned this in advance. A lump forms in my throat. What if little old Ms. Barber had a heart attack in her sleep? What if she's fallen and she can't get up? Or maybe she's napping. The last thought makes me feel marginally better.

I knock again. Harder this time and wait a little bit longer, but still nothing. It's a beautiful day. Maybe she's out by the pool and can't hear me. She loves her pool since getting down to the beach has become more difficult for her recently. She had a hip replacement last year.

With a bowl of cookie dough tucked under my arm, I round the side of the house to the backyard patio that overlooks the beach. As suspected, Ms. Barber is lounging in one of the chairs, her wide brim hat perched on her head.

"Ms. Barber!" I wave jovially and hold up the bowl. "Is it still okay for me to pop by?"

"Oh! Ri-anne! Let yourself in, dearie!" I haven't bothered to correct her on my name. She decided she didn't like that it was so much like the boy name, so she made it into two distinct words instead.

I flip the latch on the gate and step onto the patio. Updated stonework would make this the perfect oasis and the view is absolutely stunning. "How are you?" I bend to hug her.

She fans herself with a magazine. "Just peachy, dear."

"I have cookie dough, the same kind as the ones I brought you last week. Remember?"

"Oh yes! Is it already after one? I must've lost track of time. You should pull up a chair and have a seat for a while. The nice young gentleman from down the beach has stopped by to help clean the pool and he's quite fantastic to watch. He just went to get me a fresh lemonade. Oh!" She grabs my wrist and pulls me closer. "I have an idea. Pluck a handful of leaves from the bush over there, will you? Hurry! Before he comes back out."

I set the bowl on the side table and gather up a few fallen leaves and petals from the garden lining the perimeter of the pool.

"Hurry, hurry!" Ms. Barber motions me back over.

"What do you want me to do with them?"

"Toss them in the pool."

"But—"

"Just do it. Trust me."

I give her a questioning smile, but sprinkle the leaves in the pool.

"Now come sit next to me and pretend we've been talking." As soon as I'm close enough, she grabs my wrist again and pulls me into the lounger next to her. My skirt poofs up and I nearly flash my panties. At least they're nice ones, since I plan to let Pierce take them off me—possibly with his teeth—after baking time is over and we've gone on our dinner date.

"Oh, here he comes. Act natural." Ms. Barber fans her face again with the magazine.

I adjust my sunglasses and nearly choke on the mint I have stuffed in the corner of my mouth. Pierce walks across the patio, holding a pitcher of what looks like lemonade. In the other hand are a couple of glasses. But that's not what almost has me choking to death on a mint.

He's wearing a Speedo. A lime-green Speedo.

Ms. Barber gives my hand a squeeze. "Close your mouth, dear, and play it cool."

My jaw snaps closed. "Dear Lord," I mutter.

"Isn't he magnificent?" she sighs.

"He's something else." I take him in, and I'm rather shameless in my perusal. I've seen him naked, so it's not like I don't already know what he looks like in less clothing than the little he's currently sporting. But he's glistening, as if he's oiled or something.

"Is this the granddaughter you're so fond of, Ms. Barber?" Pierce asks, his megawatt smile flashing at me as he sets the glasses on the table along with the pitcher.

So that's how we're playing it. I'm sure he can see my arched brow.

Ms. Barber giggles, much like a teenage girl, and waves her hand around before she allows it to settle on his forearm. "Now you stop it with the Ms. Barber business, you make me feel old. It's just Muriel."

She's never asked me to call her by her first name. But then, I haven't offered to oil myself up and strut around her pool in the equivalent of underwear.

"Of course, Muriel. My apologies."

Her hand flutters around in the air. "This Ri-anne. She's stopped by to bake some cookies with me this afternoon."

"Is that right? I love cookies." He extends a hand, which I have no choice but to take. His fingers slide along the center of my palm. "The sweeter the better. I'm actually really good with cookies. What kind of cookie do you have, Ri-anne, is it?"

I'm pretty sure my face is on fire. "Rian, yes. I brought sugar cookies."

"Sugar cookies are my favorite." He presses his lips to the back of my hand and grazes my knuckle with his teeth.

"Well, isn't it your lucky day?" Muriel claps her hands.

"Seems that way." He winks at her.

"Do you mind pouring me a glass of that lemonade? Ri-anne, why don't you relax a little and have one with me?"

"Sure, I can do that."

I don't have much to do this afternoon apart from cookies and Pierce, and since he's already here and mostly naked, I might as well enjoy the view and the entertainment. I make a move to stand, but Ms. Barber stops me with a hand.

"No, no, Pierce will get it for you, won't you, darling?"

"It would be my pleasure to serve you both."

I have to fight a laugh, because he's seriously laying it on thick here. He poses as he pours the lemonade into the glass, every hard muscle tightening as he flexes. It's hilarious and yet, I worry he's giving Muriel a case of the vapors.

I accept the lemonade.

"Aren't you going to pour yourself a glass?" Muriel asks.

"I should finish cleaning the pool before I do that." He motions to the leaves floating close to us.

"You're too good to me." She pats his thigh.

"Anything to make it easier for you."

I take a sip of my lemonade and nearly spit-spray it back into the glass. "Is there vodka in here?"

Muriel pinches her fingers together. "Just a touch."

It tastes like a heck of a lot more than a touch. I'll have to sip slowly if I'm going to bake cookies without passing out in the batter. Or getting my cookie eaten by the pool boy later.

He swaggers—it's definitely not a walk or a strut—around the pool, grabbing the net. He starts at the other side, giving me time to ask some pertinent questions. I have an idea as to why Pierce is here—likely for a similar reason I am. We both want the house. I want to sell it or flip it, and he wants to buy it and rent it. It could end up working in both of our favors, unless Marley thinks this is a better house to flip—then I really will be sleeping with the enemy.

He's definitely got a leg up, or at least another, more enticing appendage. And showing up in a Speedo is a new level of playing dirty. I can't compete with his six-pack.

"Does Pierce stop by often?"

"Every few days or so. He helps me water the plants and take care of the gardens between the landscaping company visits. He usually brings his dog, Trip."

"Trip?" I feign a questioning look.

She laughs and takes another long gulp of her drink. "Poor little broken mutt has three legs. You'd almost think they're twins." She nods in Pierce's direction with a wink and nudge.

I stifle a choke-snorting laugh.

"Don't think I didn't notice you checking. And he wouldn't be wearing that banana hammock if he wasn't wanting us to look." She takes another hefty sip of her drink and sighs. "That boy has all the best attributes. He makes me remember I'm still a woman, I can tell you that. I haven't felt so much as a tingle below the waist since Herb passed away. Enjoy this body while you have it, and make sure you let someone enjoy it with you." She pats my leg and winks again. "That boy is a fine, fine specimen. Takes good care of himself. My Herb was the same way when we were your age. Balls hung down to his knees by the end, but gravity is a bastard like that. If I didn't have osteoporosis and my vagina wasn't as dry as the desert in the middle of July, I'd take that out for a ride."

I want to laugh, but she actually looks quite serious.

"You're in your prime, dearie. I hope you're not saving yourself for marriage or anything. You need to ride all the horses you can before you get tied to one of them."

"I'll keep that under advisement."

I finish my vodka and lemonade a lot faster than I should. I'm blaming it on the combination of the heat and Pierce in his Speedo. My favorite part is when his sunglasses accidentally fall into the pool and he has to go in after them.

His dive is virtually splashless, and when he comes up,

he's right in front of us. He slips his sunglasses back on and pulls himself out of the pool in slow motion, water sluicing down his chest. He sets one knee on the edge, highlighting his magic package.

I decline another lemonade and decide I need to get to the cookie baking. I'm unsurprised when Muriel asks if I'm okay on my own.

I head inside and turn on the oven, annoyed that my attempt to butter up Muriel has been thwarted by Pierce and his majestic peen. At least now I have an opportunity to check out the house. The interior is in much better shape than the exterior, the appliances new. The furnishings are reflective of the person who lives here, but that's easy enough to change.

I pull out the baking sheets and the parchment paper. It's a nice oven, convection, so it'll take less time to bake. I have to constantly rotate my cookie sheets at home so the bottoms don't burn.

The first batch is in the oven when Pierce appears in the kitchen. It suddenly feels like the temperature has shot up another ten degrees. "You're pretty transparent, you know that?"

He motions to the set up. "And you're not?"

He has a point. "But you're playing dirty."

"I'd like to play dirty with you later."

I chuckle. "I walked right into that one."

Pierce leans against the counter. "She's lonely."

"And horny. And you're capitalizing on that. I can't figure out if you're doing this to get something out of it or to be nice." I roll another ball of cookie dough and drop it on the pan, flattening it with a fork.

"Why can't it be both?"

"I figured it couldn't be out of the goodness of your big, huge . . . heart." I glance down, making it clear that's not what I'm referencing. "Unless you have a thing for older women."

He crosses his arms over his bare chest. "She lost her husband, Herbert, after forty-two years of marriage. They'd never spent more than a weekend away from each other in all that time. Very different from my parents, who've spent that last thirty plus years running away from each other. Half the time one of them is out of the country for some reason or other." His expression darkens for a moment, and he rubs at his bottom lip. "Muriel has three children, all boys. The oldest is Christian, he's forty and married to his high school sweetheart, Lizzy. They have three kids, Louis, Gabe, and Adele, and they live in South Carolina. The middle son is Mike. He's thirty-six and recently divorced. He lives out in Tennessee with his girlfriend, Dana, who Muriel isn't fond of. He has two kids and only partial custody."

I'm impressed that he knows all of this in great detail. I could've told him about the deceased husband and her three sons, but not the names or where they lived, or how many grandchildren they have. "The youngest son is about to have twins. I get it."

He cocks his head. "What do you get?"

"You invest time."

"It's more than that, Rian. It's not *just* about investing time for personal gain. It's about connecting with people. I've spent my life surrounded by people who are always looking for a way to get ahead or out of some shit they've stepped in. Being a lawyer means someone always wants something from you, or wants you to get them out of a mess. I love my parents, but they sure as hell didn't give me a great basis for how relationships should work, or how to communicate. I had to figure that out all on my own. All Muriel wants is to talk to someone. She misses her family and her husband. She misses having someone to love."

I don't know if he's indirectly referencing me and the way I guard myself around him, especially with what he said about his family. These seemingly innocuous revelations give me so much more insight into who this man is. I wish I could be more like him, able to let people in, to give more of myself so I can have more of someone else in return.

I cover his mouth with my palm. "You need to stop."

He grips my wrist gently and flips my hand over, pressing his lips against my knuckle. "Stop what."

"All this romantic nonsense."

"It's not nonsense. It's true. She's alone. Her family isn't here, and they don't visit very often because they all have young children and it's not as easy to travel. People want to be heard. They want to feel like they're important and cared for."

"So it has nothing to do with seeing an opportunity and taking it." It would be so much easier to maintain some kind of emotional distance with him if he fit my original perception of him, but he's proving to be the opposite.

His expression hardens and softens as quickly. "Do I want this house? Yes. I can see the value where her family won't, like you can. But I've been coming here long before Muriel even thought about selling."

"Is that why you're wearing this? Trying to seduce the elderly?" I gesture to his ridiculous body and his even more ridiculous lime-green Speedo. "I'll do anything right now to avoid making this serious. "You're shameless."

"You don't think Muriel deserves to have nice things to look at?" He runs his hand down his chest.

This is what I need, this version of Pierce, fun, silly, the joker. The serious one is more than I can handle. "You're lucky Muriel's in good shape, otherwise you'd have done all that listening for nothing. She probably has heart palpitations every time you show up. If she had a pacemaker, you'd be wearing the battery out." I gesture to the front, where the outline of the ridge is visible through the bright-green fabric. "She made comments about you and Trip being twins."

"Twins?"

"She inferred you're both tripods."

That ridiculous grin of his appears. "And did you confirm that for her?"

"As if I need to. She can see exactly what's going on behind there." I poke the head.

"You sound a little jealous, Rian." He moves quickly, planting his fists on the counter on either side of me.

I roll my eyes. "What exactly do I have to be jealous of? A sixty-five-year-old?"

"You said it yourself, she's in good shape."

I push on his chest. "That's wrong on so many levels."

"I'm kidding. Obviously. I knew you were going to be here today. Usually I show up in board shorts. I wore the Speedo for you."

I frown, aware I'd kept this meeting to myself on purpose. "How'd you know I was coming here?"

"Muriel mentioned she had a friend coming by to bake with her. She also showed me the fruit bowl in her kitchen and said it was from the same friend. I put two and two together."

I glance at the fruit bowl I brought by the other day. "Anyone could've made that."

"It looks like your style."

"Don't make fun of my pottery."

"I love your pottery." He runs his nose up the side of my neck, lips following behind. "You know what else I love?"

"Showing off your junk in a Speedo?"

He slips his hand under my sundress and finds the seam of my panties. He trails the edge, easing a finger under the fabric. "Knowing you'd be wet by the time I touched you."

"How do you deal with your ego?" My breathlessness makes it sound less snarky than I intend.

"I'm right, though." He nips along my jaw.

"Well, look at you."

"Don't try and make it so basic, Rian. You know as well as I do it's more than that. Chemistry trumps compatibility every single time, and we have both, even if your test scores tell us differently."

He's right, but his time in the Hamptons has an expiration date. I can't allow myself to get more involved than I already am.

"Where's Muriel?"

"In her lounger, half asleep. I came in to get her a glass of ice."

"Don't you think you should do that, then?" I put my hands on his chest, but instead of pushing him away, I grope a little.

"When you're finished with the cookies, are we having dinner?" He nibbles my bottom lip.

"Not if you're dressed in this Speedo."

"I might need your help with something at sixty-nine before we eat. It's currently empty." He leans into me.

"Does that something happen to be contained in lime-green spandex?"

"Why would you think that?" He rolls his hips and I fight a moan. He's so hard. I'm so glad I can hide my reaction to him better than he can hide his to me.

The sliding door opens and Pierce steps away, but he's tenting his Speedo and there's no way to camouflage it.

"Ri-anne? Are you in the kitchen?" Muriel calls out.

He mutters a curse, rushing past me and disappears into the bathroom down the hall.

Muriel peeks her head in as the oven beeps. "Oh! It smells delicious in here! Where's Pierce disappeared to?"

I point a thumb over my shoulder. "He's in the bathroom. Can I get you anything?"

"I think I might need to take a wee nap. All that sun and those vodka-lemonades have made this little old lady tired."

"I could make you coffee."

"Oh no. I'll have a glass of water. And maybe one of those cookies when they've cooled enough.

It's another few minutes before Pierce comes out of the bathroom, his problem apparently solved. He sits at the table with Muriel, accepting a glass of milk to go with the fresh-out-of-the-oven cookies. Once they're all baked, Muriel insists that Pierce take half of them home.

He helps clean up and tucks the Tupperware box full of my cookies under his arm. "I'll return this in a couple of days." He bends to kiss Muriel on the cheek.

Her smile is ridiculous. "Thanks so much for all your help today, Pierce, and thank you for the cookies, Ri-anne." She walks us to the door. Hugging me, she murmurs in my ear, "Offer to drive his fine ass home."

I choke on a laugh. I love this lady. She winks and closes the door, leaving us alone.

I shoot a glance at his crotch. "Looks like you took care of your issue." I admit I'm a little disappointed it's not currently available for use.

"It's resolved for now. Thanks for your concern." He follows me down the driveway.

"Would you like a ride? Probably safer than you wandering down the street dressed like this. You're liable to cause an accident otherwise."

He opens the driver's side door for me and saunters around the front of the car, grinning all the while. He drops into the passenger seat, spreading his legs wide in the confined space. I back out of the driveway and head for sixty-nine. I'd like to say I'm not distracted by the lime-green Speedo, or the way it highlights his assets, or the fact that we're in this small car and he smells a little like cologne, sweat, and pool water, but that would be a lie.

I deflect the sudden rush of warmth in the pit of my stomach with sarcasm. "Must've been disappointing to let loose your load in a toilet."

Pierce arches a brow. "Who said I let my load loose?"

"How else would you deflate the beast?"

"I thought about unpleasant things."

"And that works?"

"For a while."

I turn down beach house sixty-nine's driveway.

"You gonna come in and help me with that thing?" he asks.

I glance at his crotch, which has magically reinflated on the short drive. I poke at the head through the spandex. "You mean this thing?"

He groans and I shriek when it kicks behind the shiny, stretched fabric.

Seat belts click and doors slam as we both rush to get out of the car. I hit the lock button as he rearranges his erection with one hand and keys in the entry code with the other. Open door, step inside, close door.

The tsunami meets the hurricane as I'm slammed against the wood, Pierce's body flush against me, teeth clashing, tongues warring. I'm writhing against the thigh between my legs while he aggressively rubs his erection against my stomach. I shove my hand in his Speedo, gripping him tightly. My panties hit the floor, the top of my dress is yanked to my waist, and my bra gets tossed somewhere over his shoulder.

Pierce lifts me up, his cock sliding along my wetness as he carries me away from the door and deposits me on the counter, beside his wallet. We're both frantic. I pull my dress over my head. His stupid Speedo is still on but pulled down over his butt.

"What are your plans for Muriel?" he asks as he dumps the contents of his wallet on the counter. Bills flutter out.

I snatch up the condom and tear the foil open. "What're your plans? Other than to seduce a widow."

He grabs the latex ring by the tip and positions it over the head. I roll it down the shaft and his hips shift in my grip. "Lawson wants to buy it, and I agree it's a good investment. You never answered my question."

"Stop talking and get in me." I line us up, wrap my legs around his waist, and pull him forward by digging my heels into his butt.

Pierce's forehead rests against mine and he grips the counter, sinking all the way into me. "It's always so good."

I lace my hands behind his neck. "Right?"

We finish our conversations in moans and orgasms.

CHAPTER 18

FLIPPING OUT

RIAN

Pierce and I agree that Muriel's beach house has nothing to do with the sex we're having. I doubt he'll get her to agree to sell him the house without a Realtor involved, but that green Speedo is rather compelling, so it's entirely possible. As is the incredible, mind-bendingly awesome sex. The kind of sex where he doesn't require a wall or counter as support while doing it standing up. It was amazing.

I came like a tidal wave. Violent, ceaseless.

So yeah, if he wants to play pool boy while I play little Suzy Homemaker, I'm game. It makes for interesting foreplay. And Muriel is fun to be around. It's almost as though she believes she's playing matchmaker with us.

Less than two weeks after we make the deal with the Franklins for the bungalow, the paperwork is finalized, the house officially belongs to Pierce and Lawson, and the money finally hits our account. It's the benefit of a cash deal. Things happen so much faster.

The day after we get paid, Pierce's daily message fails

to come. While we've only seen each other a few times since the Franklin bungalow sale, we message consistently, so I have a moment of panic when he doesn't return mine for a twenty-four-hour span.

I immediately come to the worst conclusion, certain he's found out something about me, or my family history. It's the problem with guilt and paranoia. All I want to do is eat a pint of ice cream and worry.

Marley and I are sitting on the couch, half watching a house-flipping show while we check emails and scour the listings. "Oh my God!" Marley slaps my arm.

"Ow! What?"

"I got an email from the Paulsons, that older couple on the beach."

I sit up straighter. "You need to be more specific. There are a lot of older couples on the beach."

"I visited them last week while you were baking cookies with Muriel. They're the ones closer to the Mission Mansion. They have the place we might actually be able to afford. They'd like to meet to talk about a private sale."

I don't want to get my hopes up. This house is in need of some serious cosmetic surgery. "No market competition?"

"A straight sale. No commission, no messing around. This might be it, Rian. This could be our in. We could finally pull a flip."

"This would triple profit. We might be able to manage a second one before the high season is over."

Neither one of us says what we're both thinking. That a flip will bring us one small step closer to our goal. We have a lot of work ahead of us. But we've come back from almost nothing to get here.

I haven't seen this kind of cash flow in our account since

before our parents abandoned us, and my initial instinct is to hoard it. If we're ever going to get out of our shared duplex, we have to reinvest. It's the laws of real estate. Still, it's terrifying to consider parting with any of it so soon after it's hit our account.

We're meeting with the Paulsons tomorrow morning at eleven. We go to bed early, but nerves make my sleep restless. At one a.m. my phone buzzes with a text.

I debate checking it. Sometimes Marley texts me from her room with ideas or thoughts because she doesn't want to forget them, or she's too lazy to get out of bed.

I know who I want it to be. I need to be logical about this thing with Pierce. He's been very clear about going back to Manhattan at the end of the summer, so wanting more out of this is pointless. We're just casual, his lack of communication today reminds me of that.

It's with this thought in mind that I pull my pillow over my head and forgo checking my messages. My alarm goes off at a stupidly early hour. We have plans to bring fresh-baked muffins with us to the Paulson meeting. Bran muffins and the elderly are always a win.

My brain is already booting up as I hit the snooze button on my phone. There's no way I'll go back to sleep. Message alerts clog my screen. There are new ones from Terry—the man still hasn't given up, which is . . . unbelievable. There are ten from my sister—I was right about her messaging me with stuff she didn't want to forget. But there are also texts from Pierce. Several of them. Sent just after one in the morning; the messages I ignored last night.

I fight with myself to leave it alone and not check them right away.

Instead, I go through the ones from Terry. He would still like to reschedule our date. He would also like to know if I'm still getting his messages or if I'm ignoring them.

I move onto the messages from Marley. Basically it's a list of things we need to address with the sellers today.

My mouth goes dry as I finally click on the messages from Pierce.

> **Had a shit day. Just got home now. Had to go to NYC for a bullshit meeting that took all fucking day. Phone died at noon. You still awake? Wanna sext with me to make me feel better?**
>
> **Is sexting not your thing? I'm drinking bourbon now. Alone. It sucks.**
>
> **I'd like to sip bourbon out of your navel. I like your navel. I like you.**
>
> **Im drunk as shit. I wanna cu.**
>
> **Can u stop ignorin me pls?**
>
> **Shit. Its one in the morn. Im a ducking idiot.**
>
> **Ducking not ducking**
>
> **F U C K I N G**
>
> **Autocorrect is an asshole. I guess we have that in common 2nite.**

This isn't a version of Pierce I'm familiar with, and I can't decide how I feel about it. Last night I was trying to convince myself that keeping this dating thing casual is for the best, but there's a tight feeling in my chest over the sexting message. I'd actually like to know what made his day so bad, not just be a porny distraction, and that's a dangerous thing to want, because it sets me up for inevitable heartache when he leaves the Hamptons. It's easier when we're having fun and pushing each other's buttons. It's for that reason that I don't respond right away.

Marley and I make muffins, shower, and get ready to meet with the Paulsons. I put Pierce out of my mind until we're done with the meeting.

Except that's easier said than done, because we have to drive past his brother's beach house on our way to the Paulsons'. Pierce is pushing a lawn mower, wearing heavy work boots and jeans, a white T-shirt pulled tight across his thick chest and bulging biceps.

He looks up, adjusting his ball cap as we pass. Marley's too busy chattering away, rehearsing her spiel, to notice him.

I watch him grow smaller as we continue on. Less than a minute later, as we're pulling into the Paulsons' driveway, my phone buzzes with a message. Then it rings. I'm sure he recognized the car. Pierce and his late-night drunk texting will have to wait.

Our meeting with the Paulsons lasts three hours. We make them a cash offer, which they accept. They have their own legal paperwork drawn up, thankfully by someone reputable since they want to sell privately. By the time we're done, we're the proud new owners of a home that needs an epic facelift to bring it from the seventies to the twenty-first century.

Despite it being a private sale, the Paulsons agree to let us put up the SUTTER REALTY SOLD signs on their lawn. Marley smiles all the while as she hammers the post in with the rubber mallet. This is it. This is our opportunity to turn small profit into big financial gains. I'm so happy I could cry.

We walk around the house to the beach side, where we'll put up the second sign. That's the thing about beachfront, you want everyone to know from both sides who sold the property.

I glance in the direction of the Mission Mansion. It's so close. I can almost hear the echo of flip-flops slapping against the marble floor. The smell of cinnamon and espresso coming from the kitchen. On days like this, I miss my grandmother so much, her warm smile, her soft hugs. I wonder if she'd be proud of us for not giving up. I hope so.

"We should grab some lunch. Celebrate," Marley suggests as she sets the sign down and surveys the yard, deciding where exactly she wants to put it for the best visibility.

"Sure. We could grab something down the beach."

"We can drive over." She walks the perimeter of the yard. The yard we now own.

I glance in the direction of the restaurants close to the beach. From here I have a great view of Lawson's house. Pierce is nowhere to be seen—which makes sense since lawns don't take hours to cut. I need to return his call. I didn't think our meeting was going to last quite this long, or I would've done it sooner.

I root around in my purse for my phone and find that I have both a text and a voicemail from Pierce.

Did you just drive by?

Obviously I was right about him seeing us. The voicemail is sent less than a minute after the text:

I just reread last night's texts. Sorry about that. Yesterday was rough. I do like both you and your navel, though, and I would be totally down to sext with you. But only if that's your thing. If not, that's cool too. I'm pretty sure I just saw your car blow by. If you're in the neighborhood, you should drop in for a visit. I can make you cinnamon roll French toast again. Or take you out for

lunch. Or eat you for lunch. You know. Options and such.

I bark out a laugh. This is the Pierce I'm used to. I send him a message in response.

Rian: I'm sorry yesterday was so bad. I'm assuming lunch is no longer an option, but maybe you'd be up for an afternoon snack.

CHAPTER 19

BABY BROTHER TANTRUMS

PIERCE

It's a gorgeous afternoon. The sun is shining. There's a warm breeze coming off the water. I'd like to say I'm enjoying the awesome weather on this fine afternoon, but I'm not. I'm reading over legal documents. I've reread the same page four damn times and nothing is sticking in my head. I've taken four extra-strength painkillers and I'm still nursing a hangover. It doesn't matter if the bourbon is expensive or not, it still makes for one hell of a pounding headache the day after you drink an entire bottle of it.

Yesterday blew.

Today blows even harder, and not just because I'm nursing an epic hangover.

My father called me yesterday morning, demanding that I make the trip to the city to meet with him and the team of lawyers he has working on the botched patent.

My plan had been to talk to him about my future career plans once we were done sorting things out, and how I'm not so sure law was where I wanted to focus my attention anymore. Unfortunately, the meeting didn't go well.

The blow-up Amalie knockoff dolls are still being sold on several porn shop sites and my dad is pissed. And of course, all of this is my fault. I tried to tell him this wasn't the McDonald's of law, and that things don't happen overnight. He also didn't appreciate it when I pointed out that we'd had a spike in doll sales post blow-up doll fiasco.

Even with the small blip, sales are still declining overall. Lawson's efforts in social media outreach and our affiliation with various charities may be slowing it down, but we continue to see a consistent downward turn in the Amalie Doll market. My current fuckup has not helped us recover those losses, only slow the inevitable decline a bit.

After eight hours in his office with zero fucking progress and a ferocious headache, I figured I should make a point of stopping to see my mother. She usually accompanies my dad when he has business in the city.

It had been a couple of weeks since I'd visited, and I don't like going too long without seeing her. She had a cancer scare a few years back, and it made me aware that she wasn't going to be around forever, and that I needed to spend time with her while I could—the quality kind.

When I mentioned stopping by their New York condo, my father had adjusted his tie, cleared his throat, and looked anywhere but at me when he told me she wasn't there. It took another three minutes of prodding before he finally admitted that she was on a trip with a friend.

Which means they'd had a fight. Likely over the sex dolls.

I don't remember a time when my parents' relationship wasn't tumultuous. The two of them have always had a difficult time with balance and confrontation, and clearly this situation has created conflict neither of them can handle.

The first thing I wanted to do when I left the office was call Rian. I don't know why. We'd only been doing the dating thing for a couple of weeks. It wasn't like we were at the point where I could dump my personal problems on her, but I kind of wanted to, which unnerved me. Pushing her buttons and getting under her skin would lead to sex, telling her about my garbage heap of a day would lead to the kind of emotional connection I think scared the crap out of her.

I'd been on the way out of the office, mentally composing a text to Rian, certain I could convince her to get together tonight if I could figure out the right way to entice her.

I'd been about to step into the elevator when I came face-to-face with my ex-fiancée. And she'd been with her new fiancé—who happens to be a partner at the firm. Not a surprise, really.

The longer I'm out of the office, the more I want to find a way to keep it that way. I was pleased that seeing Stacey didn't particularly hurt in the sense that I missed her or wanted her back. She and I weren't right for each other.

I wasn't upset that she was engaged again; it had been years. It was the entire situation—the meeting with my dad, my mom having taken off somewhere, likely as a result of me, and this current clusterfuck where I felt trapped in a job I didn't want anymore—and there was my ex, all happy and glowing with her stupid-ass balding fiancé.

I suppose the one positive conclusion I came to is that Rian seems to be the exact opposite of Stacey. She's aware I have money and doesn't seem to give two shits either way. Regardless, I don't want to get screwed over again, so I figure it's probably in my best interest not to offer too much information on my family's financial status for the time being. I like how things are with Rian, and I want to keep them that way. It works for the both of us.

So when I returned to the Hamptons last night, Lawson and I got into the booze. Except he had two drinks and I finished the bottle. I'd texted Rian. Not a shining moment.

And then this morning I saw what looked like her car pass by while I was self-flagellating with the lawn mower. The Acura, not the Buick.

When I'd pulled up her contact, I'd noticed the messages from last night. All unanswered. As I read them over, I wanted to punch myself in the face. There was no way to delete them, so I called and left a voicemail. Not the best voicemail, but then again, I was nursing a hangover and half my brain cells were still on vacation.

Once I finished punishing myself with lawn mowing, I decided to shower and take a walk down the street. Mostly because I wanted to check and see if I was right about the Acura.

And I was.

Two hours later, she still hasn't responded. I tried working on the reno, but using a hammer makes it feel like my head is going to explode, and I almost smashed my thumb twice in a ten-minute span, so instead I'm trying—and failing—to review legal documents for my father.

"What the fuck?" Lawson slams the sliding door open, making the ache in my head flare. "You need to come outside and see this."

"Can you not yell, please?" I rub my temple and down the warm orange juice. So far it's not doing much to help cure this stupid hangover.

"This is bullshit," Lawson yells.

Trip makes his dying Ewok sound and runs upstairs into my bedroom to hide.

"Hey, asshole, you're scaring my dog. He's already got PTSD; you don't need to go and give him a damn anxiety attack with the door slamming and yelling."

Lawson spins around, his usual bright, jovial smile replaced by a sneer and narrowed eyes. "I'm not sure if you've forgotten or not, but this happens to be my house. You're a guest and welcome to go back to your penthouse in Manhattan at any time."

"Don't push my buttons, Law. I'm not in the mood for your righteous bullshit."

"You need to check this out." He grits his teeth and crosses to the window, motioning me to follow him. "Look at that."

I glance down the beach, trying to understand what's got him so riled up until I note the SUTTER REALTY sign, and a woman currently hammering said sign into the lawn. Rian's busy typing away on her phone. Ironically, mine buzzes from across the room as she slips it back in her purse.

"I didn't even see a FOR SALE sign and it's already sold! How the hell is that possible?"

He's got me there. I have no idea. "Why don't you go ask?"

"You ask. You're fucking one of them. Shouldn't you know what's coming on the market? What'd you do, premature ejaculate or come in her eye or something?"

"You're disgusting."

He jabs a finger in their direction. "You need to find out what's going on."

"No, I don't." He doesn't need to know about the drunk texts and the message I already left her that have gone unanswered. Although, I am very tempted to go out there and find out why exactly she's ignoring me today, other than the obvious reasons—like my sexting suggestion.

"Did you lose your balls or something? Go find out what the deal is."

"I don't understand why you even care. We bought a house a couple of weeks ago. I can't renovate two at the same time anyway."

"It's the principle. How the hell can we trust those two if they're not even telling us what houses are up for sale? They're shady."

"They're not shady." At least Rian isn't. Marley maybe. She did hit my car and leave the scene of the crime.

He points at the SOLD sign. "You can't tell me that's not some shady deal going on."

"That's exactly what we did when we bought the Franklin bungalow," I point out.

"Marley knows I'm interested in more beachfront property. She knows to call me if there's a whiff of an idea that someone is selling. I'm going over there."

"You might want to calm down first."

"Fuck that." He stomps across the living room, gunning for the sliding door again.

"Don't slam it!" I follow after him. I'd like to check on Trip, but I don't think Lawson's going to enter any kind of discussion with Marley and Rian with a level head. I also don't think he's adequately prepared for Rian's sass.

I squint as I follow him out into the hot, sunny afternoon. I'd go back in for my shades, but he's already yelling.

"Hey!" He gestures wildly to the sign. "What the hell is this?"

Rian turns slowly. Despite her sunglasses, I can already see her arched, unimpressed brow. I shake my head at my brother, because going toe-to-toe with Rian isn't something he's thought through.

Rian gives him her sweetest smile. "It's a sold sign."

Lawson glares at her and then turns his attention to Marley. "Why didn't I know about this?"

She shrugs. "It was a private sale, like the Franklin bungalow."

Rian's gaze moves to me, the dip of her chin tells me she's checking me out. I glance down and realize after my shower I didn't bother to put on anything besides a pair of board shorts. They're floral Hawaiian print. And these don't have the usual built-in twig-and-berry holder, so if I happen to get a hard-on, which is likely since Rian looks entirely too delicious, it's not going to be easy to hide. At least the flowers sort of act like camouflage.

"Those are pretty," Rian says with a half smile.

I grin back. "So are you."

Lawson throws me a disgusted look. "I would've put an offer in on this place. I would've outbid whoever bought it. Talk to the buyers and see what they want for it."

"They won't sell," Rian says confidently.

"Everyone has a price, sweetheart," Lawson snaps.

Her expression goes flat and she crosses her arms over her chest. She loathes being called sweetheart. "I can tell you with one hundred percent certainty that nothing you can offer is going to convince the buyers to sell to you."

"You can't know that. I want to talk to them."

"You are talking to them, and there's no offer that will have us handing over the property to you."

"Wait. What?" Lawson's confusion is priceless. I would be shocked, but I know this is something Rian's been working toward, so it's not a huge surprise they finally made it happen.

"*We* are the owners." Marley motions between herself and Rian.

Lawson's jaw snaps shut. I don't get why he's so pissed off about this. It's one property, and it needs a serious facelift. We don't have the time to take on another project with the Franklin renovations just getting started. As it is, I'm hiring out more than half of the work so we can get in on the vacation rental market by July, and that's pushing it.

He points an accusatory finger at Marley. "We had a deal."

Marley shrugs, blithe. "You're not my only client, and there will be other houses on the beach for sale. There always are."

"You're fucking fired." He turns and stomps off. He's like a teenage girl with his temper tantrums.

I shake my head. Annoyed. Frustrated. As if the last two days weren't bad enough. Now this. "I'm sorry. I'll talk to him."

Marley gathers up her bag of tools and slings it over her shoulder. "Don't bother. No offense, but he's a pain in the ass to work with."

This, I know. Especially since we bought the most recent property. He's been obsessive about buying more, checking the listings surrounding the Mission Mansion. While I'm on board with this new plan because it has the potential to give me an out from patent law, provided the income is consistent, his attitude about it is puzzling. I need to find out what's eating at him.

"Anyway, always a pleasure." Marley looks from me to Rian and back again, her eyebrow half raised.

A silent conversation takes place between them and Rian glances in my direction.

"Are you busy? Do you have a minute to talk?" Circumstances aren't ideal, but this would be a great time to apologize in person for the drunk texts from last night.

"No. She's not busy." Marley gives Rian a knowing smile. "I'll meet up with you in a bit." She waves brightly and practically skips up the path and around the side of the house.

Rian crosses her arms over her chest. "We don't owe you or your brother anything."

"Well, you owe me a dinner date since we never made it out of the house last time, but in terms of this," I nod at the SOLD sign, "I agree. I don't know why he has such a bug up his ass about this, and honestly I don't care."

She seems shocked at the lack of fight on my part.

"What's your plan for this place?"

"We're flipping it." Excitement makes her voice shake. "You came up with the capital."

Her fingers flutter to her lips. "We did."

"That's fantastic." She wears her pride with class. "We should celebrate." I wrap my arms around her, lifting her off the ground.

She shrieks and laughs, her smile melting away my stress. Rian is exactly what I need today, the perfect antidote to my bad mood.

CHAPTER 20
COUNTER OFFERS

RIAN

Pierce runs inside to change and returns a minute later—sadly he's covered his magnificent chest with a T-shirt and he's changed into cargo shorts, but he's still gorgeous, so I'll take it. Trip follows behind him, tail down between his legs, eyes sad and anxious.

He stays close to Pierce's legs when they reach the bottom of the stairs. "Is he okay?"

"Just nervous. Lawson's temper tantrum freaked the poor guy out." He scratches behind Trip's ear.

"Does he have tantrums like that often?"

"Not typically. He's had a bug up his ass the past week. I don't really know what's going on there."

I take off my strappy-heeled sandals and fix them to my purse while Pierce slips his feet into bright-green running shoes, and we hit the beach.

I revel in the soft warmth of the sand between my toes. One day I hope we'll be able to live on the beach again, not just buy and sell houses here. "So what happened to make yesterday so bad?"

He regards me carefully for a moment. "I'm sorry about the messages last night. I wasn't in the best headspace. The reason I have time off this summer is because I made a mistake with a patent; it caused a few issues and we're still sorting them out. I was stuck in a meeting I didn't want any part of for most of the day, and we made virtually no progress." We pause as Trip leans to one side and marks a bush, no leg lift necessary. "And then I ran into my ex." He's not looking at me as he says this. His gaze is focused off in the distance and the words come slowly, like they're being dragged out of him.

My chest grows tight; it feels a lot like jealousy. "Is this the three-year relationship you were in?"

His eyes shoot to mine, surprise quirking his brow.

"It was on your questionnaire for the dating site."

"Right. How could I forget about that? The one that deems us pretty much as incompatible as two people can get?" I'm sure he means it jokingly, but there's a dark bite to his words. He shakes his head a little. "Sorry. I'm being an asshole. But yeah, it was the three-year relationship."

"It ended badly, then?" I don't know if relationships ever end well. Mine never have.

He stuffs his hands into his pockets, seeming suddenly vulnerable. "We were engaged. She broke it off."

That's not at all what I expected to hear. I stupidly assumed he was the one who couldn't commit. Maybe I should know better by now, considering the way he's relentlessly pursued me. "I'm so sorry." I want to ask why she broke it off. What happened to make a woman walk away from him, but I don't, because I like that he's opening up to me without any prompting. I want this connection with him, even if it makes me uncomfortable.

"It was a long time ago. I'm over it. It's not like I'm still hung up on her or anything. She proved to be untrustworthy and a ladder climber, so I'm much better off without her in my life." He licks his lips and shakes his head. "What was the point of me telling you this?"

"Why yesterday was so bad," I remind him.

"Oh, right." He runs a hand through his hair, his smile sheepish. "The meeting, some stuff with my family, running into my ex . . . just a shit day. I was looking for a ray of sunshine to make it better."

"Ray of sunshine? That's a first." I drag my toes through the sand. "I meant to message you this morning, but then we had the meeting with the Paulsons. I didn't expect it to go so long."

"I can see why you wouldn't have, messaged me back, I mean."

"I wasn't ignoring you on purpose."

We pass beach house sixty-nine. The last time I was here we had counter sex. Clearly this attraction isn't waning, and I'm past caring that we've gone about this the opposite of normal. What makes me nervous is that I want to spend more time with him, and more time means I'll eventually have to reciprocate his sharing with pieces of myself.

When we reach the Franklin bungalow, Pierce pauses. "Do you mind if we stop here for a minute?"

"Sure. Are the renos coming along okay?"

Pierce nods, his face lighting up with his smile. "We're making good progress."

The smell of fresh paint and new finishes are sharp in the air as he opens the door and ushers me inside.

"Are you doing most of this yourself again?" It's a lot of work in a short span of time.

He shoves his hands into his pockets, regarding the space with a critical eye. "Since the goal is to rent and not flip, it doesn't make sense to put the same amount of time and energy into the project. We want to get it on the rental market as quickly as possible."

"You don't sound too happy about that."

He lifts a shoulder. "We could've gotten top dollar with higher-grade finishes if the point was resale. This is like half-assed cosmetics. It's not economical to go high end if we're renting. Things are going to get damaged no matter how good the renters are. Plus, I'm committed to having pet friendly rentals, so I have to take that into account with the finishes."

"Makes sense. Does that bother you?"

He runs his hand across the counter. It's granite, so he certainly hasn't cheaped out there. "I'm not big on half assing."

Flashes of how not half assed he was when we last had sex have my stomach and thighs clenching. "No. You certainly aren't."

One corner of my mouth turns up and his eyes heat. "I'm not sure you're referencing my carpentry skills anymore."

I mirror his smile. "It was sort of an all-encompassing statement."

He steps over Trip, who's plunked himself down on the floor at his feet. I have a moment of panicked conflict. The intimacy that comes with his honesty pushes at the boundaries I keep in place. The chemistry between us is ever present and undeniable, but this emotional connection scares me because it's only a matter of time before I can no longer keep them separate from each other.

His rough, callused fingertips glide gently up my arm. I shiver and my skin breaks out in a wave of goose bumps. I can handle this, the physical need. I can focus on this. He drops his head, lips close to mine. I don't dare move, already aware of how much joy he seems to derive from tormenting me. "I'm so glad you stopped fighting this."

"Fighting what?"

"Us." The tip of his nose brushes mine. "I want in you."

Panic flares at the possibility that he means it beyond the literal.

I slip my hands under his shirt, fingers gliding over bare skin as I lift my head. It's too late to stop this. Whatever the consequences, I'm already in this so much deeper than I mean to be, but I can't seem to walk away, even if it's the safer option.

Pierce's lips find mine, and my worries get lost in the spark of desire.

CHAPTER 21
ALTERNATE LOCATIONS

PIERCE

Rian's tucked into my side, her head resting on my chest. She's a limp noodle. I managed to move us from the living room floor to the bedroom before we really got going.

"Well, that was something," she mumbles. It's half slurred, like she's drunk on orgasms.

"Fun, huh?"

She snorts. "Intense is more like it."

She's silent for a minute and I close my eyes, relaxed and content to lie here and bask in the afterglow.

She lifts her head off my chest. "Do you hear that?"

"Hear what?" I'm groggy post-sex and prone to drifting off when I'm in this kind of Zen state.

"Oh shit. That's my phone. How long have we been here?" She looks around for a clock, but I haven't put one in here yet. It's on my to-do list. I need to go shopping later this week. Maybe Rian and I can go together.

She tries to push up, but I tighten my arms around her, unwilling to let her go.

"I need to get that. Marley and I were supposed to go for lunch, and I'm not sure if she's still expecting me."

"Guess you'll have to tell her we've already eaten."

"Haha. Vagina is not a meal." She pinches my nipple. "Let me up. I need to call her."

"To tell her you're sorry, but you won't be home until tomorrow." I arch a brow.

"Yes."

"Okay. You can call her." I unbar my arms.

She laughs, a little incredulous, but mostly amused. "I wasn't asking."

She slides over my body, her face still mashed into my chest as her feet hit the floor. I grin as she pushes to an awkward stand. She stumble-walks across the room and has to use the wall to steady herself.

"You all right? You need help with the walking?"

She flips me the bird over her shoulder and disappears into the hall. Naked. There are a million things I should do this afternoon, but Rian has moved to number one on my list.

I can hear her talking in low whispers to her sister. She laughs at something. "I'll be home in the morning. Not early. You'll survive boot camp without me."

She ends the call as she appears in the doorway. She saunters across the room, soft breasts bouncing and hips swaying.

She tosses my phone on the bed. "Your brother called while I was talking to Marley. Not sure if you care to respond or not."

I check the alerts. He's called three times and there are eleven messages. It's already four in the afternoon. I move my phone to the nightstand. "He needs to unknot his balls first. Besides, I'm going to be busy until tomorrow." I pat the mattress. "What do you feel like for dinner since we missed lunch?"

Rian climbs up on the bed and straddles my thighs.

"We should do delivery." She drops something on my chest, between my pecs. "Look what I found."

I glance down. It's an extra condom. I snatch it up. "Where'd you find this?"

"On the floor."

I roll her over and fit myself between her thighs. "First, we use this, then we order dinner."

"We should do Post Mates. I bet they'd make a stop at the pharmacy and pick up a box of condoms."

"You're a smart woman, Rian."

"Only sometimes."

"All the time." I kiss her neck.

"I'm a little stupid over you," she whispers.

"Same." I roll my hips and whatever worries she might have about that disappear on a moan.

I order Italian, a box of condoms, and a bottle of wine. I specify the brand and type—of condoms, that is. Rian is wearing my shirt and I'm in my shorts. We're sitting on the couch in the living room, working our way into a carb coma with takeout containers of pasta in our respective laps.

My phone lights up with yet another call from my brother.

"Should you get that?" Rian asks.

"No. He's being an asshole and completely irrational."

"Why is he so upset about the house?"

"Honestly? Your guess is as good as mine. He gets like this sometimes. Obsesses over things. He'll have ideas, and then when it doesn't go exactly as he plans, he gets pissed. Don't worry, he'll get over it."

"I'm not worried for me. I don't want this to cause is-sues between you and your family. It's obvious you're close." She spins noodles on her plastic fork, her focus staying there. I make a note to bring over some real sil-verware and dishes so next time we can eat like civilized human beings. Not that I mind this. It's refreshing not to sit at a dinner table with seventeen different utensils to choose from.

"Law and I will be fine. He's been doing this on his own for a while, and I've jumped in with both feet over the past couple of months. I have a tendency to take things over, and this is a reminder that it was his project first, not mine."

Her nose wrinkles. "You are kind of pushy."

"You like my pushy."

"*Pushy* sounds a lot like *pussy*." She slips her fork be-tween her lips, slurping up a rogue noodle, grinning as she chews and tacks on *cat* at the end.

I leave that comment. We have all night for more sex, and I plan to capitalize on the hours between now and to-morrow morning. "What prompted the sudden move into flipping houses?" I ask, moving the conversation away from the negative aspects of my personality and the similarities between words that start with *p* and end with a *y* sound.

She glances up at me. "It's not really sudden. We've al-ways planned to flip; we just needed the capital to make it happen."

"How long have you been in real estate?"

"We started pretty young. It's hard to get people to take you seriously when you look like a college freshman, but the past few years have been good. We've built a solid rep-utation and a base of clients." She worries the inside of her lip. "You don't think Lawson will say anything bad about us, do you?"

"Because he wasn't the first person you called when a

potential property came available? Unlikely, but I can talk to him if you want."

She sweeps her fingers back and forth over her lips, considering. "I don't want to ask you to do that. I don't want to be the reason for dissention between you and your brother."

"You aren't the reason for dissention. His reactive personality and my need to come in and takeover everything is."

She laughs. "You're an interesting man."

"Good interesting or bad interesting?"

"The good kind of interesting. You're kind of a walking, talking oxymoron. You've got a background in law, so you could work this supercushy office job, and make great money. But you choose to get your hands dirty instead and dabble in an unstable, sometimes unforgiving market."

"Well, to be fair, the Hamptons are pretty consistent in terms of profit and desirability, so I'm not really rolling the dice and taking chances. And if I'm totally honest, I'm only a lawyer because I'm usually good with details and facts. Recent events excluded."

"You mean the patent issue?"

I'm not sure how much I want to divulge. It's not like she can't look up my family if she wants to. Although my father has done a good job of paying people off to keep the blow-up dolls out of the direct line of the media, things slip through no matter how diligent he is. My sister happens to work for one of the biggest media corporations in New York, and the wife of the CEO adores her, so that definitely helps. "Mmm. Yes, that." I steer the conversation away from me. "Anyway, tell me more about the flip. What're your plans?"

"Well, the obvious, for starters, exterior and interior cosmetics. I want to preserve the quaintness, but bring it into the twenty-first century with a new kitchen, paint, refinished floors, you know, standard updates and up-grades. It's a great location with a nice yard and a gorgeous view, so we should be able to get top dollar for it if we manage to keep the renovation costs down."

"If you need help with trades or anything, let me know."

"Won't Lawson be angry if he finds out you're helping me?"

"He can be angry all he wants. It'll give me an excuse to see more of you."

Rian drops her head and laughs. Eventually she peeks up, smiling softly. "I had you pegged all wrong."

"People usually do. What misaligned assumptions did you have?"

"I thought you were a rich, cocky a-hole. Well, you're cocky, but you can get away with it, considering."

"Considering what?" Maybe she means the rich part. I'm sure she already has an inkling, considering we put in a cash offer for the Franklin place. Most people can't come up with a hundred grand in cash, let alone three-quarters of a million plus. If that wasn't a giveaway, my car, my suits, and the fact that I'm walking around on the beach with two grand in my wallet should be.

I'm kind of a spoiled shit, if I think about it. Which is probably one of the reasons I'm struggling to walk away from law. More than that, I don't want to disappoint my dad by bailing on him when the business is already starting to fail, or create more dissension between him and my mother, although they can always seem to find that on their own.

Rian gestures to me as if it's obvious.

I look down and run a hand over my bare chest. "I can be cocky because I have a six-pack?"

"It's not just about the six-pack."

"So, it's because I work out."

"Not exactly." She bites the end of her finger then taps my black nail. "This is sexy."

I arch a brow. "I didn't realize having a black nail that's probably going to fall off in a few weeks could be considered sexy."

She sighs. "It's not the nail. You don't look the way you do because you go to some gym and pump iron in front of a mirror with fifty other grunting men and a bunch of women in sports bras."

"Are you familiar with that scenario?" I don't like the idea of anyone other than me experiencing that view.

"Marley buys Groupons and makes me go to the gym with her." She rolls her eyes. "Anyway. You look like this because you push yourself physically. Like this muscle." She pokes my forearm. "What is that, even? It looks like you have a golf ball hiding under there."

"It's from swinging a hammer."

"See? So sexy." She runs her fingers down my forearm, skirting the healing nicks and cuts on my knuckles. "You kind of break all the molds. You have to be able to see why I was reluctant to go out with you."

"Because I fit some kind of stereotype?"

"Because you look like you're good at breaking hearts and bed frames."

"I promise the latter is far more likely than the former." I wink on reflex.

"And you have all the lines."

"That's not a line, that's me being honest. I'm not a heartbreaker. Remember, I'm the one who had my heart broken in the past."

She settles into the corner of the couch, spinning noodles on her plastic fork. "You can't tell me you didn't break any girls' hearts along the way. You must've had a sow-your-oats phase in college or something."

"I dated, but I didn't make a habit of stringing girls along." Back then I'd had freedom, at least a little, and being here now feels like I have it again, even if it's only temporary. In some ways, what we're doing reminds me of college nights spent eating takeout and putting off homework or studying in lieu of hanging out with a pretty girl. I should be working on this house, but instead, I'm spending time getting to know Rian.

"Tell me what you were like in college. Did you always have to keep Marley in line? Were you a math tutor? What did you study?"

Rian sets her food on the coffee table and folds her legs under her. "Marley can't be kept in line by anyone. I probably would've tutored if I'd had the chance. I started in math, finances actually, but it got complicated." She pauses and worries her lip before she continues. "So I ended up dropping out partway through my first semester."

She's clearly math brilliant, so that's a shock. "What happened that you had to drop out?"

Her gaze flicks up to mine before dropping again. "My, uh . . . grandmother passed away, and we ran into some financial difficulties that made college tuition a problem."

I think about the time I followed her around the grocery store and how she'd been price matching everything in her cart, about the way she'd wrangled the repair bill down and avoided insurance, how she drove a beater and her sister drove a nice car. "What about loans?"

"We were left with some debt; it took a while to sort it all out. Anyway, eventually Marley and I took real estate courses and here we are." She smiles, but she looks sad.

"Is this the grandmother who was friends with the people who owned the Mission Mansion?"

She nods. "We spent most of our summer with her. I miss her, a lot. She was an incredible woman."

I grab her ankles and pull her across the couch into my lap. "So are you." Skimming the hollow under her eyes with gentle fingertips, I expect the almost-tears there to fall, but they don't.

She shakes her head. "I'm really not."

"Stop being disagreeable."

She laughs, her eyes warming. "Says the most antagonistic man on the planet."

"That's a little extreme, don't you think?"

"At least in this zip code, then." She runs her fingers through my hair and down the sides of my neck. Goose bumps rise along my skin, a visceral reaction to the way her touch affects me. "Do you know what we should do?" she asks softly.

"What's that?"

She reaches over my shoulder and grabs the unopened box of condoms and pats my stomach. "We should work off some calories before we feed your six-pack dessert."

"Good idea. It's my best asset. We need to keep it that way."

"I don't know if it's your *best* asset." She skims my lips with her fingertip. "If we're talking physical assets, I'd say this mouth is a winner, and then of course there's one below the waist that's pretty amazing."

"I have a great idea." I slide forward to the edge of the couch.

"What's that?"

"Let's take this to the bedroom and we can do a thorough examination of each other's assets."

I wrap her legs around my waist and carry her to the bedroom. We eat dessert for breakfast.

Despite her assurance that she can get home fine on her own, I drop Rian off at her place the next morning. Well, it's close to noon, but I have all afternoon to deal with work. Trip is annoyed that he's been relegated to the back seat. He's currently resting his chin on Rian's shoulder. If she minds, she doesn't say anything. She woke with Trip between us. He was not impressed when I kicked him out so we could have sex without an audience.

"Am I sitting in your spot? I'll be gone soon and you can have our man all to yourself again."

I like that she refers to me as "our man." Purposely or accidentally, either way I'm a fan.

I drop her off at a small, quaint duplex in a decent neighborhood. It's a mix of renovated homes and older ones in need of work.

"Well, this is me." She fidgets a little, maybe unsure of herself.

I push Trip's head out of the way so I can kiss her. "I want to see you later this week. What days are you free?"

She laughs against my lips. "You realize the way you say that makes it sound very unquestion-like."

"There's a *what* in there, which makes it a question."

"But you phrase it like an order."

"It's not intentional. I want to see you, and I want to know what days you're free so we can coordinate a date. A real one. Where I take you out for dinner at a restaurant, and then I drive you home. At the end you invite me up, and I spend the night in your bed."

"I only have a double."

"That's fine. I like cuddling with you, and you can't escape in a double like you can in a king."

"What about Trip? How will he manage without you?"

"He'll deal for one night. Or I can take you back to the Franklin bungalow if that's better. Whatever works for you. I'll make it happen."

"What about Thursday night, then?"

"That seems like forever."

"It's three days from now."

"Exactly. Practically forever, but I'll take what I can get with you."

I lean in for a kiss that ends with me hard and Rian breathless. She's a glassy-eyed, slightly uncoordinated mess as she makes her way to her door. I wait until she's inside before I head to my brother's. I have to deal with him at some point, and I need to get some real work done today since I slacked yesterday. It was totally worth it, though.

I drive back to the beach in a good mood and park at the Franklin bungalow. If Lawson's being a pain in my ass, I might stay here tonight. Besides, the sheets will still smell like Rian, which is a bonus.

Trip gives me one of his Ewok barks, tongue lolling as I grab his leash and we stroll down the beach to my brother's place. He's out on the deck, taking pictures of Amalie Dolls playing tennis on a fake court.

He's stretched out on the deck, clicking away on his camera. "Sleeping with the enemy, huh?"

"Rian isn't the enemy."

"I still think she and her evil twin are shady."

"Because they took an opportunity when they saw it? Isn't that what you did when you visited the granddaughter down the beach and got the details on the Franklin house? Isn't that what I'm doing with Muriel when I drop by and water her flowers and clean her pool?"

"Not the same."

"Totally the same. I think it was a mistake to fire them."

He gives me an incredulous look. "Of course you think that since you're sleeping with one of them. You'd think you'd be using that to get insider information."

I drop into one of the lounge chairs. "Why are you so

pissed about this? It's not like we have time to start another renovation."

He snaps a few more pictures and then sits up. "I heard a rumor that the owners of the Mission Mansion are thinking about selling, so the more property we own on this stretch of beach, the better."

That gets my attention. "Where'd you hear that?"

"Does it matter?" He motions to the dolls. "You want out and so do I. If we keep doing what we're doing, it could be a possibility."

"How is the Mission Mansion going up for sale going to do that for us?"

"If someone fixes it up, it increases our property value. We buy low and sell high, bank the profit and watch our money grow. I know you don't want to go back to Manhattan at the end of the summer. So you need to keep your head in the game and your eye on the prize, which doesn't happen to be located between your girlfriend's thighs."

"Business is business with Rian."

"Is it?"

"She can buy a house to flip, Lawson. We don't need every single one of them."

"I know that, but I think you need to keep in mind that her interests are her top priority, and remember what yours are."

I guess that's the real question, because I don't think my priorities are quite the same as Lawson's. I don't want to spend my life hating what I do, but I also don't want to put myself in a position where I'm scrambling financially, or giving up what I love to make a buck.

But beyond that, I'm a little tangled up in a woman I can't seem to get out of my head. Which is clearly his point.

CHAPTER 22
SHOPPING TRIPS

PIERCE

I pull up in front of Rian's duplex and park on the street since both cars take up the narrow driveway. Rian needs to price out house supplies. It's the excuse she gave me for not having time to get together for lunch today. We have a date planned for later in the week, but I don't feel like waiting, so here I am.

She and Marley took possession of the Paulsons' two-story fixer-upper last week. Lawson got over it after he managed to snag another beach house—in better condition—a week later. It'll give her an excuse to be on the beach more often. Which will mean more opportunities for quickies. Or not so quick quickies. And sleepovers, obviously.

My excuse for showing up unannounced is that there's no way her piece-of-shit Buick can hold all the things she needs, so I'm here with my truck. To be nice. At least that's what I'm going to tell her.

I'm aware I've already got it bad for this woman. My conversation with Lawson about priorities and business made that clear. Also, my motivation for getting out of law and making renovations and rentals my full potential future has shifted to include her.

I preemptively whacked off before I came over so I won't be tempted to jump her the second I see her. I figure this is a good way to spend some time with her beyond the bedroom, which is where we end up a lot. Or any available surface, really.

"Please don't tell me you forgot the code again," Rian says as she opens the door, a saucy grin on her face. She's wearing a pair of yoga shorts, a tank, and no bra. I know there's no bra because her nipples are saluting me. Her expression changes to confusion as she takes me in. "Oh, hey."

"Expecting someone else?" I raise a brow. And suddenly I wonder who might forget the code to their house. And why the hell would that person have it? Is she seeing someone else?

We haven't framed this as anything other than two people enjoying each other's company, often without clothing. I'm supposed to move back to Manhattan at the end of the summer, so despite what she's said before, it's entirely possible I'm not the only guy she's seeing.

I should be glad that she's not all clingy and needy. I should like the fact that she's not all over my ass, texting me at all hours of the day and night. But I'm not. Right now, I'm irrationally angry.

I clench my fists, my good mood crushed by potential, unknown competition. At least until she responds. "Marley went to grab cream."

"Why would she forget the code?" I'm suspicious.

She tilts her head to the side. "Because I change it at the beginning of every month."

"Oh." That's smart. And possibly a little excessive.

"What're you doing here?" Her eyes slide from my face

down to my feet and back up. I'm wearing work boots, jeans, and a T-shirt.

I rub my chin, a little uncertain based on her reaction. Maybe this was a bad idea. She likes my pushy, but maybe I'm taking it too far. "You said you have to go house supply shopping."

"I do."

I motion to my truck. "I thought it might be easier if you didn't have to jam things in the trunk of your car."

"Oh. That's really sweet, but I've never driven a truck that big."

"I was planning to come with you, you know, to help with the heavy stuff. Besides, I have some things I need to pick up too." I'm rambling. Why am I so nervous right now?

A tentative grin breaks across her face. "You don't have anything else to do today?"

"Nah. I'm all yours."

Her grin widens and she steps back. "Wanna come up for a few minutes? I need to change."

"Sure." I have to turn sideways in the narrow hallway to get past her. Even then my arm brushes against her breast and that sweet, tight nipple saying hello under her thin tank.

I lean against the wall, wait for her to lock the door and lead the way up the stairs. It also means I get to watch her ass. I may not be here for sex, but I can still appreciate the fine specimen of woman I'm going to spend my morning with.

She opens the door at the top of the stairs and ushers me in. It smells like her, warm and sweet, a combination of flowers and freshly baked cookies. I glance around the small kitchen, searching for her signature Tupperware. As I suspected, there's a box of cookies on the counter.

"So this is our place. It's not much but it's home." She

tucks her thumbs in the waistband of her shorts and rocks back on her heels.

I survey the space, wondering how she must feel about me being here. She's aware I have money, but she's never made it a thing. Some mornings I'll find cash tucked into my wallet that wasn't there before. I only know because there's change, and the bills are always folded, the amount always half of what dinner cost, regardless of whether she saw the bill.

It's a modest apartment, the furniture older, but it's well maintained and tidy. "I like it. It's cozy."

"*Cozy*'s a good word for it." She runs her foot up the back of her bare calf, possibly scratching an itch. She's too tempting, hair pulled up in a loose knot on top of her head. Nipples still obviously hard.

"Why don't you get changed?" I really need her to be wearing something other than that tank. Otherwise my plan to spend time with her, doing something aside from making her come, will fail miserably. "The hardware store gets busy around eleven with contractors. We want to get there before then."

She gives me a cautious, questioning smile. "Okay. I'll be back in a minute. Make yourself comfortable."

I have vague memories of living in an apartment as a little kid. Lawson was just a baby. We moved to a small house when my mother was pregnant with Amalie. It was nicer, in a better neighborhood, but still not big. At least not the kind of big I've grown accustomed to over the past twenty years. We never really wanted for anything, but we also didn't have the kind of luxury I often take for granted now.

Rian and Marley clearly have to work hard for everything they have. I don't really know much about her family history. Just that she has a twin and that she was close to her grandmother. I know nothing about her parents. She's never mentioned them, not once.

Pictures of Rian and Marley together line the bookshelf. Some of them look recent, within the last year or two based on the lean angles of their faces and the curve of Rian's hips. An older photo catches my eye, and I pick it up off the shelf, hoping for a glimpse of her past that might fill in some of the blank spaces.

They're teenagers in the picture, maybe seventeen or eighteen at best.

They appear to be on a yacht, arms slung casually over each other's shoulders, huge sunglasses covering their eyes. Rian's skin is pink from too much sun, her bikini is white, but classy and pretty, the top a high halter. Marley isn't quite so tasteful in her bright-yellow number with tiny little triangles of fabric held together with flimsy strips of crisscrossing fabric. Branding tells me their clothes are expensive, as are their sunglasses.

The picture not only captures the teenage versions of the girls, but also the beach backdrop. In the distance, the Mission Mansion rises majestically behind them, in much better condition than it is now.

I scan the other framed photos, but they're only of Marley and Rian together—no parents, no grandmother, no hints of family apart from each other, which makes me wonder how literally she meant it when she said they take care of each other.

I set the photo back down beside an oddly shaped bowl. It looks like a six-year-old's pottery project and very much the same as the one she made weeks ago when I went to a class with her. I pick it up and turn it over. Rian's name is etched into the bottom in her gentle handwriting, not child scrawl.

I put it back and continue to snoop, discovering an

entire shelf of misshapen vases. I check the bottom of each one—all named and dated and belonging to Rian. That she continues to do something she doesn't seem to get better at, even after all this time is another endearing quality.

"What're you doing?" Rian's high, slightly embarrassed voice startles me, and I nearly fumble the vase. Recovering, I set it back on the shelf.

"You made all of these?" I gesture to her sad-looking shelf of pottery.

"It's relaxing."

"How many of these do you have?"

"I don't know. A bunch." She moves the vase so it's lined up with the others in all their warped glory.

"Does Marley ever go with you?"

She laughs. "No. It's not a Marley thing."

"Is it, like, something you do with your mom?" I'm fishing now.

Her eyes flare briefly and fill with sadness before resolve settles in. "Uh no, my mom isn't . . ." The doorbell rings, startling us both. She blows out a breath and laughs nervously. "That's Marley. I'll be right back."

I watch her rush down the stairs, yelling for Marley to relax when she hits the doorbell again three seconds later. I'm annoyed by the interruption. It felt like we were on the brink of a moment, and now it's gone.

She returns a minute later with Marley in tow. The sadness in her eyes is gone, and back is the slightly guarded version of the Rian I've come to know over these past weeks. "We should go before the store gets too busy, right?"

"Yeah. That's probably a good idea."

She grabs her purse and we head for the stairs, but I make a mental note to find a way back to this discussion.

CHAPTER 23

HARDWARE AND OTHER NECESSARY ITEMS

RIAN

My stomach churns with anxiety and guilt as I follow Pierce around the hardware store, pushing the cart. I'd been on the verge of either telling him the truth or a half lie, and I don't know which would be worse. He's been so open and honest, and here I am, shrouding myself in secrets to avoid letting him in. Thankfully, Marley's poor memory saved the day.

I try to put it out of my head and focus on my pricing mission. I would've done this online, but I can't see quality in an image. Fresh paint, a kitchen upgrade, new floors, and updated bathrooms is all the house needs, plus an exterior cosmetic facelift and some minimal landscaping. We have fifty thousand dollars to work with. My goal is to get it done with ten grand to spare.

We're currently in the paint section. Pierce picks up a five-gallon bucket of primer like it weighs a much as a Styrofoam cup. The muscles in his forearms flex, making the golf ball under his skin pop. I watch, enthralled by the flex and pull of muscle as he hoists it into the cart.

He ducks down so his face is level with mine. "'Sup?"

"Huh?" I blink and realize I'm probably sporting a very blank look. I squeeze his arm. "Just enjoying the gun show."

He smiles, but it's not as cocky as usual. "I can do push-ups on top of you later if you want."

"While you're naked?"

"Is there any other way?"

I push on his chest, not because I can't handle the flirting or the promise of what's to come later, but because I'm full of conflict. I want to confide in him, but I'm afraid of what will happen if I do. I'm also afraid of what it means that I want to tell him the truth, and that I almost did. I'm getting attached, which is fruitless for so many reasons.

I scan the brands of paint, anything to get out of my own head, and note an alternative to the one in the cart. "That's twenty dollars cheaper."

He glances at it, but reaches for another five-gallon bucket of the more expensive brand. I want to point out how he's wasting money, but I bite my tongue. He drives a Tesla and his second vehicle is a truck. A big truck with a push-button start and chrome everything. He's not worried about money. He's seen where I live now and is aware that we're definitely not even close to the same pay grade— I'm sure he's known that since he saw my Buick, but it still makes it more real. All of this feels more real than I want it to.

He drops the second bucket in the cart. "Cheaper but not the same quality. I'd need to use twice as much of the less expensive brand to cover the same square footage, so it would end up costing more in the long run."

"Oh. I didn't realize that." Now I feel like a jerk for thinking he was wasteful. At least I didn't say it aloud.

He points to another brand, even more expensive than the one he's chosen. The kind my father likely would've chosen based on cost alone. "This stuff isn't worth the price tag. Not when this"—he taps the buckets in the cart—"does just as good a job."

"Good to know." I check average square footage of coverage on the paint bucket, then mentally do the math for one of the bedrooms in our beach house, all four walls and the ceiling, and break it down by cost per square foot. "So this is about ten cents a square foot, but that would cost more like twenty?" I ask.

He narrows his eyes. "Did you do that math in your head?"

"Yes."

He crowds me. "You need to stop that."

I have to tip my head up so I can meet his serious gaze. "I need to stop doing mental math?"

"In public places, yes."

I bite my cheek to keep my smile in check. "Do I want to ask why?"

"Because I find it sexy, and it makes me want to do inappropriate things to you in this aisle. The kind of things that would get me arrested."

I grin. "You probably shouldn't have told me that. I'm definitely going to use that against you in the future."

He returns the smile, except his is dark. "I fully anticipate that you will, and that I'll probably enjoy it." He steps back, slips his hand in his pocket, and makes a covert adjustment. We continue down the aisle, where Pierce grabs paint rollers and a few brushes, cleaner, and cloths. I ask questions about best brands and most economical purchases.

"You know, if you want or need any help with your flip, all you have to do is ask. You can borrow whatever you need from me instead of buying new stuff, and I have trade guys I can call."

"Thanks, that's nice of you to offer. But don't you need your trade guys, and won't that piss off your brother?"

"I don't know why you're so worried about pissing off my brother. I'm not. And I don't need them all the time, so I'm happy to share contacts with you."

One thing I know about this business is that sharing contacts doesn't happen often. "Thanks, that'd be great."

We spend the next two hours shopping—well, Pierce is done picking up what he needs in less than twenty minutes. We spend the rest of the time discussing finishes and pricing out everything from kitchen cabinets to bathroom hardware.

It's fun. And normal. And coupley. It worries me how much I like it, and my guilt over my almost truth eats at me even more.

Afterward we go for lunch at a little bistro. He doesn't seem to care that he's dressed for construction among a bunch of suit-wearing business people. Pierce refuses to let me pay my share. I want to be appreciative of the gesture, but it reinforces what I'm struggling to come to terms with—that I'm invested in this man for reasons beyond his stellar bedroom skills.

Getting involved with someone who can afford luxury is scary. It's too close to what I've had before and what I never expect to have again. Until now, it's been easy. Takeout and sex in half-renovated houses or rentals don't lean toward any kind of permanence. But this—expensive meals and shopping trips where I watch him drop five grand without batting an eye—is something else entirely.

Beyond the material luxury, getting emotionally involved is downright terrifying. I don't want to get used to indulgences, even little ones, like this lunch. And I don't want to get too comfortable with him, too close, because it puts me at risk, and Marley, and everything we've worked for. If he digs, he'll find out who we really are. He's only a few well-worded searches on the internet from being able to uncover our whole sordid family history, and then what? Maybe he won't care. But if he told his brother . . . I don't know Lawson well enough to say for certain that he wouldn't use that information against us. If we're connected to our parents, it could obliterate our career in real estate. We've built ourselves up from almost nothing. I don't want to jeopardize that because I'm hot over some guy who isn't going to stick around anyway.

Pierce drags his fingertips along the back of my hand. "Everything okay?"

"I could've paid for my meal."

His lips press into a line. "I came over unannounced and coerced to you into shopping for purely selfish reasons, me paying for lunch is not unreasonable."

"You paid for takeout the other night." This is a stupid thing to be worked up about, but I'm struggling a little with how much this feels like a relationship. This is usually the point where I walk away, but in this case, I don't want to since it's going to be over soon enough anyway.

"And I invited you over then, as well." He taps the table with long fingers. "What about me paying for lunch bothers you, Rian?"

"I like equality."

"Oh." He relaxes back in his seat. "Okay. I suppose I can understand that. Sometimes my sister likes to buy dinner even though I make four times what she does. Although she is marrying a man with more money than God, so I don't usually feel too bad about it."

"That guy with the sleeve?" I motion to my arm. "What is he, some kind of mobster? I'd say MMA fighter since he's a tank and all, but his face is way too pretty and intact for someone to be beating on it regularly."

Pierce laughs. "Lex would probably get a kick out of that. He's actually—" He's cut off by his phone ringing. He flips it over and frowns at the screen. "Sorry. I have to take this."

"Sure. I need to use the bathroom anyway. I'll meet you out by the truck?"

"Perfect." He brings the phone to his ear. "Hold please."

Leaning in, he kisses me on the cheek and passes me his keys. "Thank you. I won't be long." He turns his attention back to his call and heads toward the door. "This better be important. I was in the middle of a lunch date."

I gather my purse and use the bathroom, taking my time before I head to the truck. Pierce is already leaning against it upon my return, arms crossed over his chest, eyes on his phone, expression somber.

"Everything okay?"

He glances up and his hard expression melts into a soft smile. "Debatable." He doesn't elaborate, instead he opens the door for me, his hands on my hips as I step onto the running board. I don't need his assistance, but I certainly don't mind it.

Once he's in the truck, he taps the steering wheel. "So I have to go to the city this afternoon, and I'm not sure how long I'll be there, which means we'll have to cut our day short and possibly reschedule our date."

The last time he was in the city he ran into his ex and then drunk texted me. "Is it lawyery stuff?"

"It is. It's more of a pain in the ass than anything. Can we figure something out when I come back? I don't think I'll be gone more than a couple of days."

"Sure. Whatever works." I don't want to sound too disappointed, even though I am. I like spending time with Pierce, in a bed, out of a bed, eating food, talking. I like *him*. Which is why it should be a good thing he has to cancel.

"I'm really sorry, Rian. If it's any consolation, I'd rather be with you than in Manhattan, dealing with lawyery bullshit."

"I'd rather be under you than having you deal with law-yery stuff too." A reminder to myself that I need to keep this light, not serious.

"I'm taking a rain check on that. As soon as I'm back. You and me. Sleepover. Lots of sex. Extra cuddles so I can sniff your hair without you getting weirded out."

CHAPTER 24

GNOME SWEET GNOME

RIAN

The weeks that follow become increasingly busy with the summer rush. Open houses eat weekend afternoons, and house showings consume evenings. In between it all, I'm in charge of overseeing the renovations for the Paulsons' beach house because I'm the one who pays attention to details and managing the costs.

My busy days are making it difficult for Pierce to reschedule an actual date. However, we still find time to see each other. Pierce makes himself available on a regular basis, stopping by the beach house to help with little things, which often results in quickies on dusty surfaces. I try to keep it casual, as it's supposed to be, but he's so sweet, and fun, and helpful, and all around amazing, so it's difficult not to get attached.

Usually I wind up back at whatever house Pierce is working on—they've purchased yet another property since we bought the Paulsons' and obviously we were not the realtors—eating takeout on the couch. I even started packing an overnight bag with extra clothes and leaving it in my car for such occasions, since they're rather frequent. We talk houses and renovations and sex it up like teen-agers.

He doesn't ask any direct questions about my parents again, and I don't bring it up. Sometimes he makes comments about his own family, as if he's waiting for me to take the bait, but I never do.

Last night I slept in my own bed for once, alone since Pierce had to make another trip into the city. I actually missed Pierce's overly warm body and his breath tickling my neck. I even missed Trip trying to edge his way between us. Which tells me the space is necessary.

After weeks of making cookies and watching Pierce strut around in his lime-green Speedo—it's become a weekly occurrence—Muriel is finally putting her house on the market.

If Marley and I were closer to being finished with our renovations on the Paulson house, purchasing Muriel's place might be an option, but we don't have the capital necessary to finance it. We'd hoped to have our own flip finished before Muriel's home went on the market, but there's been a delay in getting the plumber in. Coincidentally, the plumber is one of Pierce's contacts. As ludicrous as it sounds, I do wonder if the delay was intentional. However, interestingly enough, his awesome paving guys were available without a problem, so the driveway looks amazing. If I had to guess, I doubt he's sabotaging things, and it's just my paranoia that's the problem.

Besides, it would be unethical to postpone a sale for our personal gain. I owe it to Muriel to get her the best deal possible, and if I'm being honest, it wouldn't be Marley and me. Either way, we'll end up with a sweet commission, and Muriel has already found a new place in Texas, so we've scheduled an open house. I may have accidentally failed to mention it to Pierce. Not that it matters. He has Muriel eating out of his palm, so I'm sure, despite my request that she keeps the open house date between us until we're ready to announce, he'll have managed to sweet talk the information out of her.

On the morning of the open house I get up extra early and review all the important details, making sure the property specs look good. Rental furniture was delivered and set up yesterday. My plan is to head over around eleven and bake some sugar cookies so the place smells fantastic for the open house.

I drink coffee and hum to the music blasting through my ear buds as I prepare the cookie dough. Cookies and open houses are always a winner. I add cinnamon, because it's proven to make people feel more at home.

I'm in a fantastic mood when Marley and I get in the car, cookie dough already rolled out and dropped on sheets, so all I have to do is turn on the oven and wait for it to heat.

My sunshine and rainbow mood takes a sharp right turn into what-the-frack land when we arrive at Muriel's. The incredible, cost-effective landscaping, thanks again to one of Pierce's contacts, no longer looks fantastic.

"Freaking Pierce," I growl, throwing the car into park.

Marley frowns as she gets out of the car, and we walk down the freshly laid stone walkway. "What the shit is going on?"

"Son of a B!" I pull my phone out of my purse, find his contact and hit dial.

The smugness in his tone is unmistakable. "Hey, baby, how's it—"

I cut him off before he can finish, surveying the yard. There have to be more than a hundred of those hideous garden gnomes decorating the lawn. "I hope you're proud of yourself."

"I was being helpful. Don't you think it's gnomey?"

I grit my teeth as he laughs. "Enjoy the feel of your hand this weekend, because that's all the action you're going to see."

"Oh, come on, Rian, have a sense of—"

I hang up on him and shove my phone back into my purse, even as it starts ringing again. "When the heck did he have time to do this?" I was here last night.

Marley takes several pictures, snickering.

I prop my fists on my hips. "Why are you laughing? We have to clean this mess up!"

"It's kinda funny. I mean check it out"—she points to a cluster of gnomes—"those ones are having an orgy."

I throw my hands in the air. "Oh for frack's sake."

I spend the next hour tossing Pierce's perverted garden gnomes into the trunk of our car. I definitely plan to get him back for this, with more than vagina-gate. These gnomes are going to find their way back to him, one way or another.

Marley only has enough time to get one batch of cookies made before the open house begins—thanks to the pervy gnome issue. I'm a sweaty, disgusting mess, and I'm forced to blot myself with wet paper towels and use a hairdryer on cold to dry my sweaty armpits. I am less than impressed.

And of course, Pierce and Lawson are the first people to walk through the door as soon as the open house begins. I hate that I tingle at the sight of him in a button-down shirt and tie. He's wearing light-gray dress pants that conform to his magical, muscular butt. That I'd like to slap in a non-pleasurable way.

Thankfully, three other couples are right on their heels, allowing me to ignore his fine, jerkface butt. Eventually he gives up on trying to talk to me, although to be fair, I'm engaged with other, potentially serious buyers. The listing price is on the high side, as we're aware that we can get top dollar for this place since there's nothing comparable on the market. Also, Pierce and Lawson are so hungry for property, they'll pay whatever they need to own this place.

By the end of the showing we have three offers, all of them for asking or above. Of course, the highest is from Pierce and Lawson, which is the one Muriel decides to take. Despite the shared commission, on account of Lawson's new agent, we're still coming out with a significant amount of money, all of which will help with our next flip. It's after six by the time we finally leave, the SOLD sign a red beacon of success. This place might not be ours to flip, but whatever comes on the market next could be, so it's a positive no matter what.

My phone has been going off constantly all day from the confines of my purse. I know it's Pierce. I don't bother to read his messages. I just fire off one of my own.

Rian: You're on a timeout. Marley and I are having a girls' night—no penis allowed, especially not yours. I'm sure Trip will appreciate not sleeping on the floor tonight.

I get a response which I don't check. Instead, I turn to Marley. "Let's go grab a bite to eat, then we can go home, get changed, and have a night out."

Marley blinks a few times. "Excuse me?"

"To celebrate the sale."

"You're not celebrating with Pierce's peen?"

"Umm, did you miss the pervy garden gnomes this morning?"

"I didn't think you were serious about the whole 'his hand being the only action he's going to get' thing."

"Serious as a heart attack."

Marley grins. "Awesome! Girls' night!"

I pull a U-turn, heading toward the restaurants, and the gnomes clunk around in the trunk.

"What do you want to do with those?" she asks.

"Oh, don't you worry. I have a plan."

We go out for dinner—a nice one at the kind of place Pierce would take me. Before we make a stop at home, we drive by one of Pierce and Lawson's rentals, which is vacant until tomorrow morning. I know the entry code, having slept there on several occasions. It takes more than an hour to set up all the gnomes, but it's totally worth the effort.

Afterward we get bar ready. I let Marley pick my outfit—which is skimpy and revealing. For the first time in what seems like forever, Marley and I have a night out with just us. We avoid the beach bars in lieu of something closer to home; that way we don't have to drive, and there's less chance of running into Pierce and allowing him to sway me with the peen and apologies.

The cab drops us off at home at three in the morning. I'm hammered. Marley always thinks shots are a good idea. After the first one they're generally not.

I stop halfway up the front walk when I see Pierce sitting on the front stoop, elbows propped on his knees.

"What're you doing here?" I'm slurry.

"Waiting for you."

"I'mma go drink water and pass out. You two lovebirds sort your stuff out, but no domestics on the front lawn."

Marley weaves around Pierce, punches in the code, and clomps up the stairs to our apartment.

"I'm going up too." I make a move to get around him—I really need the bathroom, but Pierce jumps up to stop me.

"I've been trying to get in touch with you since yesterday afternoon. You can't seriously be this mad about the gnomes."

I give him the eyebrow. "That was a jerk move."

"It was funny."

"It was a pain in my butt. Are you coming up or what? I need to lie down. The world feels like a Tilt-A-Whirl." I have to use the railing for balance. Yeah. I'm definitely drunk. Stupid shots.

Pierce closes and locks the door, following me to my bedroom.

"I have to pee," I announce, then disappear into the bathroom. I unleash a tsunami, brush my teeth, but don't bother to wash off my makeup. Pierce is still sitting on the edge of my bed when I return. I strip down to my panties while he watches, then cover back up with a long, grubby shirt. It's not dirty, it's just old and covered in stains. I climb into bed and pull the pillow over my head. I'm not sure what Pierce is doing, and I don't really care. All that much.

The bed dips and suddenly I feel his body mold itself around mine.

"I was serious about your hand being the only action you're getting this weekend," I mutter from under the six-inch fabric-and-foam barricade.

Pierce lifts the pillow. "What was that?"

"Yesterday. I was serious. You don't get to pull the gnomery and still get the perks of my lady garden." I fight a laugh, because I think I'm actually kind of funny right now.

I elbow him in the ribs, causing him to loosen his grip. I lean over the side of the bed and nab one of the decorative pillows from the floor, shoving it between us. "Rub yourself on that."

"Are you really that mad at me? You got what you wanted, didn't you? Sold the house for over asking. Is the blockade really necessary?" He doesn't try to move it out of the way, despite it probably being uncomfortable.

"I'm not mad. I'm tired and drunk, and I want to sleep and you rubbing your penis against my rear makes that difficult."

"I won't rub myself on you. And I'm tired as fuck too. I've been waiting since midnight. My girlfriend wouldn't tell me where she was."

My heart clenches a little at being called his girlfriend. "I told you I was with Marley."

"But not where. I went to every single bar on the beach, looking for you."

"We didn't go to the beach."

"Yeah. I figured that out eventually, after I gave up messaging you and tried Marley instead. I was worried."

"About what?"

"About some guy that isn't me making a move on you. About me not being clear enough with you about what this is. I'm not seeing anyone else. I don't want to see anyone else."

"We went out dancing. That was it." Now I'm all swoony and sappy, but he doesn't need to know that.

"Last time you went dancing there was a lineup of dicks waiting to rub on your ass."

"I don't want to see anyone else either." I say nothing about being rubbed on, because that happens no matter what. "Now can you stop talking and let me go to sleep?"

"'Kay." He burrows through my hair until his nose

tickles my neck. Then his lips find my shoulder. He snuggles in, a few minutes later he shoves the throw pillow out of the way and wraps himself around me.

I feel warm and safe as I drift back to sleep. Maybe too safe, and that scares me, because it feels like I'm giving this man my heart, even though I shouldn't. Summer ends soon. And then what? Does he take my heart back to Manhattan with him while I have to go on here, alone? I have all these secrets I'm keeping, and who knows what will happen when my skeletons eventually claw their way out of the closet.

I sleep until noon. It's blissful. I freeze mid-stretch and realize I'm not alone in my bed. Memories of the bar from last night filter through. Shots. Dancing. Telling some jerk that my butt was not a place for him to grind. Panic sets in for half a second, until the familiar scent of Pierce's cologne and the perfect fit of his body against mine registers, and I can relax.

"You forget I was here?" Pierce's voice is sleep raspy.

"I thought I brought home a random, actually." Only for about half a confused second.

I grin at the sudden stiffness in his body. Then yelp when he pinches my butt. "Not funny."

"Ow. Where's your sense of humor?" I rub my rear, which means I inadvertently rub his penis, through the barrier of clothing, but still.

He exhales a heavy breath. "It disappeared with my girlfriend last night."

I roll over to face him and cover my mouth with my palm. My mouth tastes like a toilet bowl. "I didn't disappear. I went out with my sister. That's allowed, you know."

"I don't like it when you're not talking to me. And when I'm not invited."

"You're addicted to this, aren't you?" I motion to what I'm sure is my very messed-up hair. I also don't think I took off my makeup last night, so there's a solid chance my mascara is smeared in raccoon-style circles under my eyes.

"Hopelessly." He kisses the end of my nose, and then backs away so he's not breathing his sleep breath in my face. "I want to take you out for dinner tonight."

"Do you, now?"

"Mmm. In Manhattan. We can stay at my condo. I can have you all to myself."

"You can have me all to yourself right here."

"But your sister is across the hall. And all the beach houses are rented out or in various stages of reno, and not fit for a sleepover. Not the kind I want to have tonight, anyway."

"Have you forgotten that your hand is the only action you're going to see this weekend?"

"Right. Hmm." He taps his lip. "That's not a problem. We can make tonight all about you."

"All about me, huh?"

"That's right."

"Dinner and sleepover without orgasms? That should be interesting."

"Oh, there will be orgasms. I just won't get to have mine inside you."

I shiver at the thought of how creative he's going to get with that, and whether I'll be able to stand by my own boycott.

I put on a pot of coffee and Pierce hangs out in my bedroom while I shower off last night's sweat. Pierce lounges

on my bed with a coffee mug and a plate of sugar cookies—
I'm sure my bed is full of crumbs, but I'll deal with that
later—while I set to packing an overnight bag. I torture
him by parading around in a bra and panties while showing him dresses for tonight's dinner. I drag the entire thing
out for as long as I can, and I end up changing my panties
three times to make him sweat.

I think's it's probably as torturous for myself as it is for
Pierce, but I'm willing to suffer because his discomfort is
empowering.

At two thirty, as we're getting ready to leave, Pierce
gets a call from his brother. "What are you talking about?
They're what?" His eyes lift to mine and then narrow. "Can
you take care of it? They're in which rental? Fuck. The new
guests are supposed to be there in an hour. Just put them in
the shed and I'll deal with them tomorrow when I get back.
Fine. Fine. I'll come help. I'm on my way."

I smile serenely at him. "Found the gnomes, huh?"

"Well played, Rian. I suppose you wouldn't be interested in helping me get rid of them."

"Oh, I did that yesterday, all by myself."

"I'll be back in an hour. You better be ready. And I think
we might need to renegotiate the terms of tonight's date."
He kisses me on the cheek and leaves me to finish packing.

CHAPTER 25

FREE FALL

RIAN

It's almost five by the time Pierce returns. There were a lot of gnomes. And since they'd been in the garden, there was a mess of dirt to clean up. Apparently he needed a shower when he was finished. I'd like to say I feel bad, but I don't, considering what he put me through yesterday.

I'm already dressed for dinner—the gnome situation having delayed our departure, so we're heading straight to the restaurant instead of stopping at his condo first. The drive to Manhattan is rife with sexual tension, likely because I've told Pierce there won't be any scoring at the end of the night. I'm not 100 percent convinced I'll be able to stick to that. Not with him looking so delicious in a crisp black suit. Or with every other sentence out of his mouth dripping with innuendo.

It's been ages since I've been to the city. I'm nervous as we pull up to the valet and my door is opened for me. I feel like some kind of imposter when Pierce links arms with me and guides me inside. I've been to this restaurant before, a long time ago, I realize, back when Broadway theater was a regular occurrence and a night in a luxury hotel was the norm for my family.

"Mr. Whitfield, it's so nice to see you! It's been too long." The host takes his hand in both of his, shaking it warmly.

"It certainly has."

"Your father was here last week and mentioned you were spending the summer in the Hamptons."

When Pierce smiles. It's warm but his voice holds a hint of tightness. "Just enjoying the beach."

"Lovely, I'm sure." The host, whose tag reads Karl, turns his smile on me. "And who is this stunning masterpiece you've brought with you tonight?"

I laugh as he bends to kiss the back of my hand.

"This is Miss Rian Sutter, with an *i* instead of a *y*."

"Well, Miss Rian with an *i*, we're very glad you're joining us this evening." He turns his attention back to Pierce. "Give us a moment and we'll make sure your table is ready. Would you like to have a seat at the bar while you wait?"

Pierce defers to me.

"That sounds perfectly lovely." I smooth a hand self-consciously over my hip, wishing I had a nicer dress, that I could match Pierce in his designer suit, instead of my bargain-find dress and knockoff shoes and purse. I know it doesn't matter to him, but again I feel like an imposter. Someone who doesn't quite fit in this world anymore.

Pierce's palm rests against my low back as he leads me to the bar.

"How often do you bring dates here, Mr. Whitfield?" I ask quietly.

Pierce dips his head and presses his lips to my temple. "You would be the first, Miss Sutter. Usually I come here with my family."

"They won't be here, will they?"

He chuckles. "Absolutely not. I want you all to myself tonight. And there is no way in hell I would spring something like that on you without warning. My family requires preparation and shots to endure."

"Amalie is sweet."

"So she'll have you believe."

He leads us toward two open stools. "Excuse me, are these taken?" he asks, hand already on the back of the one beside a woman in a slinky black dress.

A diamond-clad hand flutters in the air, so close to my face that I take a step back into Pierce's chest to avoid getting hit. "Not at a—" Big brown eyes go wide, and her mouth forms a pouty *o*. "Pierce!"

I feel him stiffen behind me, the hand on my shoulder tightening. "Stacey."

She swivels in her chair, eyes sliding over me to Pierce. "What a surprise! I didn't think you were due back in town for a few more weeks. Has everything been cleared up with the patent?"

"We're here for the weekend." His fingers glide down my arm and settle on my hip as he pulls me possessively into his side.

Her gaze finally shifts my way, as if she's just noticing me. "Oh? Is this a friend?" Her smile is far from warm, it's assessing and judgmental as she takes me in. She's clearly very comfortable in her Louboutin shoes and her designer everything. Her hair is cut in a chic bob, lipstick perfect, lashes extended, her size-two figure maintained by God only knows how many hours of Pilates and I hope plastic surgery. I feel small under her assessment. And very much out of place.

"This is my girlfriend, Rian," Pierce practically grits the words.

I have no idea who this woman is, but my disdain for her is immediate and I have a strong urge to protect Pierce from her, which seems ludicrous considering he's clearly more than capable of taking care of himself.

"Girlfriend?" She presses her perfectly manicured hand to her chest. "Oh bless! Isn't that sweet? Do you live in Manhattan, Rian, is it? What an interesting name."

I would like to gouge this condescending bitch's eyes out with a dessert spoon. "No. I live in the Hamptons."

"Oh! Very nice. You've been playing around in the housing market out there with your brother this summer, haven't you, Pierce? Getting your hands a bit dirty." Her nose wrinkles, and I bristle at the comment, certain it's directed at me.

"And how do you know Pierce, exactly?" I ask.

Her grin widens and she bats her lashes. "We were engaged. Young love, you know how it is, sometimes it doesn't work out."

"That's so true." I thread my fingers through Pierce's. "Especially when you're a ladder-climbing gold digger with no moral compass. I certainly hope this engagement works out for you, and that your current fiancé makes you as happy as I'm sure you made Pierce." I turn and put a hand on his chest. "We should see if our table is ready. I find the bar in this place to be a little classless."

Pierce bites back a smile as he skims my cheek with gentle fingers. "I couldn't agree with you more." His eyes stay on mine, his gratitude clear as he nods a cold acknowledgment to his ex-fiancée, and we head back to the host stand.

He squeezes my hand. "I'm sorry about that. I really didn't expect to see her, especially not here of all places."

"Don't apologize. We can go somewhere else if you

want. We can even go back to your condo if you'd rather order takeout."

"No. We're here now, and I don't want her to ruin our night. I'll make sure there's no way she'll be seated any-where near us." He frowns. "Unless you want to go. I don't want this to be uncomfortable for you."

"It's not me I'm worried about. I'm more than willing to go toe-to-toe with that woman. I've been lifting sheets of drywall this summer; I'm pretty sure I can take her on if you want me to."

He laughs and bends to kiss me softly. "God, you're something else."

It turns out we don't have to wait, and Pierce has a brief, whispered conversation with the host whose brows dip and then rise. We're led to the back of the restaurant, to a se-cluded, private room and seated at an intimate table for two with a curved, high-backed bench seat, covered in plush velvet so we can sit beside each other instead of across the table.

Pierce orders a bottle of champagne, and I peruse the menu, cringing at the prices. "This place is exceedingly expensive."

He tilts his head, a questioning smile tipping his mouth. "I'm taking you out for dinner. You can do all the math you want in your head, but you're not covering half and you don't owe me anything."

I laugh but I feel too warm, too exposed. Running into his ex-fiancée, this dinner, him calling me his girlfriend, knowing I'm spending the night in his condo. I'm not prepared to deal with the serious feelings I have for this man.

"I think we're past the point of pretending I don't have money, Rian."

"I know." I stare at the menu, overwhelmed, afraid to like this, to want this.

"You deal with people who have excessive amounts of money on a regular basis. Why does this make you so uncomfortable? Is it because of Stacey?"

"No. Stacey has no bearing on anything."

"Then what is it?"

I exhale a slow breath, debating how much I can, or should, reveal. I need to give him something, maybe not the entire truth, but part of it, especially with everything that's already happened tonight. "It wasn't always like this for Marley and me."

"Wasn't always like what?" Pierce shifts so his knee brushes mine under the table.

I adjust the silverware on the table so both knives are perfectly parallel with each other. "When we were young, before our parents . . ." I clear my throat, unable to find the right words. "We had money. Things weren't always a struggle."

"You're doing incredibly well. You should be proud of what you and Marley have accomplished."

I nod. "I know. And I am. But we were in a very different place when we were teenagers. My grandparents . . . They owned a lot of property. I wasn't quite honest with you about the Mission Mansion." At his questioning look, I elaborate. "My grandparents weren't friends with the owners; they were the owners."

I've given Pierce enough information to uncover the whole truth if he digs. Who my parents really are. How my world fell apart all those years ago, and how Marley and I have had to fight our way out of debt and a ruined family name. Part of me is relieved, and part of me is terrified. I remind myself that the expiration date on us is fast approaching.

Pierce blinks, his shock obvious. "Why didn't you say anything before now? Why keep that a secret?"

I trace the edge of the steak knife. "It's hard to talk about it. Seeing it all the time and having all of these memories connected to it is painful. When my grandmother passed, we lost a lot, including the Mansion and everything in it."

Pierce picks up my hand and brings my knuckles to his lips. "God. That must've been awful for you."

"I just want it back. I know it's not likely to happen, but all my best memories are wrapped up in that house."

I can see the questions in his eyes, but the server arrives with the champagne, and any ideas I have about telling him the whole truth disappear. If he wants it, he can find it, with or without my help. And I'm okay with that. I think.

I drink champagne to calm my nerves—very expensive champagne—eat lobster for the first time in a decade, and listen to Pierce talk about how much he loves what he's doing now, and how he wants to keep it up even after the summer is over. I don't want to have hope that this will happen. And I fall. Faster and farther and deeper, because there are so many sides to him. So much I get to discover.

I'm afraid that when he eventually finds out the truth about me, it's all going to go away, and how I probably deserve to lose him for not being completely honest in the first place. Now that I've accepted this connection we have, one that goes far beyond simple chemistry, I realize I should've been honest from the start. But it's too late to take back the half truths and omissions. I tell myself that I'll find the right time to explain it all to him, maybe in the morning. But tonight I just want to enjoy him. I allow myself to pretend nothing will change and that I'm not falling in love.

By the time we're finished with dinner it's after eleven.

I'm tipsy. Okay, I'm actually pretty sure I'm drunk. Again. This is two nights in a row. My liver is going to hate me and stage a revolt.

I don't pay much attention when we reach his condo. It barely registers that we bypass the bank of regular elevators in lieu of a set with PH on it. Pierce has to punch in a code then scan his thumbprint before the doors open.

"Is this your own personal elevator?" It's supposed to be a joke.

"It's dedicated. Watch your step." He keeps his hand on the small of my back as we step inside, and he presses his thumb to an infrared keypad. The doors slide closed, and then we're moving, but the ride is so smooth it's hard to tell that we're in motion.

Since we're alone I take the opportunity to get in some elevator snuggles. I put a hand on his chest, and he backs up until he hits the mirrored glass wall. His smile is knowing, and maybe a little needy, fused with amusement. I fist his tie and tip my head back.

He grips the railing and dips down to brush his lips over mine. The whole night has been one big foreplay session, and I'm feeling a little impatient. There's an edge of desperation I can't calm, a prickling fear that this tenuous hold is about to break and tonight's revelation is going to rip this all away from me. Maybe it's because that's what happened every time I had a boyfriend who found out about my family's sordid past.

I can drown out the worry with touch. Pierce can make me forget all my fears, at least for tonight. Tomorrow I'll open the door to the closet of my past and deal with the consequences. I slide a palm down his chest, skimming past his belt buckle to cup him through his dress pants.

He's lightning quick, fingers circling around my wrists as he spins me around, clasping them in one hand behind my back. "I thought the only hand that was touching my dick this weekend was mine." He sinks his hips into mine.

"It'll be Monday in an hour. Technically that means the weekend will be over."

His grin is almost evil. "That's going to make the next hour interesting then, isn't it?"

"I like interesting." This is what I need, what I want. A distraction from what's happening in my head and in my heart.

The elevator doors slide open and I find myself lifted up. A seam tears somewhere on my dress as I wrap my legs around Pierce's waist. He carries me through his condo—penthouse, whatever—I don't remember him unlocking a door, and then I'm laid out on a bed. A big one. One that smells faintly of him, his body covering mine.

The next hour isn't interesting—it's torture. The best, most amazing torture, full of the most insanely teasing orgasms. And when midnight hits, Pierce is in me, on me, owning me, and I'm falling.

Falling.

Falling.

And I never want this to stop.

CHAPTER 26
UN-KNOW

RIAN

Pierce is the picture of sexy sweetness sprawled out on the mattress, pale-blue sheets hanging precariously low on his hips. He's out cold. Which makes sense since it's eight in the morning and he's been asleep for less than five hours.

I should close my eyes and try for a few more hours of rest, because I'm grossly underslept these days, but my brain is already on sprint mode, reviewing last night, the conversations, the sex, the everything. I shouldn't have said anything about the Mission Mansion. But I'm tired of hiding. Obviously I'm scared that he'll walk like everyone else has in the past, but if that's the inevitable end, it's better it happens now than later when my heart is totally locked up in him.

I glance around his bedroom. It was dark when we arrived last night after dinner and my focus was on Pierce. The mattress I'm lying on is cloudlike, and the bed frame is solid cherry. The sheets are satin soft, the pillows definitely feather. This bedroom screams money. Lots of money.

I throw off the covers and carefully leave the bed without disturbing Pierce. Nabbing Pierce's shirt from the floor, I pull it over my head. I need to use the bathroom, but I don't want to risk waking Pierce, so I slip out the door and wander down the hall. The floors are dark hardwood. Possibly Brazilian cherry. I find a second bedroom two doors down, smaller than the master, but at least three times the size of my own.

I use the private bathroom before I continue my self-guided tour.

The morning sun almost blinds me when I enter the living room, the wall of windows showcase a gorgeous skyline. The décor is a fusion of modern minimalist and antique rustic. It's very Pierce. I run my hand along the back of the vintage leather couch—at least it looks vintage, but based on the buttery smoothness of the leather it can't be very old, and like everything else in here, it's expensive. I need to look up this building. My purse is where I dropped it when we arrived last night, by the dedicated elevator to his penthouse.

That's right. A dedicated elevator. That small detail tells me all I need to know about how much it costs to live up here. I root around in my purse and find my phone. I log into my account on the listing site and punch in the address for the building. Only two condo units are currently available for sale. They aren't corner penthouses and they're listed at two million dollars each. "Good God," I mutter, flipping through the pictures. Based on square footage and location, this has to be at least twice the cost.

I rub my forehead, my stomach knotting. A patent lawyer salary can't afford this penthouse. I mean, I'm sure he makes excellent money as a patent lawyer, and the rental properties are probably helpful, but this doesn't quite jibe.

I continue my exploration of Pierce's penthouse.

I stumble across his office, which is a grand, gorgeous space, one wall lined with ornate, hardwood shelves filled with legal books. On each shelf is a wooden sculpture of some kind, and I have to wonder if they're Pierce's creations. His office desk faces the wall of windows. I cross over to the executive chair and drop into it. This is where lawyer Pierce must sit and do lawyery things.

I picture him dressed as he was when he approached me in the grocery store. Tom Ford suit hugging his sculpted body. Tie begging to be yanked. I run my fingers along the edge of the desk. I bet it would be fun to play lawyer with him in here. He could wear his suit; I could be his naked desk ornament.

I sigh and swivel in the chair. There are several folders stacked to the right, all labeled with his neat printing. A few pictures line the shelves to the left—of him and his family based on Amalie and Lawson's presence, and there are a couple that seem to include his brother-in-law-to-be.

On his desk is a copy of *The Moorehead Review*, a magazine dedicated to the upper crust and their financial dealings. It's not the most reputable news source, but there are some interesting, although biased, articles in there on occasion. I flip to one about real estate in the Hamptons.

It seems to be about a huge hotel mogul coming in and buying up properties, particularly in Hamptons Bay. I turn the page and my stomach drops as I scan the image and then the article. One page is taken up by a glossy color image of a very familiar face. A very attractive familiar face. I scan the byline and a name pops out. Lexington Mills. Lex. The MMA fighter-superhero who's engaged to Pierce's sister stares back at me with his shockingly blue eyes and wide, almost smirky smile. He's ridiculously attractive, even in a two-dimensional magazine photo.

He's leaning against a desk and beside him is a man

who must be his father. To his left are two other equally attractive men. The Mills family. Mills Hotels. They're massive. Like the biggest. They were who my father wanted to
be. The competition he could never catch. The same competition who brought him down. Because he scammed
them along with everyone else, Marley and I included.
And I'd unknowingly helped him do it.

I read on, devouring the article, snagging on a line about
the Mission Mansion. There's no reference to the shady
dealings of my father, but there is a mention of the prime
location of the rundown mansion, its sadly vacant state,
and its buyer appeal. I flip back to the beginning and read
it all over again. There's conjecture that the Mills family
would like to put up a hotel in the Hamptons. While this
would ultimately drive up the housing prices, there are
drawbacks with that plan. Excessive tourism, overcrowded
beaches. And a huge gaudy hotel would ruin the landscape.

A sick feeling crawls up my throat. How long ago did I
tell him about the Mission Mansion? It's been weeks since
I mentioned my summers spent there, and last night I finally
came clean about my real connection to it. Pierce had more
than one opportunity to mention this, especially knowing
how important it is to me.

Is this what they've been planning the entire time? To
buy up all the property around the Mission Mansion, put
enough time and money into renovations to increase property value, and then sell it off to the Millses so they can
build a huge hotel?

I want to believe it's too elaborate a ruse, but at the same
time, there are so many red flags flapping in the breeze.
And this is exactly the kind of thing my father would've
done to get what he wanted.

My stomach churns with the myriad possibilities, none
of which are good. Pierce is far too close to the people in

this scenario to be in the dark, and I've been so wrapped up in him and the Paulson renovation that I haven't been staying on top of much else. I don't know what to do, what to believe. I need to talk to Marley. My head has already gone to the worst places. I need perspective and I need out of here, before Pierce wakes up and this entire thing collapses. I don't want to accuse him of something that isn't true, but I also can't ignore this feeling of doubt that's twisting up my stomach.

I tiptoe back to his bedroom. He's hugging my pillow, his spectacular bare backside on display. I quickly and quietly gather my clothes from the floor and dress in the spare bathroom. I pull my hair in a ponytail and fix my makeup as best as I can before I head for the elevator.

I call for an Uber on my way to street level, relieved when it arrives not two minutes later. I consider calling Marley on the trip to the train station, but I don't think it's the best plan. I need to be in front of a computer when I have this conversation with her, so I can figure out what the heck is going on and how Pierce is involved in this.

I bite my fingernails, tears pricking my eyes. He seemed so genuine last night. Things felt different, like maybe he's serious about me being his girlfriend, and not temporarily. Or maybe it was a ploy to get me out of the Hamptons and keep me distracted, from what, I'm unsure. The train ride from Manhattan to the Hamptons seems to last forever. My phone is at 30 percent and draining fast. I didn't bring a charger so I have limited battery life with which to search Pierce Whitfield.

I don't know why I haven't bothered to do this before now. Or maybe I do know. I liked getting to know him without dissecting a dating profile. And I don't want him to search me. Although, to be fair, Sutter isn't my last name by birth, and Marley and I have done everything we possibly can to separate ourselves from our father's infamy. But sometimes things slip through. An old article, pictures, things that could easily lead back to us if we still lived in Long Island instead of the Hamptons.

The first Pierce Whitfield link takes me to his law firm. Halfway down the page are several Facebook profiles for various Pierce Whitfields—who knew it was such a popular name—but after that there are endless articles connecting him to a line of popular children's dolls. I consider typing in *Whitfield family net worth*, but I don't want to know that yet.

I'll come back to that. When I'm ready. Next I search *Mills Hotel* and *Mills Family*. The name is actually rather common, but the familiarity lies with my father's disdain for them, because they always had what he never could, and eventually they took it all by uncovering his endless scams and lies.

I pull up article after article on their family dynasty. They're worth an insane amount of money. The kind of money that could buy up an entire strip of homes in the Hamptons without even blinking. Hundreds of millions of dollars.

I think for a moment about Amalie, Pierce's sister, and how normal she seems to be considering she's marrying into what is likely one of the richest families in New York. But then, her family has money too. I'd be surprised if the Millses don't have their own private jet.

I flip back to the Whitfield family who hold the patent for Amalie Dolls. And dear God, they have an app. It's crazypants. I click on a link that takes me to a website with endless varieties of those creepy dolls with the blinky eyes that are more often than not the demonic, possessed stars of horror movies.

I've seen those dolls in stores. They're a huge deal during

every holiday. Easter, Fourth of July, Halloween, Thanksgiving, Christmas; there's a new doll with a new outfit and new app add-ons. It's no wonder Pierce can afford to buy a three-quarter-of-a-million-dollar house with cash.

It's ten thirty when I arrive home, and it's a Monday, which is typically a slow day in real estate, so I don't expect Marley to be awake, particularly since she went out last night with friends. It's possible she has company. I hope not.

I pull up the article I read in *The Moorehead Review* on my laptop and send a text to my sister before I knock on her door. Then I send another one three minutes later because she still hasn't answered. "Mar? Are you awake?"

I get a grunt in response.

"Are you alone?"

It takes several long seconds before I get a groggy "Yes."

I feel a pang of guilt for my surprise. Marley after a night at a bar is usually accompanied by some guy, random or not, taking up space in our apartment and making things awkward.

"I'm opening the door," I warn, in case she's lying about her alone status.

She glances at the clock on her nightstand and frowns. "What're you doing home this early? Shouldn't you be having a sexathon with your lawn boy?"

I lean against the doorjamb, laptop propped against my hip, and attempt to feign calm. "I'm a little worried about my lawn boy."

She sits up, rubbing her eyes, her frown deepening. "Uh-oh, did the condom break?" I shake my head, and she exhales a relieved breath, but it's short-lived. "Are you okay? What happened? What did that asshole do?"

I love that she immediately makes him the villain, even

though I'm unsure whether or not that's true. I sit down on the mattress beside her and turn the laptop toward her. "Read this."

"He's not married, is he?"

"No, but it might be the same level of bad."

She scans the article, eyes darting to mine when she gets to the part about the Mission Mansion.

"Is this even a credible news source? Isn't *Moorehead* into those clickbait scams? And what does this have to do with Pierce?"

"His sister is engaged to Lexington Mills. Son of the CEO of the Mills Hotels. I met him at Lawson's the day after we sold them the first house."

Marley scrolls through the article again. "And you think Pierce is somehow involved?"

"I don't know, but I told him a long time ago that we used to spend our summers there, and last night I told him our grandparents used to own it. He's going to figure out how we're connected to it sooner than later. What if he's had a plan this whole time? What if he and Lawson are biding their time until the Millses start buying up property and he never said anything? Think about it: They've done minimal renovations on their properties this summer. We both know flipping is far more lucrative than renting, but they suddenly change gears and choose to hold onto every-thing they buy? What other reason would there be?"

"That they want to build a rental base? They obviously have money to play with. I don't know that it has to be as sinister as all this." She motions to the magazine spread out before us.

"The Mills family is beyond rich, though. They could buy up every single damn property on the beach and it would barely dent their bank account."

Marley chews on her bottom lip and regards me with

quiet speculation. "I don't know, Rian. I mean, I guess I can see how you might think there's a connection here, but Pierce doesn't seem like the kind of guy to do something like this. It doesn't seem logical, and honestly, he's so into you. He sat on the front porch for hours waiting for you to come home."

"How many properties have they bought this summer? Every time something comes up they're right there, putting in an offer. It can't all be a coincidence."

She exhales a slow breath. "Okay, but if they're going to sell it anyway, why put any money into renovations at all? Why not sit on it?"

"So they can rent until the Millses jump in and buy it up? Maybe it wasn't their plan at first and then it changed when this article came out." It's a few weeks old. God, how long has Pierce known about this and not said anything?

"Pierce wasn't all that excited about that plan, though, was he? I think you need to talk to him before you start jumping to conclusions."

I run my palm down my face, hating the panic and the twisted feeling in my stomach. "I'm going to have to tell him how we're connected to the Mission Mansion."

"You can't hide it from him forever."

"Our dad screwed dozens of people out of their homes and money, including the Mills family, who he's directly connected to, with my help." Less than six hours ago I was sure I was falling for this man, and now the half truths are biting at my heels.

"You had no idea what he was doing, Rian. You can't keep blaming yourself for something you didn't do."

"But I gave him what he needed to do it, which is just as bad." And I've lied by omission, which is almost worse than lying outright. My phone buzzes with messages from

Pierce. I don't look at them. I'm pretty sure I know what they'll say. He woke up to an empty bed.

Marley sighs. "Does he even know where you are?"

"He was asleep when I left."

"What if he's not involved? What if this is all on Lawson?"

"What if he is involved? What if he's known this whole time and he's been stringing me along, keeping me occupied while he and Lawson make deals with the Mills family."

She sighs, her eyes sad. "Maybe you're trying to make him into the bad guy so you can feel justified in walking away."

"What about all these connections? It can't be coincidental."

"I think you need to ask yourself if you're forcing them to be there because you're afraid to tell him the truth. You have to talk to him, Rian."

She could be right, but she could be wrong. Either way, there's a real possibility I'm going to lose something important at the end of all of this. I hope it's not my heart.

CHAPTER 27
EMPTY BED

PIERCE

I nuzzle into a pillow that smells like Rian, and slide my palm along the mattress in search of the real thing. Except all I get are ten-thousand-thread-count Egyptian cotton sheets under my palm. I crack a lid, close it because it's too bright beyond the back of my eyelid, and wait a few more seconds before I open it again.

In the space where Rian's body should be are rumpled sheets, cool to the touch. I assume she woke up and decided to let me sleep. If she's hungry, we can do breakfast, then each other. Then we'll figure out what to do with our day. I'm voting for Naked Monday, but I'll give her a say. Except when I get to the kitchen, she isn't there; she's also not in the living room.

I rub the back of my neck to ease the hot feeling as I wander through the penthouse. The coffee cups on the counter are clean and unused. I backtrack to my bedroom and glance around the vacant space, noting the absence of her clothes, which most certainly had been strewn all over the floor last night. That prickling sensation on my neck becomes a sinking feeling as I call Rian's name but get no response. Her heels aren't by the door and her overnight bag is gone.

Maybe there was an emergency. Maybe an impromptu showing came up and she needed to go and didn't want to wake me. But I'd like to think she would've left a note.

I check my phone for a message, but there's nothing, so I fire one off, asking where she disappeared to. I worry last night was too much for her. I'd considered telling her how I felt about her, especially since she'd opened up to me. But in the end, I'd held back, aware a declaration like that might make Rian skittish. Getting close to her hasn't been easy, and I've been trying my hardest not to push for more than I feel she's willing to give.

While I wait for a response, I put the coffee on, but even after it's finished brewing I still haven't heard back from her, so I leave her a voicemail and head to my office. Since I'm in Manhattan, it makes sense to clock a few hours of work and see if there's been any progress on revising the patent so the knockoff blow-up dolls are no longer a concern.

On my desk is a *Moorehead* magazine from a couple of weeks ago. I don't generally put much stock in the articles, since the Mooreheads tend to spew a lot of biased garbage, but I still get a copy every week, mostly so I can keep tabs on my sister's ex-husband's family dealings. It's lying open rather than stacked neatly on the corner of my desk, as I would've left it. An article about my sister's fiancé and his family fills the page. I'm sure the Mills Hotel empire is getting ready to put up another five-star resort somewhere in the near future. They have projects all over the world. I assume *Moorehead* is covering this simply because it gives her ex-husband a reason to dig into Amalie's life.

I spend a couple hours reviewing emails and paperwork that have been forwarded to me as a courtesy, more than anything else. What I really need to do is revisit the discussion with my father about my future at the firm.

I mentioned it the last time I was in Manhattan to feel him out, but I don't want to push too much when the patent issue is still unresolved. We're close to putting it to bed, but it's been tricky since my dad would like to avoid court and drawing more attention to the problem than necessary. Which means settling. And settling costs money.

Regardless, I don't want to put this off any longer.

I call his office, but discover he's out of town with my mother for the week. I suppose it says something about where I'm at mentally when I don't even know what's going on with my parents.

After two more hours of silence from Rian, in which I review my personal finances and determine that without my trust, walking away from the firm will be exceedingly difficult on my bank account, I decide to head back to the Hamptons. All this ruminating is getting me nowhere, and I need to find out what's going on. I try Rian's apartment first, but neither car is in the driveway and no one answers the door.

By the time I arrive at the Paulson renovation it's well into the afternoon. Worry dissolves into anger when I find Rian's car in the driveway. I don't knock before I open the door and walk inside her half-finished reno—one I've put a lot of hours into personally.

Rian's standing on a ladder in the middle of the room with a can of paint and a paintbrush, ear buds blocking out the world. It pisses me off that she's here, and I've spent my entire morning and most of my afternoon worried about what the fuck I did wrong to warrant her disappearance and her silence.

I startle her when I appear in her peripheral vision. She fumbles the paint can and nearly tumbles off the ladder trying to keep it from tipping over on her. I take it before it falls and set it on the floor.

Rian yanks her ear buds out. "Pierce! What're you doing here?"

"Looking for you. Wanna tell me why you disappeared this morning with no message, and explain why you're avoiding my calls?" I gesture to the phone tucked between her breasts in her clingy tank.

"I couldn't sleep and I had work to do." She motions to the paint, eyes darting everywhere, but avoiding my face.

"Shovel or bulldozer?"

"What?"

"What would you prefer for your bullshit, a shovel or a bulldozer? Because I'm not buying it. What the fuck is going on, Rian? We had a great time last night. Better than great, and I wake up to an empty bed and no indication as to where you went or why. Do you have any idea how worried I was?" My anger is gathering steam instead of dissipating, maybe because she's mirroring my pose, arms crossed over her chest defiantly, chin tipped up, but her eyes say something different—they tell me she is scared, and I have no clue why that would be.

"I needed some space."

"Space from what?"

She motions between us, eyes darting around. "From this. From us."

"I don't get it. I thought we were finally getting somewhere and then you pull a disappearing act this morning? How'd you even get home?"

"I took the train. I needed to think."

"Think about what exactly? I'm really fucking confused

right now, so if you could explain this so it makes some kind of sense, that'd be great."

"Why didn't you mention that Amalie's fiancé is part of the Mills empire?"

"You mean Lex?"

"Yes, Lex."

I get a sinking feeling in my stomach. The kind that makes my gut feel like it's trying to turn itself inside out. "Because it has nothing to do with us, and it's irrelevant."

"But it does." She's so cagey and I don't get why.

"I don't see how my sister's fiancé's family has any bearing on our relationship."

"It does when they want to put up a new hotel in the Hamptons." Her anger seems to match mine.

"They're always talking about putting up another resort. It's what they do. It still doesn't explain why you pulled a runner this morning."

"I found that magazine in your office this morning, Pierce. The one with the whole article about the Mills family and the Mission Mansion. You can't tell me you don't know anything about that."

"Are you talking about the *Moorehead Review*? Because I generally don't read or believe whatever bullshit is spewed in there."

Her eyes narrow. "So you read the article."

"Sure. I'm still not understanding where you're going with this."

"That magazine is weeks old."

"I read it this morning. I told you, I don't generally put much stock in the content."

"But you were in Manhattan a few weeks ago when that magazine came out."

"Is there an accusation in here somewhere? Because that's how it's starting to sound."

"You keep buying all these properties on the beach. Are you holding onto them so you can sell to the Mills family?"

"I'm sorry, what?"

She plants her fist on her hip. "You knew how I felt about the mansion. I told you weeks ago, and now you're trying to play it off like you had no idea any of this is going on." She motions between us. "Why all of a sudden are you calling me your girlfriend? Why take me to Manhattan? To get me out of the Hamptons so your brother is free to hatch some scheme?" Her eyes are wild, hands flailing as she paces around the living room.

Incredulous isn't a strong enough word for my current state. "How the hell do you make such a wild leap? I don't get how you can believe I'd do something like that."

Rian throws her hands up in the air. "It makes sense, doesn't it? Get close, be a distraction so you can get what you want and get laid in the process."

I scrub a hand over my face. None of this is making sense. "This is what you think of me? You know, maybe I could understand if all we were doing was fucking each other, but come on, Rian, what's going on between us is a lot bigger than that."

"You're going back to Manhattan in a month. How is this supposed to be anything more than a summer fling? You can't tell me I don't have a reason to question this, Pierce. I mean, look at me and look at you." She gestures between us, eyes darting around, her panic rising. "Your situation and mine aren't exactly the same. You live in a penthouse and I live in a crappy duplex. You wear two-hundred-dollar pairs of jeans to mow the lawn, and your sunglasses are worth more than my car."

"That's what you want to make this about? My financial situation versus yours? Do you really think I'm that much of a shallow prick?" Her silence is like a nail-gun shot to the chest. My jaw tics and I take a step closer. Rian, being Rian, doesn't back down at all. She tips her head up, eyes flashing with defiance and under that, fear and devastation. "Let me tell you something. I grew up in a two-bedroom apartment in Long Island for the first seven years of my life. Then we had to rent a three-bedroom house when my sister came along. I know what it's like to eat peanut-butter sandwiches for dinner when money's tight, so don't box me into some shitty stereotype that doesn't fit me, Rian. I'm not that guy. I've never been that guy, even if you want me to be, even if it makes this, *us,* easier for you to dismiss."

She swallows thickly, seeming vulnerable and small. She blinks a few times, eyes clearing, determination winning out. She stalks across the room, grabs a sheet of paper from the island, and holds it up in front of my face. "Look at this."

It's a black-and-white printout of an aerial view of Mission Mansion and the surrounding properties, several of which are circled in red. "What is this?"

"You and Lawson own all of these." She pokes viciously at the red circles.

I take the sheet, inspecting it.

"What does that look like to you?" Rian demands.

I take in the strategic locations in which Lawson has pushed to buy properties. We have beach houses flanking all sides of the Mission Mansion. He's been talking to Lex a lot on the phone lately; I've seen his contact lighting up his phone. I didn't think anything of it because he's going to be our brother-in-law.

"Look at how many of the properties you own close to the mansion, Pierce." Her jaw is tight, eyes hard and yet they appear glassy, as if she's fighting tears. "I told you weeks ago how I feel about that place, and two of these properties have been purchased in the last month. Why wouldn't you tell me if you were making plans? Why would you keep that from me knowing how important the mansion is to me? You call me your girlfriend and then you do this? Tell me I don't have a reason to be paranoid."

"I can't believe this." And honestly I can't, and then again, maybe I can. I've been so caught up in Rian, in spending time with her, and enjoying the fact that I don't have to deal with bullshit patents and paperwork, or snobby assholes who think the sun rises and sets on them, that I've missed all the goddamn signs. Fucking Lawson.

"I'm right, aren't I? You stopped with the big renovations and started the quick cosmetic updates because renting makes more sense if you're planning to sell them off to the Millses."

I exhale a frustrated breath. "Whatever Lawson's plans are, he sure as hell hasn't shared them with me." Clearly I need to talk to him, because now that I'm holding this piece of paper, I have to wonder how long this has been his plan, and why he kept it from me. "I wouldn't have kept it from you if I'd known the Mission Mansion was actually coming up for sale and more than just a rumor. *Moorehead* is good at feeding rumors, not truths. You should've talked to me before assuming the worst."

Rian chews on her thumbnail for a second before shoving her hands into her pockets. "What was I supposed to think when I found that magazine in your office? Lex's face is all over it and you're connected to his family!"

"So at no point did you even stop to consider that maybe you could be the slightest bit off base? That in all this time we've been spending time together—"

"—giving each other orgasms," she supplies.

"You're un-fucking-believable." I bark out a humorless laugh. "You could've walked away instead of trying to make me into the villain." I turn and head for the door.

She grabs my arm. "Pierce, wait."

I shake her off. "For what? You to accuse me of something else? For you to decide I'm worth more than just a fuck? No, thanks."

I grit my teeth, the pain in my chest growing as I realize two very important things. One, I'm totally, hopelessly in love with Rian, and two, based on her reaction, it's completely one-sided.

I'm in a foul mood by the time I reach my brother's house. I sit in the car for a good twenty-five minutes, scouring recent articles on the Mills family. They're often in the news because they're constantly expanding. While some of the articles are based solely on speculation, there's enough of a common thread for me to believe they want to invest in property in the Hamptons. I'd be more likely to assume that Lex wants to either build or buy Amalie a house, not bulldoze a bunch of beach houses to put up a monster resort. Besides the city council probably would have a lot to say about that. I wonder if Lawson even thought about that when scheming up his master plan, if he even has one.

I find my brother lounging on the deck with his laptop flipped open, dicking around on social media. It's his job, taking care of that side of things, but half the time the messages are propositions from women, or boob shots. It's creepy.

I toss the printout of the properties with all the ones we own circled in red on top of his keyboard.

He glances up at me, annoyed by the interruption. "What's this?"

I hand him the magazine, open to the article featuring Lex, and drop down in the lounger across from him, crossing my arms over my chest.

He glances at the article. "Why are you giving me this? And what's with the pissy mood? Didn't you ball your girlfriend's brains out last night? Shouldn't you be happier?"

"I'd be happier if you weren't planning shit behind my back."

He has sunglasses on, but he can't hide the tic in the corner of his right eye. It's his tell. Everyone has them, and as a lawyer, I've had to learn how to watch for those. Rian was a signal flare for all kinds of sketchiness today. I gesture to the papers and the magazine. "Tell me how these two things are connected."

He frowns, inspecting the printout. "They're not. The circled properties are the ones we own." He tosses the magazine back to me. "This is publicity for a Mills Hotel project."

"Which happens to be in the Hamptons."

"And?" He closes his laptop and taps on the arm of his chair.

"What kind of deals are you cutting with Lex behind my back?" No point in tiptoeing around the issue.

"Who said I was making deals?"

"For fuck's sake, Law, be straight with me." I motion to the documents in his lap. "Is this the reason we're holding on to all these fucking properties? Are you waiting to sell them off when the time is right?"

He sighs. "Think about the financial logistics, Pierce. We own all these homes on the beach and they're anchor points around the Mission Mansion, which is rumored to be going up for sale this fall. Having all these properties makes sense, especially if the Millses get zoning flexibility. And even if they can't, imagine how much these beach houses are going to be worth if that mansion is renovated, or it's turned it into an upscale resort. It's been sitting

empty for years, and there are ten bedrooms in that monster home. That's not even taking into account the outbuildings. Think about the bank that could come out of
that. And if they want to buy out the homes around it, then
we're looking at killer return on our investments."

"How long have you been planning this with Lex?"

"I haven't been planning anything with Lex. It's just
been conversations. Look, man, I don't want to spend the
rest of my life fucking around with dolls"—he points to
the pair of plastic sunbathers to his right; today they have
Frisbees—"just like you don't want to be a patent lawyer.
I'm trying to find a way to make bank and get out, exactly
the same as you, and this is a way to do that."

"And you didn't think to mention any of this to me?
Rian thinks I've been in on this."

"Which is why I didn't say anything to you. I mean, I
figured you'd kind of clue in eventually, but you've got
your face buried so deep in that pussy—"

I'm out of my chair and hauling him up by his shirt. The
laptop hits the deck with a crack. "Don't finish that sentence unless you want a black eye and some missing teeth,
brother."

He holds up his hands. "Jesus, Pierce, calm your shit."

"You're fucking this up for me." I shove him back into
his chair.

"How? By buying property? They could've been making a shit-ton of commission if they hadn't played it shady
with that flip of theirs."

I give him a look. "It wasn't shady and you know it."

"It sure wasn't above board."

"The Paulson house doesn't matter right now; the Mission Mansion does."

"Why is this such a big deal?"

"Because Rian's family used to own it."

"What?" Lawson frowns. "How is that possible? That family was loaded."

I don't have enough background on Rian to really understand the connection. "She'll be devastated if the Millses plan to tear down the mansion so they can put up another hotel."

"I doubt that's their plan, if they even really have one. They have something like five new hotels going up in the next two years. It's not like they have any shortage of projects to keep them busy. I'm trying to make the best investments so I can get out, Pierce. Amalie Doll sales keep dropping every quarter, let alone every year. This train is going to go off the rails eventually."

"Dad built this company and made room for us. Won't he be disappointed if we jump ship when it's sinking?"

"Dude. Dad needs to retire, us bailing would give him a reason to let go and sell out. Half the reason he's holding on is because he wants us to have an easy life since his wasn't, you know?"

I take a few deep breaths, the tightness in my chest a distraction. I can see what he's saying. I know he's right about the dolls. It's why my father pushed for the life-sized doll patent and why my screwup was such a big deal.

We need alternatives. Something so my father doesn't feel like he has to keep reinventing the wheel to keep us employed.

So many things seem to be up in the air, and while I don't want Rian and I to be one of those, I'm too angry to get over her accusations.

It's barely seven in the morning and I'm sitting on the deck, facing away from Rian's half-renovated beach house, drinking coffee and going through Amalie Doll reports. I'm distracted, as seems to be the theme lately.

I have unanswered messages from Rian on my phone. Yesterday she asked if we could talk, but I'm not ready to deal with her without going off yet.

"I think you need to see something, bro." Law drops down beside me and holds out his laptop.

It's an article on the history of the Mission Mansion. "Why is this important?"

"Click the next tab." He taps the screen.

An image pops up that has nothing to do with houses. He cocks a brow. "Those twins look familiar to you?"

A pre-teenage version of Rian and her sister smile at me on the screen. The shot is grainy, having been taken from a magazine article more than a decade ago. It's a family photo, apparently, taken with the late Deana Mission, her daughter, Stephanie, and son-in-law, Nelson Fisher.

"Deana Mission was born a Sutter."

I rub my forehead. "Which explains why they go by Sutter, I guess?"

"Possibly, but they're technically Fishers."

"I don't get it."

"Do you remember Fisher Estates?"

It sounds familiar, but I'm not sure why. "Should I?"

"A decade ago Fisher was huge; they represented some of the biggest real estate buyers in the area. Except Nelson turned out to be a real criminal. He screwed all sorts of people out of money, including the Millses. Harrison was the one who took him down. Bankrupted the family from what I know. And when Deana died, Nelson sold the mansion and fled the country with his wife."

"So Nelson is Rian's father?"

"Ding, ding, ding!" Lawson slaps the arms of his chair. "You got it. He and his wife left two teenage girls with a huge mess. Their bank accounts were frozen and all their assets were seized. My guess is they go by Sutter to avoid being connected to the Fisher name."

I sift through the tidbits of information that Rian has given me about her family, which is admittedly very little. "Are her parents still alive?"

"I have no idea. Apparently they got something like three million for the mansion, since they needed cash fast, had it transferred to an offshore account, and disappeared. If they're alive, they're staying under the radar, because if the federal government finds them, they'll be in prison for a long time."

I think back to first time I was at Rian's house, to the pictures on the bookshelf and my question about her mother—the one she never answered. As the pieces start to come together, I realize how much she's kept from me.

"Hey, you okay? I figured this would be helpful, answer some of those questions."

I rub the back of my neck, the muscles suddenly tight. "What kind of parents leave two eighteen-year-old girls to clean up their mess? And with nothing to survive on?"

"Shitty ones, I guess. Makes ours look like saints, doesn't it?"

I huff a humorless laugh. Our parents are far from perfect. They haven't been the best relationship role models, but they've never left us to fend on our own, financially or otherwise.

I consider the life Rian once had. Her upbringing had been the opposite of mine. She came from everything and had it all ripped away from her. She was abandoned by the people who were supposed to take care of her. No wonder she's so guarded. Her secrets are the walls between us.

I push up out of my chair.

"Where you going?"

"To get some answers." And break down some walls.

CHAPTER 28
TRUTHS

RIAN

I flip my phone over in my hand, waiting for a message I'm not sure is ever going to come. I feel ill. The same kind of ill I felt after my parents left Marley and me alone, with almost nothing.

If it's over between me and Pierce, I have no one to blame but myself. Maybe I should've been honest with him from the beginning, but I was doing what I thought was right. I was protecting me and Marley. It's what I've always done. And he's supposed to be temporary. A fun summer distraction, not someone I want to keep around.

Regardless of whether or not I'm right about Pierce being in on whatever Lawson may or may not have planned, we're so closely connected by all of these invisible threads. I'm sure he's already figured it out by now, which might explain the silence on his end. The pieces of my past that I've kept hidden threaten to destroy this brief blip of happiness.

Instead of putting trust in Pierce, I villainized him. I accused rather than asked questions, and now I'm facing the consequences. He has every right to be angry with me because my omissions are as bad as lies. In trying to protect myself, I only ended up hurting us both.

Last night I slept on the couch at the Paulson reno. Because it still smells very faintly of Pierce. I'm so pathetic.

The knock on the sliding door startles me. It's almost eight, and the finish carpenter is supposed to be here at nine to take care of the last little details, but I expect him to come to the front door. I peek over the end of the couch, mortified that I'm still in my pajamas. Except it's not the finish carpenter. It's Pierce.

My heart stops and then beats double time. I throw the comforter off, no longer worried about my sleepwear, or the fact that I probably have pillow lines etched in my face. I've slept like crap the past two night and based on Pierce's stubbled chin and cheeks and dark eyes, so has he.

Maybe I'm not alone in my misery. And I'm definitely miserable.

My stomach clenches, and not in a good way as I open the door. He looks angry. Maybe angrier than he did the last time I spoke to him. "Hi."

I don't get so much as a smile in response. He glares at me with stormy eyes, full of confrontation. "Why didn't you tell me who your family was?"

I clasp my hands so I don't fidget under his rightfully angry gaze. "I didn't think it was important," I say meekly.

He purses his lips, eyes moving over my face. There's no warmth, just hurt. "You didn't think it was important to tell me that my sister's fiancé's family were responsible for exposing your parents?"

"I didn't put it together until I saw that article when I stayed at your place."

"Is that part of the reason you bolted then? Was everything else just a way to push the blame off on me?"

Shame and fear make it hard to speak. Shame over who my family is, fear that my omissions are going to cost me so much more than some embarrassment. In hindsight, maybe I've made a bigger deal out of it than necessary, but explaining who my family is and what they did is mortifying beyond belief.

"Where are your parents, Rian?"

I look down at my feet, unable to see his disdain for me. "I don't know."

"You don't know or you don't want to tell me?"

I curl my toes under, hating the way my stomach knots. "I haven't heard from them in three years." They could be dead, although I have a feeling if that was the case, I would probably get a call.

"Three years?" His voice is laced with disbelief.

I twist my hands, remembering the last time I heard my mother's voice; the sound of her laughter, the music in the background, the crashing of waves. "The last time my mom called was our twenty-fifth birthday." There's bitterness in the memory I don't want.

His face falls, his anger ebbing slightly. "And you've had no contact since?"

I bite the inside of my lip, trying to keep the tears they don't deserve from falling. "They said it was too dangerous, someone could trace the calls. We had a small trust come due that birthday, so . . ."

"They called to get money out of you?" I loathe his pity because it confirms what I already know—my parents are beyond horrible.

There's no point in keeping any of this from him anymore. Whatever his reaction, I'm done hiding the truth. "When we wouldn't wire them money, they tried to redirect it into their account. Of course, it didn't work because the money was in our names. After that Marley and I changed our phone numbers and switched over to new accounts so it wouldn't happen again. It was too painful to hear from them, especially when we knew it wasn't because they cared or were worried about us, but because they wanted something." I smile, but it's pained and my throat feels tight. Marley's been my only person for so many years. I haven't let anyone else in; I'm haunted by a legacy anyone would be ashamed of.

Pierce's lip curls. "That's disgusting."

"It is," I agree. "You see why I wasn't eager to share any of this? My parents are bad people. They're cheaters, liars, and thieves. My dad used me to swindle people. I didn't know what he was doing, and when I realized I'd helped him . . . it was devastating. Marley and I did everything we could to separate ourselves from them. We legally changed our last name to sever the ties. My dad left us ten thousand dollars in cash and no way to contact them. Why would I want you to know that about my life? Tell me it doesn't change how you see me."

He shakes his head, and I despise how sad he looks, because it makes me feel pitied. "I can't, because you're right, this most definitely changes the way I see you."

I drop my head and wish my hair wasn't in a ponytail, that it could provide a curtain of protection for the pain I can't hide. I hate that I have to carry this past with me forever. I press my palm to my mouth, fighting back a sob, because even though they've disappeared from my life, my parents still manage to ruin all the things I love.

"Hey." Pierce's rough, callused fingers skim my jaw. I can't handle this gentle affection, not when I know it's coming from a place of pity, and that the end is inevitable.

I twist my head, unwilling to see how this truth changes everything. And it's now that I recognize how much I

wanted to keep this, us, him. I want him to want me regardless of who my family is.

"Rian, you need to look at me."

"I don't want to." I sound petulant, and my voice cracks.

He ducks down so his face is right in front of mine, and
his nose brushes the tip of mine. "I think you need to ask
me *how* what you've told me changes how I see you."

"I already know."

"You think so?"

"You feel sorry for me. You're going to tell me how awful that must've been, but I'll understand if you can't be
with me anymore. I know I should've told you the truth
right from the start, or maybe I shouldn't have gotten involved with you in the first place. But I didn't think it was
going to get complicated like this. I thought—"

"Can you shut up for a second?"

"You don't need to explain. I get it, P—"

His mouth crashes down on mine. I keep my lips
pressed together because I haven't had a chance to brush
my teeth, and I do not want his tongue in my mouth. Well,
I do, but not until I've had a breath mint.

"Open."

I shake my head. "Nuh-uh."

"Yes."

"I can't," I say through gritted teeth.

He backs off a bit. "Why can't you?"

I hold a hand in front of my mouth to prevent him from
launching another lip attack. "I need to brush my teeth."

He rolls his eyes and sweeps his fingers gently along
the hollow under my eyes. They're damp, I realize. Because
I'm crying.

"Stop being so sweet when you're supposed to be
running the other way."

He smiles softly and brushes the tip of his nose against

mine. "There's my girl. I'm not going anywhere. How many times do I have to tell you that?"

"But you're angry and I lied to you."

"I am and you did, but I understand why."

"I'm sorry."

"I can see that you are. It hurt, that you could think the worst of me, Rian. I hated knowing I was missing something, and I wanted you to feel like you could tell me, but I get why you couldn't. I needed some time to manage my own emotions. Needing time doesn't mean I'm going to walk away. How pushy do I have to be to get that through to you?"

"Marley's been my only constant for the past decade. When people find out who we are, they tend to walk away, and I can't blame them. We've worked so hard to get where we are and make our own name so we aren't connected to our parents. It's just so shameful."

"It's not your shame to own, though." He threads his fingers through mine and leads me to the couch. Pushing the blankets aside, he pulls me down with him.

"I helped my dad. I knew numbers. I didn't know what he was doing. He stole so much money from so many people."

"You were a teenager and you trusted the people who were supposed to take care of you."

"I don't need you to rationalize this for me, or feel sorry for me, or pity me—"

"I'm not doing any of that. I'm cutting you the break you can't seem to cut yourself. And it's not pity, it's awe. You did all of this on your own. You made a life, you protected yourself and your sister, and built your own career. That takes an incredible amount of resilience and determination."

I want to sink into him, absorb some affection, and

forget that my past still creates so much turmoil in my present. "So what now?"

He stretches his arm across the back of the couch. "We talk."

"About me?" I say it slowly, as if the words are made of lead and painful to spit out. I've worked so hard to stay focused on the present, on the now and not the then, even though my past has shaped me, and not always in a good way.

"Well, yeah. I think it's about time, right? I want to understand, so I know how to handle you moving forward."

"I don't know how to deal with it when you say things like that."

"You'll get used to it, like you've gotten used to me being a pushy asshole."

I laugh and then sigh, considering how I want to approach this. "I've spent the last decade trying to separate myself from my childhood. I think the most painful part wasn't losing things, because it's just stuff. It's physical comfort, but the emotional comfort, not having people to rely on, that was devastating." And now here's this man, who knows who my family is and what they've done, and he's still here, still wanting me even after the omissions and the accusations I threw at him. I need to trust that he's not here to screw me over. God, I wish my parents weren't such fuckups and that I could believe in the good in people.

"I can't imagine how hard it was for you to go from that kind of life to something so—"

"Pathetic?" I smile sadly.

"No. Not pathetic at all. You went from having everything to having almost nothing at eighteen. That couldn't have been easy."

"I used to take so many things for granted. My parents bought me a Range Rover for my sixteenth birthday. What sixteen-year-old needs a freaking Range Rover? Also, it had a roomy back seat, not ideal for preserving teenage virtue. Not that my parents cared, either way."

Pierce's expression darkens. "Are you speaking from personal experience?"

"Marley was the defiler of the back seat. I wasn't really a get-it-on-in-the-back-of-the-car kind of girl."

"You like dryers and beaches better." He winks.

I appreciate the moment of levity. "Well, dryers anyway. Maybe not the beaches." After a few moments of silence, in which I'm sure my face turns red at the memory, I continue. "My parents would drop us off as soon as school finished for the year, and they'd come back and get us before it started up again."

"So you didn't see them all summer?"

"No. But that wasn't unusual. We didn't see them much, period. We had nannies and housekeepers. So while other teenagers were getting part-time jobs and doing meaning-ful things, we were hanging out on yachts. Well, that's not completely true. I did a lot of volunteer work in the sum-mers, thanks to my grandmother. She was big into charity work, and she taught me to give back where I could. I prob-ably would've been a complete spoiled brat otherwise."

Pierce fingers the end of my ponytail. "I can't imagine how hard it is to be so close to something you know so well, with so many memories attached to it."

"Painfully nostalgic, I suppose. Some of my best mem-ories are there. And worst. It's why I wanted this flip. I feel close to what I once had, I guess."

"I get it. Sometimes I go back to my old neighborhood to see the first house we had. A reminder of what life was like before. But for you, it's the opposite."

"The fall is hard. You find out exactly who's real and who isn't when your grace is gone."

"You lost a lot more than financial stability and your parents."

"We lost everything and everyone. And honestly, I couldn't blame anyone. My father swindled so much money out of people. It didn't matter if they were friends or not, he destroyed a lot of lives. In a lot of people's eyes, our family got what we deserved."

"No eighteen-year-old deserves to have her entire life turned upside-down like that."

"People experience losses far worse than what we did, who deserve it far less than my family did. Like I said, I took a lot for granted until I had to go without, and I don't want to do that again."

"You really are incredible," Pierce says softly.

"I'm really not. Mostly I'm just good with numbers, and I hurt a lot of people because of that."

"Don't take that on, Rian. You're a hell of a lot more than good with numbers. You were taken advantage of by someone you loved and trusted. You're phenomenal and brilliant, and that's nothing to be ashamed of."

I expel a slow breath, wanting to tell him he's wrong, that I'm none of the things he thinks I am.

"I can see you trying to form an argument in that head of yours, and you need to stop. How I see you is not up for debate."

"None of that changes where I came from."

"You think that matters to me? I don't give a shit who your parents are, or how much of a spoiled rich brat you think you were as a kid, or whether you messed up your dating profile questionnaire so we ended up as a two out of ten on some ridiculous compatibility test score when we should be a ten." Pierce takes my face between his palms, his expression determined and serious. "I'm one hundred percent in love with you, and there's absolutely nothing you can do to change that."

For me, love has always been such an unstable, conditional emotion outside of my twin. Except as I look at Pierce, I can see that he means it, that it's real and warm and comforting. Stupid tears well and track down my cheeks.

Pierce wipes them away gently, his smile an echo of that tender touch. "I'm overwhelming you with the declaration, huh?"

I laugh, but the sound ends on a half sob. "I love you back." It comes out a broken whisper.

He places a soft kiss on my lips and pulls back. "That was hard, wasn't it?"

I nod. He gets me in a way no one else does, not even Marley sometimes. Saying it out loud makes it so much more real. Telling the person who owns your heart that you love them gives them power—the kind that can make you whole or shatter your world.

"I promise I'll take good care of your heart, Rian. And I promise it'll get easier if you keep saying it." He kisses me again, whispering against my lips, "I love you."

I give up caring about brushing my teeth and try to keep our mouths connected, but he holds me firmly between his palms. "Your turn."

I bite my lip and meet his earnest, patient gaze. My God, this man.

"I love you." This time the whisper isn't broken.

"See how much easier it is already." This time when he kisses me, he doesn't stop.

We make love; those whispered words turn into moans and sighs and pleas for more. And I allow myself to fall completely, hopelessly in love.

CHAPTER 29

MISSION

RIAN

I've probably slept in my own bed twice in the past four weeks. Post-fight and love declaration, Pierce decided the best way to get the flip finished was to move in to the Paulson reno with me and do as much of the work himself as possible, while also overseeing the hired trades. He insists on working for free and just having us pay for supplies. I make it up to him in the bedroom.

The good part about Pierce staying with me is that we see a lot of each other, apart from his weekly trips to Manhattan. Sometimes he's gone for a night, and sometimes he's gone for two. He's been putting a lot of work into cleaning up the patent issue and tying up loose ends there. He's mentioned more than once how much he'd like to stay in the Hamptons, and how he's broached the subject with his father. If he does end up leaving law, he'll have to train someone to take his place. While I'd love for that to happen, I'm trying not to get my hopes up too much.

I suppose in some ways those trips are preparing me for

the possibility that he'll have to move back to Manhattan. He's always stressed and preoccupied before he goes, and needy when he returns, which makes me nervous. I've been busy with the flip, and it's really all work when he's there so accompanying him seems pointless. Not that I've been invited. I try not to let it get to me, but sometimes my paranoia takes over and I have to remind myself that Pierce isn't going to screw me around.

We're two days away from finishing this renovation. It's nine o'clock in the morning on a Thursday, and we have an inspector coming to check the electrical and plumbing upgrades before the flip officially goes on the market on Saturday.

While we wait for the coffee to brew, Pierce decides we should pass the time by making out. It escalates quickly— until I end up on the island with him between my legs, looking to get inside me. As if I'm going to say no to a little morning lovin'.

I'm three well-angled thrusts away from coming when the door slams open and Marley's voice echoes down the hallway.

My eyes go wide and I whisper, "Oh no, I'm so close."

"Stay where you are!" Pierce shouts. He's already holding onto the back of my neck to keep me in place.

"Oh, for fuck's sake. I'll be outside," Marley yells, and the door slams shut again.

I'm too far gone to care or be embarrassed. Pierce crushes his mouth to mine as I come. Less than two minutes later, my clothes are back in place, and Pierce is disposing of the spent condom.

I open the front door to find Marley sitting on the steps, fiddling with her phone.

"Why didn't you call to let me know you were coming by?"

"Because it's my house too. Why can't you two screw in a bedroom like normal people?"

"Good point."

"Ya think?" She stalks past me, clearly annoyed. "I have news."

"What kind of news?"

She crosses over to the coffee and fills two cups. When Pierce comes around the corner, looking relaxed and smug, she rolls her eyes and grabs another cup, filling that one too. "The kind of news we've been waiting a long time for."

"What's going on? Is everything okay?"

"I actually need a few minutes alone with my sister. Do you mind if I take her for a walk?"

Pierce frowns. "Sure. As long as everything's okay."

"It's fine. Just family stuff." Marley smiles tightly.

For most people, family stuff isn't a huge deal, but for us, in the past it meant very bad things. My stomach clenches and I half expect Marley to tell me she's heard from our parents despite having changed our phone numbers more than three years ago.

I take the coffee Pierce has doctored for me. He kisses my temple. "Take your phone. Let me know if you need anything."

I nod and follow Marley outside. We head down the front walk to the beach and sit in the sand. "What's going on? Is this about Mom and Dad? You're making me nervous."

"It's not about Mom and Dad."

I exhale a sigh of relief, and the tension in my shoulders eases a bit, but not much. She looks so serious.

"I got word this morning that the Mission Mansion is going up for sale."

"What? Are you sure? When?" I glance over my shoulder, back at the beach house where I've left Pierce. I hate the sudden suspicion and the conflict over this news and what it could mean for us, for him, for his brother, for the Mills family.

"The email came a couple hours ago. I know the representing agent."

"What's it going for?" I sip my coffee in lieu of chewing on my nails. It's perfect, the right amount of sweet and the right amount of cream. Pierce is definitely a detail-oriented man. He pays attention. It means there's logically no way to keep this from him, not that I want to anyway. Things have been so good these past weeks; I don't want anything to change that.

"I don't have anything concrete, but the agent is saying somewhere around five million I think. It needs a lot of work."

Even with good credit and a solid return on our flip, it's doubtful the bank would approve us for a mortgage that size. "It's too much, isn't it?"

She lifts a shoulder. "There's an agent viewing tomorrow afternoon. I know how much you love that place, and you have all these good memories tied up in it, but it's really rundown, Rian. The only maintenance has been on the landscaping over the past decade."

"I know." And I do. Maybe it's not completely rational to want it back, but it's the one piece of my grandmother I can't seem to let go.

"I managed to secure a spot so we can go, just to see, at the very least." She sips her coffee, maybe waiting for my reaction.

I squash the pointless hope blooming in my chest. "There's not really a point in talking to the bank about financing, is there?"

Marley doesn't tell me no, even though we both know

my question is rooted in nothing but nostalgia and a dream that's never going to come true. "I think we should look at it first, see what we're up against."

"Okay." At least one of us is pragmatic. "Do we have anyone who would be in the market to buy it?" God, just saying it aloud makes my stomach twist.

"I'm going through our list of contacts this afternoon. If nothing else, the commission would be enough to finance another flip."

I swallow back my sadness. Seeing the Mission Mansion empty all summer has been difficult, but seeing it full of life again might be even harder. "What day is the open house?"

"The agent is saying Sunday." She picks up a tiny shell and flips it between her fingers. "But that could always change, depending on the seller. There's a lot of interest in the property, Ri, so even if we went in as buyers, and I'm not sure that's logical or feasible at this point, there's no guarantee we'll get it. And if we did, I don't know that the upkeep will be affordable."

"I'll still go through the numbers tonight." I run my fingers along the rim of my cup. "If it was a year from now, we'd be in a better position."

"I know," she says softly. "And we don't know when or if it will be on the market again."

I dig my toes into the sand. In my head I had this amazing plan for the Mansion. We'd turn it into a bed-and-breakfast and live in one of the outbuildings. My eyes burn as the dream I've held onto all this time seems so far out of reach, dissipating into vapor.

We watch the waves break against the shoreline in silence for a few minutes.

Marley sighs. "Sometimes I miss our old life. I know it'll never be like it used to, but I don't ever want to worry about being able to afford to pay the credit card bill at the end of the month again."

"We won't let that happen." I feel a pang of guilt over the fact that in the past few months I've spent more time with Pierce, and some of the luxuries we'd lost have been mine again. The stability and security have been nice, better than nice. I worry about Marley, because she's a lot like me. We've only been close to each other, which means she's all alone now.

"I hope not." She rests her cheek on her knee. "Are you going to tell Pierce?"

"Keeping it from him is pointless."

"Are you worried he'll tell his brother and that the Mills family will get their hands on it?"

"That's a risk, regardless. We just have to hope there are other projects that are more lucrative for them."

"I'm going to cross everything that that's the case."

Marley leaves me to tell Pierce. One benefit of the Mission Mansion coming on the market is that we'll definitely be able to price our flip on the higher end, because of its proximity and desirable location.

Pierce is rearranging the rented furniture for staging purposes when I return. Amalie sent him with a load of supplies, and aside from the inspection, our job today is to set up the house. Tomorrow the cleaners come, and then we're show ready.

He shifts the couch around, biceps flexing, then steps back to inspect its placement. He knocks it with his hip a couple of times before he seems content, then notices me standing off to the side. His gaze moves over me, assessing, as he grips the back of the couch. "Lawson called while you were outside with Marley."

I cross the room and stand on the opposite side of the sofa. "So you know the Mansion is coming up for sale."

"I do." He hops over the back of the couch, spreads his legs wide, and pulls me between them, palms wrapped around the backs of my legs.

I run my fingers through his hair. "Who told him?"

"I'm assuming his agent."

I note that he never refers to Lawson's agent as *our agent*. Maybe for my sake. I don't really know. "There's an agent open house tomorrow. Marley and I are going."

"Are you going as a buyer or an agent?"

I lift a shoulder and admit what I don't want to acknowledge. "Likely as an agent. I'm not entirely sure we could afford to take it on as a project."

"Do you want me to come with you? I'll understand if you'd rather I not be there."

I consider how it would feel to have him with me while I revisit my past, possibly for the last time. Probably is more like it. "I think I want you there."

"Think about it. Sleep on it. And in the morning, if you want, I'll come with you and if not, I'll be right here, waiting for you when you get back."

The following morning I find a brand-new dress that probably costs more than two months of mortgage payments hanging in my closet and a pair of strappy sandals. I almost cry, but manage to rein in the tears.

Pierce assures me it's not meant to guilt me into letting him come along, but I want him there. Last night, I mentioned his offer to come along to Marley to see how she'd respond. She didn't seem upset about it, but then, sometimes it's hard to tell with Marley.

Pierce looks like he craps gold bars in his tailored Tom Ford. I'm nervous when we pull up to the Mansion and pass over our keys to the valet. There's a six-car garage,

because one or two cars is clearly not enough when you
have an eight-thousand-square-foot mansion.

I've gone over the figures, run the numbers a dozen
times, lowballing the potential profit on the flip, trying to
make it work. Making an offer is a bad financial move.
Even if we could afford it, the renovations alone would
sink us.

The seller's agent offers to show us around the Mansion, obviously unaware of our history with the home, but
with so many agents coming through, it's easy to decline
and tour on our own.

It's almost exactly as I remember it, but everything is
dated and worn. Even the furniture is mostly the same—a
shrine to a lost life. In the interest of selling quickly, my
father had opted not to hold a contents estate sale. He sold
the Mansion and everything in it. Once the money was
transferred into his offshore account, he and my mother
disappeared.

No one has lived here in the past decade; the owners
purchased with the intent to renovate, but they lost interest and moved on to other pursuits. Now that the market
is hot again, they want it off their hands.

My heart feels like it's in my throat as we pass through
familiar rooms. I run my finger along the edge of the massive table in the formal dining room, set with my grandmother's china—she would roll over in her grave if she
knew they'd used it to stage the showing. I remember afternoon tea with her friends, crustless sandwiches and petit
fours, pinkies in the air as we sipped tea, and my grandmother winking over her cup at the ridiculousness of it all.

In all of these years, I haven't really allowed myself to
miss her, this place, having lost too much all at once. I
glance at Marley when she reaches out and skims the edge

of one of the teacups and see the same sadness reflected back at me in her eyes.

There are so many memories caught up in this home, mostly good, and a few bad. Like when my grandmother passed, and the day the SOLD sign went up.

A bead of sweat trickles down my spine when we pass through to the west wing. We nod hello to the other agents, who murmur about the lack of upkeep, only able to see the dollar signs and prospective profits. The second door on the right lies open, and I step inside the bedroom, Marley on my heels, Pierce following a respectable distance behind.

Two huge double poster beds still occupy the space, and I have to take a deep breath, the heaviness in my chest hard to handle. We spent our summers sharing a bedroom in our teen years. Talked into the wee hours of the morning more nights than not. Sneaked out to the kitchen after midnight and raided the pantry while everyone was sleeping.

Marley threads her fingers through mine and squeezes as we step farther inside. "Nothing has changed," I murmur.

But that's not true. While the mansion has stayed the same, Marley and I haven't. We've made a life beyond this place, forged our own path.

We unlink hands when we reach the beds and separate, mirrors of each other as our fingers drift over the intricate wooden bed frames, recently dusted and polished. Even after all this time, the ridges in the grain are familiar, small imperfections left in the wood from tossing things to each other and missing.

I move to the dresser, where an old jewelry box sits. I try to lift the lid, but it's locked. Marley meets my shocked gaze in the mirror, and I know she's thinking the exact same thing I am. I tug the second drawer down; it's empty and my chest constricts as I reach inside and lift the edge of the decorative liner, sliding my fingers along the back of the drawer until I feel the cool metal against my fingertips. "It's here," I whisper.

Pulling the key free, I flip the tarnished silver between my fingers, then slip it into the lock. Inside are trinkets, worthless baubles as far as anyone else would be concerned, but among them are two heart-shaped lockets, one for Marley and one for me.

I lift them from their velvet home, feeling very much a thief, even though they belong to us—gifts passed down from our grandmother, left behind the last summer we were here. Possibly locked away purposefully. I'm sure my grandmother thought we'd have a chance to claim the things that were ours all those years ago. I hold it against my heart, feeling full in a way I haven't in a long time. I finally understand why Marley never seemed to be as attached to this place as I was. It's the people not the place that hold the memories.

I lock the jewelry box again, running my fingers over the surface before I slip the necklaces and key into my purse for safekeeping.

Pierce is standing in the doorway, an unreadable expression on his face. It's exposing to have him here with us, giving him more than a glimpse into a life that's no longer ours.

As we move from room to room, and pass over to the east wing where the staff quarters are, the memories that fill my heart make me aware that I need to let this go. Marley wanders through the rooms, fingers trailing over smooth finishes and fine details.

Pierce's hands rest gently on my shoulders, and he dips down to press a soft kiss against the side of my neck. "I could buy it."

I drop my head and exhale a breath. It would be too easy to say yes. "I can't ask you to do that."

"You're not asking." He looks so earnest in his offer.

"This place reminds me of the good parts of my family, but I don't need the Mansion to keep the memories." I tap my temple. "Everything is already up here." Then I move my fingers down to my heart. "And in here."

He caresses my cheek, eyes soft and questioning. "So you don't want it anymore?"

"Buying it isn't going to bring my grandmother back, and it's not going to make my family whole again." I lace my fingers with his. "I already have what I need."

Pierce leans in to kiss me. It's brief and chaste, possibly on account of my lipstick. "Good luck today."

I pause with my fingers wrapped around the door handle. "You're not coming in?"

"I have a couple of errands to run this morning." He glances at his phone, which has been buzzing nonstop since we woke up.

"Oh." I assumed he'd stay for the open house considering how much time he put in on this project. He's freshly shaven, dressed in a suit, not a hair out of place, but he looks tired and restless. "Is everything okay?"

"Fine. Nothing you need to worry about." He flashes a smile, but it seems off, and his gaze doesn't quite meet mine. "I'll be back before the open house is over."

"Okay." I don't move, though. Something's up. Something's been up since we visited the Mission Mansion the other day.

His phone keeps buzzing, and he taps the steering wheel. He misreads my anxiety. "It'll sell today. I have no doubt."

I nod and expel a breath.

This time his phone lights up with a call. He checks the screen again. "I gotta go, hotness." He gives me another peck on the cheek, and I have no choice but to get out of the car.

He gives me a tight smile and a quick wave as he puts the car in reverse and backs out of the driveway like his ass is on fire. What the heck was that all about?

I don't have time to fixate—much—because the open house on the Paulson home begins in less than an hour, and I still need to put the cookies in the oven.

The showing ends up being the best we've had this summer. An endless stream of potential buyers tour the property, keeping us busy the entire time. Despite the influx of interested parties, I still notice that Pierce doesn't return prior to the end of the open house like he said he would. Disappointment settles under my skin and irritates like an unscratchable itch. He's been such a big part of helping make this happen. I would've thought he'd want to be here to see it sell. And it does sell. By the time it's over, we have four offers, all well over asking.

Marley's phone rings while we're reviewing offers at the kitchen table. I'm still irked that I've yet to hear from Pierce and the open house has been over for half an hour already.

"Who is it?" I ask absently, still punching numbers into my calculator. Our profit on this one is going to be incredible, the money we'll make on the flip far outweighing any commission we could've made. I ran the figures out of curiosity, and we still can't afford the Mission Mansion, beyond the down payment.

"Oh? But I thought the open house wasn't until tomorrow?"

I glance up from the calculator, taking in Marley's stiff posture. The unsettled feeling that's been plaguing me all day hit again, making my palms sweaty.

"Do you know who bought it? Right. Of course. Okay. Well, thanks for letting me know. Congratulations on the sale."

She ends the call and sets the phone on the table, eyes slow to meet mine. I don't say anything, waiting for her to say what I already know.

"The Mission Mansion sold to a private buyer."

I knew this was coming, but I didn't think it would be until tomorrow. As prepared as I thought I was, it still causes an ache to bloom in my chest. I clear my throat. "Did she say what it went for?"

"A hundred thousand over asking." Her eyes are soft, assessing my reaction.

"That would've been a great commission." Tears prick my eyes and I fight to keep them from falling.

"Are you okay?" Marley gives my hand a squeeze.

"Rationally, I know it's better this way. We couldn't have afforded to manage the property, but it still hurts to know it's gone already."

"I get it. I know how much you loved that place." She comes around to hug me. "Why don't we deal with the offers in the morning?"

"Okay." I help Marley gather up the papers, straightening them into a neat pile and returning the promotional materials to the folder.

"Are you okay on your own for a bit? I kind of feel like going for a walk." I push up from the table, sadder than I thought I'd be.

"Do you want me to come with you?"

"I think I need a little time alone."

"Sure. Of course."

"I won't be gone long, then we can have dinner or something to celebrate."

I leave her at the kitchen table with the paperwork and head down the beach. Marley has never had the same connection to the Mansion I do. While she would've taken on that venture with me, it would've been because I wanted it and she loves me enough to make that sacrifice.

Even from a distance I can make out the bold red letters of the SOLD sign. I stop about fifty yards from the Mansion and stare up at one of the best parts of my past; a place full of love and happiness and good memories. I let the tears fall for the family I lost all those years ago, and take comfort in the fact that all those things still exist inside my heart.

CHAPTER 30
LITTLE GIFTS OF LOVE

PIERCE

You know those days when you're in a rush to get something done, but the whole world seems like it's against you? I'm having that day. I'm finally on my way back to the beach, but Rian's open house is long over. I'm disappointed that I've missed the whole thing, but I'm hoping my absence will be forgiven shortly.

I pull into the driveway, grab the flowers from the passenger seat and head for the front door.

I find Marley sitting at the kitchen table reviewing paperwork. She doesn't look up. "Rian went for a walk about twenty minutes ago."

"Is she okay?"

"She will be."

"Is she upset that I missed the open house?"

"She'll get over it." She gives me a small knowing smile and nods to the flowers clutched in my fist. She pushes up from the table. "Pretty sure we both know where she is, so you should go find her."

I head for the sliding door and step out into the warm summer air. I'm still wearing a suit and dress shoes, which quickly fill with sand as I make my way down the beach toward the Mansion and the lone figure staring up at it.

Rian's dress flaps lightly against her legs, hair fluttering in the breeze, arms wrapped around her as if she's hugging herself. I come up behind her and slip an arm around her waist, holding the bouquet of flowers in front of her. "Congratulations on the sale."

She startles and runs her fingertips along the petals of a peony. She twists in my arms so she can look at me, her head resting on my chest. Her smile is soft and questioning, eyes shimmering with sadness. "Well, it's not official yet, but thanks."

"I'm sorry I missed the open house." I stroke her cheek and move so we're face-to-face. "I had to take care of something important this afternoon."

Her eyes shift, following her fingers as she traces the lapel of my suit jacket. "It must've been pretty important."

I hear the questions in that statement, feel her despondency in the weight of her palm on my chest, and I know I've done the right thing today, even if right now it's making her sad. "Why don't we go back up to the house and I can tell you all about it?"

"Sure. Okay." She gives me an uncertain smile as I lace our fingers together, and looks over her shoulder at the Mansion one last time as I guide her back to the house with its own, matching SOLD sign.

I don't take her inside the house. Instead, we sit on the deck. It's peaceful out here this evening, the breeze warm and light. The sun hangs low in the sky, heading for the horizon. I've grown attached to this, both the view and the woman. "So I did something today, and I need you to hear me out before you get mad at me."

Rian looks away from the ocean and frowns. "What kind of something?"

"Just promise you'll listen before you go off." I'm nervous right now. This could go two very different ways and one of them ends with Rian very pissed off. I'm hoping that's not what happens.

"This approach is not reassuring, Pierce."

"Yeah. I get that." I run my hands down my thighs. They're damp and clammy. "So you know how I've been in Manhattan a lot recently?"

"Clearing up the patent issue."

"Yeah. Well, that's part of it, but I've been taking care of a few other things."

"Okay." Rian clasps her hands and waits. "What kind of other things?"

I need to spit it out. "So a lot of the reason I've been in Manhattan a lot lately isn't just about the patent. I've been training someone to take over at the firm for me."

"You're quitting?" Her eyes flare with surprise.

I nod, lick my lips, run my hands down my thighs again. I need to cut the fidgeting. "I talked to my father and explained the circumstances."

"Circumstances?"

"That I wasn't happy practicing patent law, that I wanted to be here instead, doing something I love."

She sits up a little straighter. "And he was okay with that?"

"At first I think he was surprised, but yeah, he understands and mostly he kept pushing the business because he wanted there to be something for me and Law and Amalie. He wants to slow down, so he's talking about selling the majority of the company off, but we'll see what the logistics are."

"Wow, that's . . . wow." Rian exhales on a whistle. "This is good then, yes?"

"It is."

Her expression is soft and hopeful, which is reassuring. "So does that mean you're staying here? In the Hamptons, I mean?"

I feel like a bobble head with all the nodding. "Yeah. I, uh, put my penthouse on the market."

Her eyebrows shoot up. "Oh? When?"

"A few weeks ago. It's already sold, which brings me to the thing I did that I don't want you to get mad at me for." I turn my head and clear my throat. "So I know you said you didn't *need* the Mission Mansion."

Rian's eyebrows furrow as confusion turns to understanding and then disbelief. "Tell me you did not buy the Mansion." And there's the anger I was expecting.

Rian likes to do things on her own. She's strong and independent and fierce, which is why I'm so hopelessly in love with her. Buying her the Mansion and presenting it as a gift was never going to fly, so I had to figure out how to frame it so she gets that it's not a gift—well, not exactly. "I can't tell you that."

She purses her lips. "You can't buy me a mansion, Pierce."

"I don't think the bank is going to give me a refund." I raise my hands when she opens her mouth. "Just hear me out before you get upset. Or more upset. I didn't buy it just for you. I mean, yeah, you're clearly one of the reasons I bought it, but it's more than that. Selling my penthouse freed up a lot of money, and I need a project and a place to live, especially now that you've sold this one." I motion to the deck we're currently sitting on.

"So you thought you needed more than eight thousand square feet of rundown living space?"

"It's a smart move, Rian. I can fix it and live in it, and when it's done, if you decide you don't want me to keep it, then I can sell it and probably get twice what I paid for it. But if you decide maybe you don't want to get rid of it, then we could turn it into a B and B like you talked about. Like *we* talked about. It could be ours, and we could do it together."

I can't read her expression, and it's unnerving. I take her hand in mine and lick my lips, my mouth suddenly dry. God, I really hope she's ready for this. "Look, Rian, this has been the best summer of my life, particularly the past month. Being here with you, working on this project with you, being part of it, this is what I want. I have all the things I love right here, and I don't want to give that up, and I didn't want you to have to give up a dream if you didn't have to."

"That's a lot of money to spend on my dream."

"Well, it can be our dream now, can't it?"

A hint of a smile appears. "What about Lawson?"

"He knows this is my plan and that I wanted to do this on my own."

"And he's okay with that?"

"He has plenty to keep him busy."

Rian props her chin on her fist. "I can't just leave Marley."

"I talked to her too."

Rian's eyes flare. "What?"

"I wanted to make sure I was doing the right thing. She thinks it's smart too. It's a huge house; there are plenty of outbuildings. There are lots of options. We don't have to settle on any one decision right now."

"Wait. So Marley already knows you bought the Mansion?"

"She knew I was going to put in an offer."

"I can't believe she didn't tell me!"

"Well, to be fair, I asked her not to, and there really wasn't a guarantee that I was going to get it, so . . ."

Rian huffs a laugh. "You know, most boyfriends buy their girlfriends flowers and jewelry, not mansions."

"I did the flowers thing, so I got that part right. I think we both know I'm not most boyfriends, and like I said, I needed a project. Besides, this seemed like a pretty fool-proof way to get you to move in with me."

She throws her head back and laughs. "You're a little crazy, you know that?"

"Crazy in love with you." I kiss her, but pull back before either one of us can deepen it. "So that's a yes, right? You and me. Nightly snuggles, waking up beside each other every morning. Cinnamon roll French toast. Me driving you nuts. Naked Sundays. You in?"

She smiles up at me, eyes soft and warm. "How can I say no to that?"

"I told you we had something, didn't I?" I stand and hold out a hand.

"You did. Many, many times." Rian slips her palm in mine and lets me pull her up.

I tug her toward the house. "Come on, it's almost Sunday, we should get a head-start on the naked part."

EPILOGUE

CINNAMON TOAST CRUNCH SURPRISES

PIERCE

One year later

"Can we make a quick stop on the way home? I just remembered a few things we need."

"Sure." Rian looks up from her phone, head tipped a little to the side. "Everything okay?"

"Yup. Yes. Everything's fine."

Her eyes narrow the tiniest bit. I suck at keeping secrets. Especially from Rian.

"Are you sure? Because you've been all kinds of sketch today."

"I haven't been sketch today." I most definitely have.

I've been trying to get Rian home all afternoon, but it's been stop after stop in little antiques shops to pick up whatever decorative thing she falls in love with. Rian sometimes likes to take a hundred dollars with her and see how far she can make it go. Today the trunk of the Tesla is full of her kitschy, fun treasures for the Mission Mansion, which we converted into a bed-and-breakfast as planned.

We also live on the property, in one of the newly renovated outbuildings. The past year has been incredible, and I'm hoping to make the rest of the ones ahead of us just as amazing.

"You're all . . ." She gestures at me. "Sketch."

"You're imagining things." I keep my eyes on the road because if I look directly at her, there's a good chance I'm going to give myself away and then my whole plan will go up in flames.

"I don't think I am, but if you're committed to pretending you're not being all weird today, then have at it."

I grin, despite the way my stomach is all knotted up and how sweaty my palms are. I turn right into the parking lot.

Rian frowns as she takes in our location. "What are we doing here?"

"I need a few things." I pull into an empty spot by the front doors.

"From here? Why not stop somewhere closer to home?"

"Because here has what I need and it's on the way." I open the driver's side door, expecting her to do the same, except she just sits there. "Aren't you coming with me?"

"I figured I could wait in the car."

She sure isn't making this easy for me. "I could use your help."

I get another arched brow, but she unbuckles her seat belt. I pat my jacket pocket, making sure I have my wallet and the other important and necessary item. When we get inside the store, I grab a cart and hand Rian a basket. As expected, she heads directly for the cereal aisle, as if drawn to it by some invisible, magnetic force.

"Hey, I thought I'd make cinnamon roll French toast tomorrow morning. Can you head over to the bakery aisle and get what we need for that?"

Rian hesitates, glancing first at me, and then at the

cereal aisle with the same kind of longing I often experience when I'm teasing her in the bedroom and refusing to give her what she wants. "But—"

"You always pick the best buns. Oh, and can you grab some eggs while you're at it? I think we're almost out." I lean down and kiss her softly. "When we get home, I have plans for you." I give her ass a little squeeze, so she knows what kind of plans I'm talking about. Although, if my current plan doesn't go the way I want, then neither will my naked plans later. "I'll meet you in the fun food aisle."

"Okay." She glances over her shoulder, looking a little skeptical as she nabs a store flyer and heads in the direction of the bakery aisle.

As soon as she turns the corner, I rush for the cereal aisle, tossing a few things in my cart so it looks like I'm actually shopping. I come to a stop in front of the Cinnamon Toast Crunch, throw five boxes in the cart, and hastily slide my finger under the flap of one. God, my palms are ridiculously sweaty, even with the air conditioning pumping through the store.

I wipe them on my pants so my fingers aren't slippery. I quickly tear open the bag, then slip my hand inside my pocket and find what I'm looking for. I manage to get it into the box of cereal and withdraw a handful of the sugary, cinnamon squares when Rian comes around the corner, basket tucked into her side.

Her brows knit together and her perfect, pouty lips turn down when I stuff the handful of cereal into my mouth. "What're you doing?" she asks, incredulous.

"I got hungry."

She drops the basket with the eggs and the cinnamon rolls into the cart and snatches the box from me. "You haven't even paid for that yet!"

"What do you think is going to happen, the grocery police are going to take me away in handcuffs? It's not like I can't afford to buy it." I try to stick my hand back in the box, but she shifts it out of my reach. "Besides, there's a prize in that box, I wanted to see if it was any good."

She inspects the box, looking for the advertising that indicates there's something special contained within. "There's no prize in here."

"Yeah, there is, look inside."

Her eyes narrow, but she reaches in and pulls out the tiny box, now covered in a dusting of cinnamon and sugar. "What is this?"

I pluck it from her fingers, take a deep breath, and hope like hell she's ready for this.

I flip open the small box, revealing the contents as I drop to one knee. Her eyes go wide and the Cinnamon Toast Crunch slips from her grasp, landing on the linoleum and scattering across the floor around us.

"Rian Mission Sutter, a little over a year ago you came crashing into my life, and every single day since then has been better than the last. I love you, I love everything about you, even your obsession with Cinnamon Toast Crunch, and I plan to spend the rest of forever loving you. Will you marry me?"

Her fingers flutter to her mouth, a tremulous smile turning up the corners. "You're proposing?"

"I am."

"Here?" She motions to our surroundings, including the mess of cereal at our feet and the sudden crowd gathering at the ends of the aisle.

"I figured we might as well go back to the scene of the crime." I really hope she plans to say yes soon, considering this isn't the private moment it started out as.

"I love you. Of course I'll marry you." Tears make her eyes glassy as I push to a stand, cereal crunching under my feet.

"She said yes!" I shout to our audience, including a teenage employee armed with a broom, looking less than impressed.

A few cheers and whistles of approval follow as I slip the ring on her finger, my hands almost as unsteady as hers.

"It's beautiful, perfect."

"Just like you." I cup her face and tilt her head up, brushing a kiss over her lips. "You had me worried there for a second."

She arches a brow. "You thought I'd say no?"

"I was banking on a yes. I mean, we've been living in sin for a year already, and we co-own a business together. I know chemistry is a big deal, but with the whole two of ten on the compatibility scale, I was a bit worried, yeah."

She laughs. "God, I love you."

"Just remember that when you find the empty boxes of Cinnamon Toast Crunch in the cupboard." I kiss her through her laughter.

She tastes like love. She feels like my future. Rian is the beginning and the end. She's the fight I won't give up. She's the forever I won't let go.